SWEET SUMMER

Sweet Summer is the second of Frank Ryan's acclaimed thriller trilogy, which began with *Goodbye Baby Blue* and is completed by *Tiger Tiger*, all featuring Sandy Woodings. With his perceptive eye for background and character, Ryan has created a thriller masterpiece.

"Magnificently tense . . . "   *The Sunday Times*

"The page-turning and spine-chilling ability of a good novelist."   *The Sunday Telegraph*

"Powerful atmospherics . . . Impressive storytelling throughout."   *The Literary Review*

"A riveting thriller."   *Publishers Weekly*

"Well written . . . Recommended for libraries."
Library Journal

"The twists and turns from which he extricates his characters are very clever. To call (this book) a psychological thriller would be to understate it. The novel is a work of genius."   *Liverpool Echo*

"A riveting book . . . "   *Elle*

Frank Ryan

One of today's more exciting and gifted of writers, Frank Ryan is equally adept in fiction and non-fiction. He came to widespread international acclaim with thrillers such as *Goodbye Baby Blue*, *Sweet Summer* and *Tiger Tiger*, and his groundbreaking non-fiction, *The Greatest Story Never Told* and *Virus X*. His books have attracted front page reviews in the *New York Times* and *Washington Post*, in addition to lead reviews in the *Daily Telegraph*, the *Sunday Telegraph*, *The Scotsman* and *Irish Times*. They have also been translated into a dozen languages and have been the subject of features in many television documentaries in Britain and America. A play, based on *The Greatest Story Never Told*, featured the Oscar-winning actor, Jason Robards. More recently, he has added fantasy to his fiction repertoire, with the publication of *The Sundered World*.

SWEET
SUMMER

Also by Frank Ryan

In Fiction

GOODBYE BABY BLUE
TIGER TIGER
THE SUNDERED WORLD

In Non-Fiction

TUBERCULOSIS: THE GREATEST STORY
NEVER TOLD
VIRUS X

FRANK RYAN

—

SWEET SUMMER

SWIFT
PUBLISHERS

SWEET SUMMER

A Swift Book

First published in hardcover by Quartet Books Limited 1987

Swift edition published 1999

1 3 5 7 9 8 6 4 2

Copyright © Frank Ryan 1987

The author asserts the moral right to be identified as the author of this work

A catalogue record for this book is available from the British Library

ISBN 1–874082–01–4

Typeset at The Spartan Press Ltd
Lymington, Hants,
Printed in Great Britain by
Caledonian International Book Manufacturing Ltd
Glasgow

All rights reserved. No part of this publication may be reproduced,
stored in a retrieval system, or transmitted, in any form or by
any means, electronic, mechanical, photocopying, recording,
or otherwise, without the prior permission of the
publisher, nor be otherwise circulated in any form of binding,
or cover other than that in which it is published
and without a similar condition including this condition
being imposed on the subsequent purchaser.

Swift Publishers
PO Box 1436, Sheffield S17 3XP
Tel: 0114 2353344; Fax: 0114 2620148;
Website: www.swiftpublishers.com

For Barbara

1

It was, he thought, the sound of the sea which had woken him so early. That, together with the unfamiliar surroundings, and dawn, at 5:50 a.m., breaking through the small aluminium-framed window of his rented caravan. All the same, Detective Chief Inspector Sandy Woodings enjoyed the simple pleasure of the holiday feeling, the peace of the attractive little North Devon resort of Croyde Bay. Three hundred and forty miles to the north, in the South Yorkshire village of Dossage, Emily Pendle was similarly awake, in the reassuringly familiar surroundings of her own bedroom, enjoying that same peaceful moment. Although they lived no more than twenty miles apart, the detective and the sixty-year-old woman had never met. There had never been any reason for their meeting – before this morning.

Mrs Pendle was the first on her feet, crossing the floor of her bedroom and throwing open the curtains on to the cottage garden, on the same level as her bedroom window. This she did with a flourish, admiring the beautiful morning, the sky a milky white at horizon level, merging into a Prussian blue above. Without bothering to wash, or to change the underwear in which she had slept, she threw over her head a sleeveless black top – something she had knitted herself in a chunky careless kind of weave – then pulled up a pair of black corduroy trousers, before proceeding to coat her fingernails and toenails with a fresh layer of a lurid purple. Into the holes in her ears she pinned two chunky and pendulous ear-rings in the shape of horse-shoes, while over either wrist she slipped in apparent random order at least half a dozen heavy gold bracelets, from which hung dozens of lucky charms, figurines of animals and signs of the zodiac. Her bracelets tinkled merrily as she smoothed her eyebrows with a saliva-tipped finger; then, with toilet complete, she walked barefooted out of the bedroom on to a wide landing of broad bare floorboards, varnished over Edwardian brown paint, and opened a second door of the landing, calling out:

"Here, Harry Tom! Who's a good old boy then! Who's a good old fellow-me-lad, then!"

In the centre of the second bedroom, rousing himself with a self-indulgent bleary look, was an enormous pig with a large black patch over his back. Harry Tom made little grunts of delight as she raked his coarse hair with her newly painted fingernails. It was about this time that Sandy Woodings padded out through the thirty-foot awning in which his four children lay sleeping, zipped up a hole in the awning after him, and then, wearing a navy and red track-suit and trainers, set off on the first morning run of his family holiday.

Taking his time at first, he picked his way through a field sparsely dotted with brightly coloured caravans and tents, and emerged on to the empty road that separated the caravan site from the beach. He walked across the road, looked to his right where the way led to the pleasant cliff-top walk of Baggy Point, but then decided to make directly towards the beach. Walking down a concreted approach, he began running slowly through the deep soft sand, then, once beyond the dry outer fringe of the beach and on a firmer surface, he picked up pace.

Today was Tuesday, May 8th: four days previously he had granted his wife Julie a divorce, so that she could marry the husband of her erstwhile best friend, Mary. The holiday was in part to get away from all this. But now, alone with the

2

morning, he couldn't stop himself thinking about it. The divorce was all her doing. He had never wanted it. Now he realised that there was nothing at all he could do about it, nothing he could do that would simply erase his feelings.

Mrs Pendle had also started out on her morning journey. With the pig in front of her and wearing the same clothes she had put on after getting out of bed, she followed the pig's ambling pace down a main road, keeping to the white line on the crown of the road, now and then banging on a pot lid she held in one hand with a wooden ladle she wielded with the other.

"Tup!" she said crisply, when his curiosity wavered. "Come on now! Tup, Harry Tom!"

The unusual couple passed an old converted farmhouse and turned right. The sun had risen a few degrees above the horizon and the beauty of the morning had increased commensurately. She tupped Harry Tom past hedged exuberant with forsythia and cherry blossom, nothing of which was lost to her curious brown eyes. Past banks of daffodils – she could smell each individual clump of honeysuckle – but most especially for Mrs Pendle the embryonic pink genitalia of the sycamores. The Sycamores, regarded by the villagers as the native weed, were closer to her in their unplanted naturalness, their wildness.

Four hundred yards from the corner she came to a small modern brick-built house which she evidently disapproved of, for she banged even harder on the pot lid than before. It was equally evident that whoever lived there shared the antipathy because the front bedroom window came down with a clatter. Soon she followed Harry Tom, who now needed no prompting, into another right turn, through an open gate, into a council recreation area. The pig's feet moved a little faster now, as he came within sight and smell of the woods.

To their left was a slope planted with young hazel and birch. As they manoeuvred themselves over a small stile,

3

Harry Tom gave a squeal of delight. His nose darted left and right in rapid succession, and his excitement was suddenly so great that she made no effort to direct or to control him any longer.

Panting and sweating, his trainers wet with surf, Sandy Woodings was staring out to sea. The sound was strange, like that of human breathing and not made any the less so because so many people before him had used the comparison. The analogies with the human heart seemed so obvious. Like it, the sea could conceal whatever lay at its core, so that its emotions and reactions remained a mystery. You could not trust the sea. And Sandy Woodings would find difficulty in trusting any other woman.

He began to walk slowly, following the tide, listening to the rhythm of it, while Mrs Pendle followed a clay path deeper into the wood, her keen ears and sharp brown eyes easily finding the wake of the pig. And then she saw him and horror started to rise in her, twisting into a ball in her throat.

"Oh, Lord! Oh, Lord, Harry Tom! Get back out of it. Get back out of it. Back! Back!"

In his simple confusion, the pig might have been shaking his head at her, as she battered him about the snout in an effort to dislodge his grasp of a blood-stained human hand.

At 8:17 a.m., a very tall, heavily built man with grizzled iron hair showing just a trace of its original red, stood unmoving in the morning sunlight and watched an olive-green Peugeot slow for the uniformed policemen at the entrance to the recreation area and then pull in with a graceful sweep to park immediately in front of him. Detective Superintendent Georgy Barker opened the driver's door with a minor flourish and greeted the tiny dapper figure inside with a lopsided smile.

"Good morning, Doctor. Glad we managed to get you personally on this one."

"Good morning, George!" Doctor Atkins, chief forensic

pathologist to the city's police force, was the only person who did not call him "Georgy". The doctor lifted his case from the passenger seat as he emerged, then placed it studiously on the seat of a rough-hewn picnic bench before extricating a square handkerchief in which was neatly tucked a nasal insufflator. Into each nostril, with a dainty movement, he squeezed two puffs, folded the whole away again as neatly as it had emerged into the side pocket of his dark-blue pinstripe, and then allowed the detective to lead him in the direction of the woods.

"How much do we know about it already?" the doctor enquired in a cultured and polite voice, as they crushed tiny blue forget-me-nots in the sloping lawn of grass. Their steps were curiously disharmonious, the smaller man having to make various corrections of stride to keep up with the giant's limp – Georgy Barker suffered, among many other ailments, from osteoarthritis in his right hip.

"Murder. There's no doubt about it. A young woman, possibly no more than a girl. Nice long fair hair. Not possible to go for identity yet because she's lying face down. Multiple wounds. Blood everywhere.'

Uniformed policemen searched on all fours among leafless oaks and tall fragrant pines. The pair arrived within minutes under a twenty-foot holly tree and were filmed in motion by a photographer with a video camera. The superintendent stood and watched, his face dappled with sunlight, as, within the strict privacy of the screened-off enclosure, the doctor opened his case and began his methodical task.

The cameraman captured the doctor, framed against the deep evergreen of the holly, as he pulled on his surgical gloves in that curiously practised fashion, continuing the film as the small dapper figure stood at the foot of the body, dictating in short crisp sentences into a hand dictaphone. He described the scene, the time, the ambient temperature, the climatic conditions which had prevailed in the preceding twenty-four hours. The young woman's body lay more half turned than truly face down, with her legs extended, her left arm concealed beneath her and her right arm flexed and held aloft above her head. The superintendent had not exaggerated about her hair – it was fair, long and attractive, now matted with dust, and, above the right ear, clotted with blood. A ribbon about an inch wide surrounded her forehead. The colour of the ribbon vaguely matched that of her mauve sweater. She wore a tightly fitting white cotton skirt, no stockings, one white sandal still on her right foot and the other foot bare, pathetic in its innocent nakedness. There were signs of a considerable struggle, with, as the detective had intimated, a great deal of blood.

"I shall have to disturb her."

"Carry on – we've taken more than enough pictures."

Having taken a "core" temperature, the doctor lifted the back of the sweater to display a bra-less back that was dotted and lacerated with puncture wounds.

"Cause of death – multiple stab wounds." Chief Superintendent Barker's voice was a little tight as he spoke for the first time in many minutes.

"It would appear so,' said Doctor Atkins evenly.

Between them they turned the body over, and in doing so demonstrated for the camera a fully developed rigor mortis. The flesh resembled something solid, quite inhuman, more like a plaster window model. It was immediately obvious, even without disturbing her clothes, that the main frenzy of attack had taken place from the front. Avoiding the face and extending from the neck downwards was a mass of stab wounds, following a vague but sinister trail. They encompassed the pointed girlish mounds of the breasts and extended in a wide fan out on to the abdomen, to the most severely and extensively insulted focus on the lower trunk just above the pubic bone. Yet it was her face, now exposed, which caused the two men to take a simultaneous step backwards, in a mute and quite involuntary expression of pity. Her face was indeed young, perhaps that of a teenager, and to an unexpected degree pretty – more than pretty, it was an extraordinarily beautiful young woman's face.

2

The incident centre for the murder enquiry had been set up in an old building at the heart of the village, which was once the village school, because there was a stone over the door which said so, dated 1821. At 8:30 a.m. Detective Inspector Jock Andrews was glad to leave this organised chaos, and set out on foot, walking down an attractive lane skirting the village green. The village had discovered wealth as a result of its proximity to the city. The lane along which he now walked had over the previous thirty years been entirely bought up by commuters. The cottages and farmhouses had been expensively modernised, and their generous gardens erupted on to the lane in a carnival of floral hedges.

Jock Andrews walked at a steady pace, arriving at the bottom of the lane a good five minutes after he had left the old school, and now he paused again to check his bearings, looking at the address in his notebook, finding difficulty with the numbering of doors which was anything but logical. The cottage he inspected must once have been the living-quarters of the farm labourers, since, although now it evidently formed a single home, there remained the two original carved stone doorways. There was no name on the ornate stone entrance posts and there appeared to be no numbers at all on either door. However, the address in his notebook was 1 Vicarage Lane, so this had to be the place. As he walked along the paved path to the entrances, he was flanked on his left by the cottage, which showed signs of considerable age, with heavily mullioned windows and leaded glass set direct into the stonework, and on his right by a four-foot drystone wall, capped by long flat coping-stones. The wall appeared as old as the house, with an extraordinary variety of alpines creeping over its lichened surface. In the garden beyond the wall were two very old but still blossoming pear trees, their trunks twisted and deeply fissured, while in their shadow was one of the most unusual vegetable gardens he had ever seen. He didn't recognise most of what was growing there – in face he had an impression that many of the plants were weeds, out of place. Even more unusual, and which caused him to break into a cackle of laughter as he leaned in real astonishment with his hands flat on the coping-stones, was the menagerie that scratched and scuttled at will throughout the vegetable beds. He recognised a hen-pheasant, guinea fowl, one Canada goose and what looked, at least on first glance, to be a rather clumsy cousin to the common chicken. He would have enjoyed a closer look had it not been for the fact that his presence had been noticed through a spy-hole in the door. It opened before he had time to rattle the brass knocker, and a plumpish woman with dyed black hair and ostentatious gold ear-rings dangling from her ears demanded to know who he was and what he wanted.

"Mrs Pendle?"

"Yes."

"Detective Inspector Andrews." He smiled at her, and went on in a strong Glaswegian accent, "If you wouldn't mind, I'd like to ask you some more details of how you found the body."

She invited him to sit down in a room with a beamed and raftered ceiling in black oak. Influenced by the accumulation of animal hairs and the smell emanating from the upholstery, he elected to sit on the arm of a sofa, a large tear in which had been repaired with elastoplast. Placing his notebook on the seat of the sofa, he passed her a photo-graph, and asked her if she recognised the young woman in it.

Although it was of a standard size, three by five inches, and a good-quality colour print, the light entering the sitting-room through the small leaded panes was so poor that she had to take it across to the window and peer at it in a way that suggested she needed spectacles.

"It's poor little Angela."

"I'm not asking you who it is in the photograph, Mrs Pendle. I'm asking you if you think it's the same lass you found in the wood."

"I don't know – I mean, I should think so, wouldn't you? Or, rather, you wouldn't be showing it to me if it wasn't the case, now, would you, Inspector?"

As she handed him back the photograph, he noticed that her hand shook.

"The young woman in the photograph is Angela Hawks-worth, who has been missing from her mother's house here in the village since yesterday evening. But you're telling me that you didn't recognise her at all when you found her in that state – is that it, Mrs Pendle?"

"I didn't. I mean, oh Lord – I don't know half of what I think. I'm in such a state of shock. But it is Angela. Poor young Angela – and so pretty! It's a ghastly tragedy, a terrible tragedy."

"We're still waiting for full and proper identification. We can't really do that where her body is now. We have a proper way of arranging that. But you must know the lass. You live together here, in this small village. Do you think it likely that the girl you found is the same one in the photograph?"

"Yes. Yes, it must be, mustn't it? Oh, poor girl! You see, I've known her since she was a mischievous little child – with her lovely hair."

The detective sighed and noted her comment in his book,

then suddenly lifted his foot in fright, because the floor had moved, and a tortoise, who seemed none the worse for the experience, crawled from under his shoe.

Mrs Pendle was resting her head against the back of a green dralon armchair, with her face concealed behind her painted fingers, but he had the impression she was watching him curiously through the gaps. "Poor, poor, Angela. Oh, it's horrible, ghastly – awful!" she murmured, while with every slight movement the bracelets round her wrists gave a sibilant high-pitched tinkling. "I don't suppose, inspector, that it was some kind of terrible accident?"

"She was murdered all right. That's the single thing we can feel very sure about. But then, maybe you have some ideas about that. You knew her very well, from the sounds of it. Perhaps there is something you should be telling me, Mrs Pendle?"

"Oh, no – nothing. Absolutely nothing – no reason at all. What reason could there be?"

"You must tell me anything at all you do know about the girl."

"What do you know about anyone else? You can live in the same village. You can share the same house and the same bed and you don't know what's happening inside somebody else's head. Now that's the truth, isn't it, inspector!"

Jock Andrews sighed again. His attention was distracted for a moment by something that glided by the window, an animal as big as a dog or a sheep, but which looked more like a patchwork quilt on four legs.

"I wouldn't like to think that you were being unco-operative with me, Mrs Pendle."

"Certainly not, Inspector."

"An attractive girl, aged twenty. You know we've spoken to her parents – you've guessed that, haven't you, because how else could we have the photograph and the fact that she's been missing since yesterday? So tell me about her.

11

Boyfriends. Attractive lassie like Angela would have boy-friends galore, or else the world has changed since I was twenty-one."

"Boyfriends? Yes. Oh, I'm sure she's had plenty of boyfriends."

"Do you think we could have the name of at least one of them, love?"

"You mean Paul. Oh, I shouldn't go thinking what you're thinking about Paul. Paul wouldn't do a thing like that to Angela. Oh, no. Heaven forbid!"

"Paul who?"

"Paul Thorpe of course. But I shouldn't go thinking – ."

"Does Paul Thorpe live here in the village?"

"Yes, of course he does. A nice young man – one of the old village families, you know."

"What was it – a quarrel? Did they fall out over some other boyfriend perhaps? What are you trying to hide, Mrs Pendle? It's just wasting our time hiding things, because you know we'll find it all out from everybody else."

"Oh, yes, you're right, aren't you. You see things so very clearly. Yes, of course everybody in the village knows that they fell out with each other. But it wasn't another boy. It wasn't that at all. It was much worse than that. Oh, dear! Poor little Angela. Everybody could see she was making a big mistake. But you can't tell them, can you, Inspector? I mean, you haven't a daughter of your own, have you, by any chance? Well, it's a phase of growing up. It only happens to girls, I should imagine."

"So there was another boyfriend?"

"Not a boy. A man. That crazy artist twice her age. Or so he calls himself. An artist, hah! More than twice her age, if you ask me. But you won't let on that it was me who told you about him. I can do without any more enemies, thank you very much – especially such a violent kind of man. Oh dear, what am I saying?"

For the first time since entering the room, Jock Andrews

noticed the parrot. It was watching him from the backrail of a dining-chair, as still as a ghost, dilapidated, its green feathers moulting.

3

Chief Superintendent Georgy Barker spoke in a measured and reasonable tone of voice. "You don't have to answer any questions here and now, if you don't want to. We're not ready to take down a formal statement. You could look upon this as a sort of preliminary enquiry. We're not accusing anybody of anything. All we want is to get to know a little bit more about Angela."

"If you're not accusing me, why bring me here then?"

Paul Thorpe was sweating. He had been sweating from the moment of sitting opposite the superintendent. Georgy Barker studied him a moment and wondered if he was sweating because he was upset or if it was because of the heavy black leather jacket he was wearing.

"Would you like a cigarette? We'll fetch you a cup of tea, if you want one."

Paul Thorpe touched the wisp of moustache over his mouth but didn't reply, then, after a moment's deliberation, he took a cigarette packet from a breast pocket, put one between his lips and lit it.

It was 4:15 p.m. on Thursday, May 10th and they faced one another across a small oak table in one of the temporary booths that had been partitioned off in the big classroom of the old schoolhouse. Sunlight streamed over the young man's shoulder through the tall mullioned and transomed Georgian windows, which faced west. Behind the bulky seated figure of the superintendent, who had removed his coat and draped it over the back of his chair, stood a silent Detective Inspector Andrews, while from behind the honeycomb of partitioning came the cacophony of typewriters, the voices of the six-man switchboard and the rhythmical clicking of daisywheel printers.

"You're very upset. Naturally you are. But you'd like to help us catch whoever did that to Angela now, wouldn't you?"

Paul Thorpe opened another of the buttons on his black shirt, exposing a vee of white tee-shirt. "I'm not upset – I'm glad. I am. Personally I'm glad."

"I don't believe that you're glad."

"But you suspect me and I didn't do it. I'm glad but I didn't do it."

"Nobody has accused you. I haven't accused you, have I?"

"I could never harm Angie. Never! I just couldn't. Ask anybody. Ask Mrs Hawksworth. She'll tell you I could never harm Angie."

"Sometimes we do hurt people we feel deeply for, you can see the sense in that, can't you, lad. Sometimes. Sometimes it just happens. Everything blows up in our face. All our plans. I mean to say, you and Angela, you had plans – there was a time when you made plans, wasn't there, Paul?"

"We were always making plans and then she'd go and cancel them again."

"But you were never actually engaged, were you?"

The young man shook his head. He had a long heavy chin under the wispy moustache. A head full of black curls, two prominent bosses in that perspiring forehead over soft, watery-blue eyes. Not over-tall, but awkward and powerful, with broad thick hands tipped with a mechanics's finger-nails.

"Did she have any enemies?"

"Nothing like that!"

15

"Nobody threaten her? Phone calls? Something she put down as silly?"

"Don't be daft!"

"Why don't you tell me what happened – between you and Angela. There it was, everything going well for you – !"

"The way you talk, you know everything already anyway."

"I'd like to hear your side."

"I'm sure you would."

"You both went here to the village school. You met only a hundred yards from where we're sitting right now. Just over there, across the road, on the playing-fields. She was two years below you. She was always daring you to do things, wasn't she?"

"Me and Angie – it was always up and down. We've been broken off for two months. I know nothing."

"What did she dare you to do, Paul?"

"She never dared me to do anything."

"That's all right. You're not telling me the truth but I'm not even annoyed. You don't have to tell me anything you don't want to. But maybe you'll think about it, see how you feel when you've given it time for thought. But let me tell you something I think about you, Paul. I'll bet you that you're good at sports. Now am I right about that? I mean, you like to play around. You can enjoy a good laugh?"

"What's that supposed to mean?"

"Practical jokes. Don't tell me you never get up to that sort of thing?"

"I'm not telling you nowt."

"I've heard different, Paul. Let me tell you what I've heard. I've heard that you're the village practical joker. For instance, there was something about putting an extra little decoration into the flower picture on the village green on May Day?"

There was a pause, during which the chief superintendent

16

thought he could smell peppermint on Paul's breath. Probably the lad had been drinking.

"Are you denying it? After all, it's not very important."

"I didn't touch the well-dressing but I got blamed for it. Like I get blamed for a lot of things in this place."

"For instance you might have gone out there, maybe to meet up with someone. Maybe you didn't meet up with that someone. It's possible, isn't it? Anything is possible. Maybe you knew she was meeting someone else. A practical joke, maybe just to show her how serious you were. Because you were serious, weren't you lad. You've just told me how serious you were. You loved her. And she treated you very shabbily. Running off with what's-his-name."

"Martin!"

"Old enough to be her father. And married too. That wasn't a very nice thing for Angela to do to you, lad."

"Angie wasn't always such a nice person."

"Ah!"

"No! You're tricking me into saying things I don't mean to say. All I meant is she did crazy things now and then."

"Don't we all."

Paul Thorpe took a long pull on his cigarette without answering.

"Like going out into the woods after dark, with some sort of knife. You only meant to frighten her. To show her you meant business. Maybe showing her you meant business would make her take you seriously instead of a middle-aged married man."

"I wouldn't need no knife to do that." The curly head nodded with infinite slowness on the strong red muscular neck.

"I'm not convinced, Paul. You see, I can understand it. I'm not just sitting in judgement. I think I could see how it might feel. A middle-aged married man. I mean, it couldn't have been an easy thing to accept."

The head on those strong shoulders simply continued to

17

nod. Almost imperceptibly at first, but very soon it was nodding up and down, quite fast.

"Let's be more specific then. You know what I want. Tell me where you were between six in the evening and twelve midnight yesterday."

"I've already told *him*."

"Certainly. And the inspector has written all you told him down in his book. But I want you just to tell me again, just the same."

"I was with me mate, Jacky Arber. A quarter past six we set out for a run on our bikes."

"A quarter past six? As early as that?"

"I just told you."

"Then somebody else must have seen the pair of you?"

"Likely they did."

"Somebody who could vouch for you?"

"There's nobody in this place would vouch for me, I reckon."

"What time did you come back in from your run on your bikes?"

"After eight. Half past, or thereabouts."

"So somebody would have seen you then? Seen you parking. Maybe you stopped and said hello to somebody in the village, or whistled at a girl?"

"We wheeled the bikes straight into our yard. Nobody saw us. Nobody I noticed anyway. Nobody except me mam."

"And then you stayed in watching television all night?"

"We watched it when we felt like it."

"What programmes did you watch?"

"We watched a bit of the news. And something about Italy. The trouble with the car factory in Milan."

"You must have watched it very closely to have remembered that much about it."

"I wasn't very interested. Who cares what's on the box anyway?"

"Yes, lad. So what else did you do with all of those three and a half hours?"

"We talked."

"You must be better at talking than watching."

"That's right."

"It must have been interesting, whatever it was that you talked about. Interesting enough for you to tell me what it was about then?"

"It wasn't that interesting. As a matter of fact it was boring. It wasn't anything in particular. Bikes mainly. Bikes and grumbling about the job stakes. That's not very interesting, is it?"

"Everything is interesting. It's all very interesting to me. Right now I'm very interested in when you last saw Angela."

"Two days ago – she passed me in the street and didn't speak."

"The large man appeared to stare in almost a fatherly way at the youngster. He said, "And you never saw or heard from her again in the two days?"

"Nothing!"

"All right – that's your story, at least first time round."

"That's it full stop. Can I go now?"

Chief Superintendent Barker merely waved a hand, with his wrist still at the level of the table top. "You can go and have a cup of tea. Then come back and we'll start right over again from the beginning!"

When the lad had gone he stared after him for a moment silently, then lifted a tape recorder from his lap from under the table surface, and switched it off carefully, before placing it down with a long deep inhalation in the centre of the table.

The evening was quite as lovely as the day, with the sun setting behind stone cottages. There was a comfortable warmth rising from the ground outside the murder headquarters as Georgy Barker leaned against the door jamb to heave and wobble in the effort of finding his pipe, while Inspector Jock Andrews stared with a mild interest in the direction of the triangular village green opposite.

"I'll grant Sandy Woodings something – he certainly knows when to take a holiday."

Jock nodded, putting a tablet of gum in his mouth and starting to chew.

"What's your verdict on old Mrs Pendle, then?"

Jock considered with amusement the fact that the woman was only a couple of years older than Georgy himself, and, if anything, looked younger. He said, "I'm not sure if she's mad pretending to be sane or sane pretending to be mad."

Georgy hee-hee'd, gripping the stem of his briar between his teeth. "And the youngster has only two alibis, one his best friend and the other his mother – !"

Jock watched the superintendent light his pipe, and puff for several seconds, until the evening air was filled with the aromatic smell. "When are we going to talk to this Martin character?"

"All in good time, Jock. You don't know him. There's something about him seems to worry the top brass. Orders are to take it slowly, get all of our facts. We'll need all our facts together before we get round to calling on our friend, Simon Martin, the English Bernini."

"Angela Hawksworth. Age – twenty years. Artist's model. Unmarried. External examination. Height – five feet five inches. Build, medium. Eyes brown. Hair fair. Stigmata of pre-existent disease or surgery – nil. Marks of violence – stab wounds to neck, limbs and trunk – in excess of fifty separate entry wounds. Wounds consistent with a sharp-bladed instrument of unusual type and shape. See drawing of typical wound. Blade approximately three-quarters of an inch wide and crescentic in section. Wounds on both hands and upper lower arms consistent with attempts to ward off injury. Tendency of wounds to converge on the region of lower abdomen, where nature of reaction suggests the wounds in this region were inflicted after death."

It was 8:30 a.m., on Friday, May 11th: through the window of the schoolroom, Georgy Barker's gaze drifted to the mustard fuzz that was the blossom on a berberis hedge. In the room, twenty-one detectives sat facing him as he paused in addressing them across a table, with the post-mortem report of Doctor Atkins spread on the surface in front of him. Lying next to the report on the bare table was his unlit pipe, which he would fiddle with and lift and stab at the air or tap on the desk surface as the mood took him.

Jock Andrews sat close to the back, next to the uniformed figure of Assistant Chief Constable Meadows, who leaned his folded arms on the back of the empty chair in front of him, and listened with his well-groomed white-haired head gravely inclined and attentive.

"Examination of internal organs. Starting with thoracic cavity. Heart – penetrated by five stab wounds. Penetration of both right and left ventricle. Penetration of root of aorta. Penetration of both right and left lungs, with bilateral pneumothorax. Blood filled pericardial cavity. Blood and air filling of both pleural cavities. Any one of the stab wounds to the heart or to the great vessels would have been sufficient to cause death from haemorrhage or cardiac arrest.

"Abdominal cavity. Remains of light meal of vegetable salad in stomach. Stomach ruptured as a result of several wounds, with contents spilling into peritoneal cavity. Liver and spleen punctured with slight evidence of haemorrhage, indicating that subject was close to death when wounds were inflicted. Bowel perforated in many places, with no evidence of peritoneal reaction. Kidneys and bladder perforated by similar wounds. Uterus penetrated by two post-mortem wounds. Subject was approximately three months pregnant."

It was characteristic of the superintendent that he read the post-mortem reports to the team personally. Also that in the reading of them he would pause at intervals, either to allow some point to be reinforced or maybe to register his sense of shock or outrage. Because this too was another of his characteristics. A life spent in dealing with crime of all manner and viciousness had still left him the facility to feel a sense of outrage. This was such a moment of outrage and his eyes glistened in their bleary red-rimmed sockets and he tapped monotonously on the desk surface with the mouth-piece of his pipe.

"Conclusion: death caused by multiple stab wounds using a sharp weapon of unusual blade design. Judging from the maximum depth of wounds inflicted, blade length at the minimum was eleven inches. Time of death, judging from rectal temperature and degree of rigor mortis, between six and twelve midnight, May 7th. The nature of the wounds and their number would suggest that the attack took the form of frenzy. The convergence of wounds on chest and abdomen, the large number inflicted in these regions, would indicate that the attacker inflicted these when subject was lying dead on the ground. The body was turned over after the attack, probably by the attacker but possible by some-one else at any time up to discovery. There was no sexual interference or evidence of intercourse."

Silence reigned in the large well-lit room, apart from the scratching of ball-point pens as people made their own notes, during which Meadows ran his fingers through his hair without appearing to disturb its white grooming.

Within fifteen minutes the room had emptied, except for the three senior officers. The chief superintendent, with a loud sigh of deliberation, told Inspector Andrews to go and pick up Martin.

"For God's sake, Georgy!" Meadows screwed up his mouth in protest.

"I'm not in the mood to be careful," replied Georgy,

stuffing his unlit pipe into his mouth and making a grinding noise as he chewed the ebony mouthpiece.

The assistant chief constable ordered two cups of tea and then sat silently in the sunlight-filled room, while Chief Superintendent Georgy Barker lit his pipe and ignored the cup of tea.

"This fellow has national, even international, connections. If we act clumsily, we could not only cause a lot of friction, but we could lose him altogether in the smoke-screen he could fan around himself.

Georgy looked unimpressed and angry. He stalked across to the window, and stared out at the massive stone on the green which proclaimed some past historical event, but his eyes naturally wandered away from the monument to the clouds of daffodils. In his own garden earlier this morning he had inspected the swelling blossom buds on his four apple trees. Then the telephone was ringing and it took seconds to register. When Georgy turned, Meadows had the receiver in his hand, his cup of tea hastily placed on the table top by the side of his saucer.

"Martin," said Meadows, without attempting to conceal his annoyance, "is refusing to co-operate."

"I wonder why!"

Meadows put his hand over the mouthpiece. "Listen to me now, Georgy –"

Let me talk to Jock, Arthur."

Meadows didn't hand the receiver over. Instead he murmured into it: "Stay parked outside, inspector. If Martin leaves, follow him. Otherwise stay there and we'll get back to you."

"Bloody hell, Arthur!" said Georgy, standing to his full six feet three and his trimmed-down sixteen stones.

"You're not fit for all this running about any more, Georgy. Why not leave this one to Woodings?"

"Woodings isn't here right now."

"Where is he holidaying?"

23

"Never mind where. His wife divorced him only days ago. Let him be. He has his four kids with him."

"Call him up, Georgy. The case is too urgent for compassion."

"I couldn't do that to him, sir."

"May I remind you, Georgy, that Andrews is sitting in a car waiting."

"What does it mean, Dad? Does it mean that we can't go for a walk to Baggy Point and see the gannets?"

"No. We'll go and have our walk. Don't you worry."

Sandy Woodings stood and waited in a short queue at the small public call-box on the road to the beach. A local patrol car had relayed the message and he had declined the offer to be taken back to the local station and make his call in privacy.

"Woodings here." He watched the children squabbling. Children, who always seemed to sense when their pleasure might be about to be spoiled.

"It's Meadows here, Woodings. Where are you calling from? It sounds like a public call-box."

"It is a call-box, sir. What's the matter?"

"You must have read about the murder here two days ago?"

"I heard – on the car radio."

"It's an awkward one, Woodings. When are we expecting you back here?"

"8:30: Monday morning."

"Now listen to me. I'm going to send a brief down to you there. To be delivered by hand by the local people. I want you to be already acquainted with things before you return."

Sandy Woodings made no reply. If he had said what he was thinking it might have cost him his job.

"I suppose if I were to ask you to break – or postpone – your holiday – ?"

"You'd be wasting your time."

"Presumably you arrive back here on Sunday?"

"I arrive back on Saturday, but I'm officially on holiday until Monday morning."

"I'd like you to come in on the Sunday, if that isn't absolutely impossible. Get started on this case straight away. Be fully conversant with all the developments from day to day while you're down there. That should enable you to carry on with your holiday and still lose no time."

"I suppose this is all absolutely necessary, sir?" Through the glass he could see sand-dunes; beyond the dunes, a glimpse of sea.

"I'll assume you didn't need to ask me that question, Chief Inspector."

At 11:00 a.m. that same morning, Sandy Woodings lay back in a carpet of wild flowers at the extremity of the short walk to the point and listened to the children arguing.

"Backside," exclaimed Gerry's still childishly high-pitched tones, "can't be a swear word because it's made up of two ordinary words, back and side. Isn't that right, Dad?"

He ran his hand playfully through Gerry's hair and then Marty, his youngest daughter, who was the opposite side in the argument, pointed to where a hundred feet below a line of gannets dived one after another, like a collapsing pack of cards. The twins stood together a short distance away, arms linked, watching some young men abseiling down the cliffs behind them.

"So!" he exclaimed with a sudden rush of astonishment.

"So!" also exclaimed Georgy Barker, back in Dossage, but much more softly, so that the men who were climbing out of the second car couldn't possibly hear him.

He nodded to Jock, who had also climbed out of his unmarked car, still parked where he had been waiting fruitlessly for a good three hours, and who now spoke softly to the four burly detective constables, giving them very careful instructions.

The garden wall was built of masoned stone, as was the house within the extensive garden. Now, leaning over coping-stones prettily decorated with dry feathery lichens, and by standing on tip-toe, Georgy Barker watched the five men approach the house, knock on the door, then produce their search warrant.

"So – dammit!"

His hip ached. There was a bulge at his waist, which was due to the presence of a small pump connected to a tube that ran under the skin of his abdomen, a new kind of medical experiment for pumping insulin into you at a constant rate. Georgy Barker suffered from diabetes and they had not so far been able to control it with tablets or the aid of a diet.

Nothing! They had found nothing in the house. All five men emerged, and then split up, two going clockwise and the other three anti-clockwise round the large heavy ornate building. Silence for a while and then a cry – more a shout of bloody-mindedness, he thought – followed by some cursing and what was obviously an arrest effected without co-operation. It was confirmed when all five men appeared again round the nearside of the house, one of the constables sporting a bloody nose, and carrying, with one limb apiece, a struggling man whose hair was white with marble dust. Jock walked along behind them looking distinctly uncomfortable, telling them now and then to take it easy. They wanted no injuries to Martin, never mind a broken nose or two on their side! They manhandled him bodily up to a rear door of the squad car, then prised his hands free of collars and door rim to bundle him inside.

Suddenly there was a commotion from the path leading from the house, as four figures appeared. One was definitely female – Georgy Barker guessed this must be Mrs Martin – but now, seeing them closer, he had to presume that two of the other three were also female, older than Mrs Martin, and dressed oddly, in men's trousers and shirts, one of them with a monocle hanging from her neck. The fourth and last was only just male in Georgy Barker's estimation; the superintendent put him down as some kind of effeminate artist.

The car with Martin was already moving away so they turned their attentions on the large man staring at them in some amazement.

"Who the hell do you people think you are?"

"Bloody Gestapo!"

"What do you think you're going to gain by arresting Simon?"

In his vision they were a blur of angry faces, open mouths, gypsy scarves round necks, that anachronistic monocle!

But Georgy Barker hardly registered them. In his mind he was recalling Meadows: that look of intense irritation on his face when Georgy had forced the arrest of Martin on him. *Tread warily, Georgy!* He'd jolly-well show them how to squeeze the truth out of a villain – even if he had to wring his famous artistic neck personally!

4

Mrs Pendle had noticed the arrival of the tall man from the corner of her eye, but as yet she pretended she had not. In his turn the man was quite content to watch her, leaning with one elbow on top of her heavy stone wall so that he was facing the garden and the morning sunlight. She was crouching patiently in the shade of one of her pear trees, on both knees, with a large upended glass jar in her hands. Suddenly she pounced, diving with her jar over something in the garden. Then with great care she slipped a small square piece of blue slate under the upended neck of the jar and transferred the whole a distance of no more than eighteen inches before easing the slate away and sliding the jar downwards, so that it completely enveloped what for all the world resembled an ordinary garden weed.

"Mrs Pendle?" the man enquired politely.

"Another policeman? Oh dear!" She stood up, taking her eyes resentfully from what was happening inside the tiny world of the jar.

"Detective Chief Inspector Woodings!" He maintained his tone of deferential politeness.

"Hmph!" she exclaimed, suddenly lifting the jar and waving excitedly at the bee which she had just liberated, as if to clear it from her hair.

"Coltsfoot!" he knelt down and brushed a large flat leaf. "And here – knitbone! And chickweed!" He laughed, straightened up and looked Mrs Pendle direct in the eye. "It's been a long time since I've seen a real herb garden."

"Oh, it's just amateur dabbling – it runs in the family – always kept a few."

She approached him with fussy determination, leaving the garden through the home-made gate with its pale-green spars and green-painted chicken wire. But he appeared to block her way to the cottage door.

"And I see you keep a Gloucester old spot."

"Oh, Harry Tom! He's just one of my collection, you know."

"What kind of collection is that, Mrs Pendle?"

"You certainly ask a lot of questions!" she exclaimed, turning her face away so that he couldn't study her quite so closely. "And you seem to know all sorts of things I wouldn't expect a policeman to know about. Here now – I haven't seen your identity card, have I?"

With a smile, he handed her his card, which she held at arm's length, with her bracelets jangling. "Chief Inspector Alexander Woodings! Hmph!" She returned the card to him, while maintaining a wary avoidance of his shrewd blue eyes. "Chief Inspector, eh? I'm not about to be arrested or anything?"

"Of course you're not going to be arrested, Mrs Pendle!"

"That's what you say now. Maybe that's what you said too to that Martin fellow. But then you came along in a car and threw him into it and from what I hear about it he didn't much care for the experience."

"Mr Martin has been released."

"Yes – and I expect that caused a few red faces down at your headquarters! But I don't suppose you'd care to talk to me along those lines, would you." She really didn't know quite what to make of him, since he seemed quite friendly really. Nice eyes. More violet than blue, a bit like Elizabeth Taylor's, it occurred to her. She had already decided that when he smiled his eyes said that he meant it. "I've already made a written statement about finding poor Angela. And I've been questioned by Inspector Andrews even after that."

"This will not be quite so formal. I just wish to ask you a few questions."

"I suppose you'd better come in like all the others and fire away with your questions, then."

"It's a nice enough morning. Would you mind if we just strolled about your garden?"

"I suppose not." She allowed him to lead her back through the green-painted gate, watched him close it carefully after her. "I daresay you do what you like with people anyway."

"Shall we start with when you last saw Angela Hawksworth alive?" he asked as they began to walk slowly down the garden.

Mrs Pendle looked across to where Harry Tom lay on his side, lazily basking in the sun next to her manure heap. "A week – I think so. About a week before –"

They passed a nanny goat, tethered with its white kid nearby. "For the children at the city hospital," she explained. "I pass on the milk I have over. Some of them are allergic to cow's milk."

"Where did you see her? Under what circumstances?"

"Here! Here in the lane – outside my cottage. It's central in the village, you see." Passing a big old elderberry, she involuntarily picked a sprig, rolled it hard between fingers and thumb. "Keeps away the midges," she explained, but in the moment of crushing the soft green leaves, he thought he might have seen her lips move as in prayer. It was difficult to be sure since she was such a nervous kind of woman, some part of her always twitching or on the move – now she touched his sleeve with that same hand and he could smell the plant's astringent aroma on her fingers.

Stopping before some pens containing long-haired sheep and a donkey with peculiar-looking ears and what looked like a horse's mane, he asked: "Why did she visit you here? What did she want, Mrs Pendle?"

"Oh, heavens – it wasn't anything but casual. I just happened to see her out in the lane. She was on her own. We said hello."

"This herb garden – ?"

"You mustn't read too much into things, Inspector – if it's all right to call you Inspector, since Chief Inspector is such a mouthful?" She hesitated and when he didn't appear to mind, she continued. "Merely my collection. I like to preserve the unusual, both plant and animal. People give me the tip when there's something coming up at the livestock auctions. Anything that other people wouldn't know what to do with."

They had completely circled the house, and he had had a reasonably comprehensive survey of a garden which comprised about two acres, divided into many compounds by walls and hedges in which Noah would have found an occasional surprise.

"Did you supply Angela Hawksworth with a herbal treatment – for any illness or symptom, Mrs Pendle?"

"No, I did not. And if that's the end of your questions, I've got a lot of work on my hands."

He ignored her attempt to terminate their conversation. "Where were you on the evening of Monday, May 7th, between six in the evening and midnight?"

"Here in my cottage."

"Have you any witnesses to that?"

"Only Bunter, my donkey, and Harry Tom and Coddles."

"Coddles?"

"My parrot."

With a smile, he pulled home the bolt on the green-painted garden gate, turned, then touched his forehead, as if in an absent-minded afterthought. "I believe Harry Tom was also the name of your late husband, Mrs Pendle?"

31

"Goodbye – Mr Tricky-the-Loop, Chief Inspector!"

At 5:15 that same evening Sandy Woodings sat in front of a green-covered table, behind Chief Superintendent Barker, who threw his voice back over his shoulder, standing silhouetted against the big schoolroom window.

"You look well, Sandy. The holiday must have suited you."

"Thanks, Georgy. A month would have suited me better."

"Just look at this weather! Like California. Went out there once on the department's expense sheet. Evenings like this, hot as noon, blue sky."

It was a kind of thinking interval for the three detectives after listening to the tape of Georgy questioning Paul Thorpe. Sandy Woodings was sitting with the recorder in front of him, Jock was next to him, with his elbows on the table, Georgy by the window. A tea lady interrupted them, bringing in a tray. Georgy's pint mug without sugar, tea in polystyrene cups for Andrews and Woodings.

"Well then – what's the verdict on Paul Thorpe?" Georgy turned on Sandy, inhaling deeply.

"You kept it remarkably brief. Why make such a point of not asking him about the pregnancy?"

"At the time I didn't know about the pregnancy. But all the same, maybe that's one ace we should hold up our sleeve for the present?"

Sandy tried the tea, wincing, simultaneously watching Georgy light his pipe. He felt mildly desperate for a cigarette. But he had made a resolution on holiday and now he was determined to stick to it.

"Thorpe interests me," he said. "But you were the one to actually interview him."

"Yes," admitted Georgy, without saying anything at all. "So where do you intend to go from here?"

"I want to see the scene of crime for myself."

"You'd better take Jock along with you and pick his brain of all he knows – since Meadows is so keen to have him off the case!"

"He calls it manpower shortages. All the uniformed boys on the miners' pickets."

Sandy shook his head. "You still haven't said what you thought about Paul Thorpe, Georgy. What was the actual feeling you had at the time of the interview?"

The chief superintendent took an almighty swig from his unsweetened tea and hardly seemed to notice the taste. He placed the mug back on the table with a clump, inhaled, puffed a second on his pipe, then lifted it out of his mouth again and looked askance in Inspector Andrews's direction, while still saying nothing.

"Yes," said Jock, "I had a go at him too. He's very touchy. But then he would be – it's only to be expected."

"I think," said Georgy slowly, "that he likes to put a tough front on it. I had the impression he was very deeply involved with the girl."

"With all due respect, the two are not incompatible, Georgy. It doesn't matter how tough a fellow can be."

"But to kill a girl, to kill her in that way. If you loved a girl, could you do that to her?"

Jock, having downed his entire plastic cup of tea with one disgusted gulp, said emphatically, "For what it's worth, I met a lot of young Paul Thorpes in the slums of Glasgow. All with that same awkwardness. It's a kind of stupidity – like a flatness in the eyes when you try to get through to them. If what you're asking me, chief, is if Paul Thorpe could commit murder, then the answer is, yes, Paul Thorpe could commit murder! I haven't the shadow of a doubt about it."

5

Sandy felt puzzled not just by the murder, but also by the way in which the enquiry had been conducted before his return. There seemed to have been some palpable brake on things. Something hard to define. Meadows telephoning him on holiday! Georgy! Something about Georgy!

He slept at Josie's apartment after a five-course dinner and two bottles of hock. On Tuesday morning, May 15th, he left her asleep with her dyed blonde hair fanned artistically over the black satin counterpane, her face turned on its side towards him and her mouth, with its well-formed lips, somewhat agape, gently snoring.

As he drove into Dossage, there was news on the car radio about striking miners throwing rocks through the windows of their former workmates. He met Jock at the school and they started out on foot for the scene of crime. Sandy took the time carefully, 8:21, on his watch when they left, and as they walked, at a deliberately normal pace, he asked Jock exactly what had gone so disastrously wrong when they had brought Martin into headquarters.

"A complete shambles! He simply refused to talk and there was nothing we could do to make him," Jock replied phlegmatically, chewing gum.

He felt uncomfortably hot, so he appreciated the moderate wind. He also felt slightly guilty finding himself admiring the beauty of cherry and almond blossom in the gardens.

34

Dossage was eight hundred feet above sea level and spring came late and lasted longer.

"How do you mean exactly, Jock? He must have communicated something?"

"He simply claimed that we brought him into head-quarters under duress and with no good reason and that if we wanted to discuss the matter further, we could do so through his lawyer."

There was no footpath, so they had to stand in a bramble hedge which had burst out over a tumble-down drystone wall, before risking a quick dash across the surprisingly busy road outside the picnic area.

"I wonder why he was so awkward?"

"Search me!"

"You see, I know him, Jock. I saw quite a lot of him about three years ago on an evening course on art and philosophy at the university."

They entered the picnic area through a wide gateway marked by upended granite paving-setts and paused under a coppice of young birches. Jock frowned, stroked his chin, then remarked:

"That was what Meadows was worried about. Playing our hand too soon as far as Martin was concerned."

"Meadows!" Sandy exclaimed, more to himself than to Jock.

"That's right. But you know the super when he gets an idea into his head. If you ask me, there's no love lost between him and Martin. You know how he feels about intellectuals. I think he got really mad. It was straight after we got the post-mortem report."

They continued to walk up an undulating incline of grass dotted with forget-me-nots. They walked in silence, during which Sandy considered Jock's explanation. Georgy losing control of himself? Georgy so indignant after reading the post-mortem report? It was possible, he told himself. But he didn't know if he quite believed it. There was something

35

about Georgy all right. It was certainly true that he had noticed a definite edginess about Georgy ever since he had returned from his holiday – something now about the memory he had of him, standing with his back to them both, staring out of the schoolroom window with yesterday's light spilling back over his shoulder.

They were following a definite path. The ground sloped down again. There was slightly brown grass on the edge of the slope above a thin coppice of trees, a much thicker and more mature coppice to their right, then a low stone wall, a stile made of those same reused granite setts as the outer gate posts, followed by the wood proper. Sandy immediately looked at his watch – 8:40. Allowing for the fact that Angela Hawksworth's home was about the same distance away on the other side of the school, and her mother had said that she had left home on the evening of the murder a little after 7:30 – assuming 7:15 – and a walking-time which he now estimated at thirty minutes, then she must have arrived at this spot very close to 7:45. This was the last occasion when she might easily have been spotted; minutes later she would have been completely hidden by the wood proper.

They entered the wood, which was thickly forested with oak, beech and pine.

"The video showed a great deal of blood."

"That's right," said Jock, as they stood gazing down on the marked spot under the twenty-foot holly. Sunlight filtered easily down through the pale-green as yet immature leaves.

"So it would have been obvious if there had been a chase. If she had had the opportunity to run?"

"As far as we could determine, it was only from the nearest point on the path to here. Twenty yards at the outside."

"You searched very hard for the murder weapon?"

"We searched and we didn't find it. But in a wood this size –."

"Funny!" Sandy touched his forehead, stared at bluebells growing through the remains of last year's leaves, acorns, pine cones.

"Why do you say that?" asked Jock, following him as he wandered about a little, then retraced his steps in the direction of the path.

"I was trying to think it through, Jock. Maybe somebody saw her cross the picnic area. From there, crossing the grass, she would have been visible, even from the road. Not a sex attacker, according to the report. Yet somebody who definitely knew her – was probably aware of the fact that she was coming to this very spot."

He pondered it again, turning full circle, moving the brown fronds of last year's ferns with the top of his shoe. "How far would you say we've come into the wood?"

"Four hundred yards or thereabouts."

"Completely invisible from the road here. Invisible to anyone even at thirty yards' distance. If you look at the nearest spot on the path – . I haven't the slightest doubt about it – this is where she confronted her murderer. On the path. So either she expected to see him there and was taken by surprise by the attack, or she was followed and somehow noticed something, she saw something – something which frightened her. Something which made her run. She ran off the path – "

They were walking again: back into the wood to the side of the path, to the spot where, if you looked carefully enough, you could see residual brown stains within the roped-off circle under the holly tree.

"So why didn't she run back the way she had come? She ran blindly into the wood."

"What would you expect, Jock? Whoever it was must have been facing her from this direction. Perhaps from a short distance away. Ten, twenty yards. Impossible to dodge round him. But not blind terror, not necessarily. There would have been no point running along the path, that would only take her deeper into the wood. Off at a right angle, then she might lose him and make her way round him on to the way she had come."

"Whatever way you look at it, it didn't do her any good," said Jock phlegmatically.

Sandy stood very still. There had been a soft crashing noise in the undergrowth, something following them. Now, with a chuckle, he caught a glimpse of a bright-yellow triangle of beak – a blackbird!

"Something bothers me about those wounds, Jock. Did you notice anything unusual about them? You saw the pattern."

"Homicidal maniac, in my opinion."

"Perhaps." He clenched his teeth, not in anger but in absolute concentration. "I must have a word with Doctor Atkins. As soon as we get back to the old school."

6

From the scene of crime they walked a good deal more briskly back to the old school, where Jock bowed out of the case. Sandy gave Georgy Barker a curious glance as Jock left and Georgy watched Sandy with equal curiosity as he telephoned the medico-legal centre in the city centre only to discover that Doctor Atkins wasn't in. The forensic pathologist's secretary suggested that he try again in two hours.

Sandy spent a couple of hours reading carefully through the written statements taken by the murder squad in their door-to-door enquiries. Nothing dramatic came of this, although there were a number of minor points of interest and one important omission. Nobody had witnessed Paul Thorpe leave the village with his friends, but there had been two or three possible sightings of two leather-clad motor-cyclists later in the evening.

At 11:50 he telephoned the medico-legal centre again and managed to get hold of Doctor Atkins. Once again Georgy made a point of listening in to his conversation from a few feet away, his enormous thighs splayed and his pipe billowing smoke, as Sandy spoke urgently into the mouth-piece.

"In the post-mortem report on Angela Hawksworth you mentioned that the remains of her last meal were still in the stomach and had spilled out as a result of her wounds – so you would know exactly what kind of meal she had eaten?"

"Yes. Some sort of vegetable salad."

"Could you tell me how recently she had eaten it?"

"I would think no more than an hour before her death."

"You can be that precise?"

"The stomach is completely empty of a meal four hours after you have eaten it, Chief Inspector. In fact the food is processed even more rapidly than that, the part lying nearest to the exit from the stomach being pushed through in little fits and starts quite soon after eating it. Virtually all her meal was still fresh and intact within the stomach itself – it was so fresh you could have put it on a plate and eaten it."

Sandy winced at the sight of the sandwiches and coffee just deposited on the table close to the telephone. "So all we have to do is find out when she took the meal?"

"That was why I took such care about the food. Find the time of that meal and you will be able to pinpoint the time of the murder much more accurately."

"That shouldn't prove too difficult. Just one further query, doctor. I wonder if you've kept a sample of the stomach contents for further analysis?"

"That is routine."

"So – no problem if we wanted it examined by an expert? I mean, you wouldn't mind, would you, if we took that out of your hands?"

"How do you mean – are you suggesting some kind of toxin? We've done all of the routine toxicological screens on the serum and it proved entirely negative."

"No – I don't mean toxicology, Doctor. I was thinking more of a botanical expert. An identification of the actual plants that formed the salad."

There was a pause, during which the doctor considered what this could mean, and during which Georgy Barker gave a slow blink, with a curious half smile.

"Very well – if that's what you want. No need for you to arrange it – we'll do it for you. We'll liaise with the forensic botanists in the North Yorkshire Laboratory and get back to you."

"That would be very helpful. Thanks a lot!"

"But just before you hang up, can you be any more specific – I mean, precisely what are we asking them to be on the lookout for?"

"If you don't mind, I'd prefer it if we just left that open for the moment."

Immediately he put the phone down, Georgy murmured with deceptive calm through a mouthful of tea and Cheddar sandwich: "So you're already on to the village apothecary!"

"How did you guess?"

"An hour tasting the bitter with the locals in the Drunken Duck."

"You never mentioned it before."

"Your investigation, Sandy. Yours to conduct in your own sweet irregular fashion. Meadows's very own instructions. Nice touch that – about the meal. Hadn't so much as occurred to me." Georgy nodded his appreciation, then lifted his pint mug of tea to his lips and imbibed thirstily.

Sandy wasn't hungry. He tested the cup of tea, eyed somewhat sceptically Georgy's clowning performance then picked up the receiver again and dialled the number of police headquarters, where he asked to be put through to his secretary.

"Mrs Parks!" He sounded pleased just to hear her sigh of recognition. "Glad I managed to catch you before your lunch."

"Now listen to me, Mr Woodings – before you start! People have been calling for you. You're very popular this morning."

"Never mind the calls, Mrs Parks, there's something I want you to do for me."

"Not another of your favours!"

"How did you guess, Mrs Parks? Just a little trip to the central reference library. Two kinds of books, both from the botanical section. The first a good compendium of all of the common or garden British plants and flowers. Wild flowers – and I don't mean the horticultural variety."

"And the second?" she sighed, while he visualised her look of resignation over the spectacles halfway down her nose.

"Anything you can find on herbalism. Particularly books of the older sort. Have a word with the assistants. Not the modern prissy stuff like dandelion leaves and so on. Try to get hold of something from the days when they really believed in the stuff."

There came the clatter of Georgy banging his pipe carelessly on the table, then a blowing action of those floridly veined cheeks as he scooped the contents of the bowl into the palm of one spade-like hand, before allowing the ash to fall in a fine shower downwards into the green cube of the bin.

Sandy had a second cup of tea before walking out into a warm noon sun with less breeze than earlier in the morning. He took the right turn immediately outside the old school, and had time to look at the village church with churchyard, immediately behind the old school. In architecture the whole complex was obviously contemporary, all late Georgian. He then passed some very old stone cottages, a stretch of brick-built houses, flats and bungalows, before reaching the edge of the village proper. Here, a matter of only three hundred yards from where they had set up their murder headquarters, the road dipped and narrowed and a sign indicated a footpath which ran over a wooden stile into a rough hillocky field to his right. Climbing over the stile, he walked along by a tall and ancient hedge, followed a straight path strewn with cowpats, then emerged on the main road again in a deep hollow about two hundred yards further on. He heard running water – it sounded like a small waterfall – to his right, while immediately ahead was a small stone-built bridge over a wide flat-bottomed stream. Curiosity took him as far as the bridge, where he looked down into the water, followed it across to the right of the road and placed the small waterfall above what must have been a watermill, before retracing his steps fifty yards, to find himself standing precisely where Georgy Barker had stood on tip-toe in order to inspect the Martins' house.

It was one of the most attractive older properties in the village, situated diagonally opposite the wood where the murder had taken place. Presumably there was some connection with the stream lower down, because there was a large fish-pond in the garden in which live fish could be seen rippling the surface. A tarmac tennis court was strewn with the yellow fall of forsythia blossom, which had also blown into the poorly tended pond, giving an impression of rakish neglect which seemed true, too, of the large garden which surrounded the house on all four sides. Overgrown docks poked their seedspikes out of the lawn, nettles abounded near fences and walls, weeds sprouted between the white marble chippings on the paths, giving the house and surrounding grounds a strange, even suffering presence.

The house itself faced away from the path at a slight angle, so that the front door wasn't quite visible from the gateway. He opened the gate in the finely masoned gritstone wall, walked past the fish-pond and a rockery, which had been quite invisible from the outside because it was immediately under the wall and to his right as he came through the gate. He could only appraise things fleetingly before climbing a step and then pressing the bell on the white-painted heavily panelled door, which was placed eccentrically in the front façade between three square massive stone-jambed and bowed windows.

The woman who opened the door was tall, with straight brown hair tied back severely from a high forehead. Around her neck on a black string was a monocle, which she held with incongruously damaged and roughened fingers. Her voice was unfriendly as she demanded to know what he wanted.

"Chief Inspector Woodings." He handed her his identification card, then asked if he could speak with Mr Martin.

"Have you either a search warrant or an arrest warrant?"

"No – but I believe Mr Martin will agree to see me," he replied firmly, without impoliteness.

"On what grounds, might I ask?"

"On the grounds that Bertrand Russell would have found a more subtle trick than drunken brawling to outmanoeuvre a hard-pressed police force engaged in a murder enquiry," he answered with a faint smile.

Simon Martin himself appeared behind her, glanced back up the path to confirm that Sandy was alone and then turned his attentions to the policeman.

"You look familiar."

"My name is Alexander Woodings. You did your best to tutor me in the philosophy of twentieth-century art some three years ago."

"But that was Woodings the pupil and this is Woodings the policeman?"

"Detective Chief Inspector," he acknowledged calmly. "I'd appreciate it if I could come in and have a talk with you – without the histrionics."

"That's fine, Lennie." Martin nodded to the reluctant woman. "Please come in. And I do apologise to your people for the trouble I caused a few days ago. Although I won't pretend that I didn't enjoy it at the time."

He led Sandy Woodings into a large high-ceilinged drawing-room with the original Georgian wall-panelling, doors, ornate ceiling mouldings and rosettes over two enormous cut-glass chandeliers.

"This is my wife, Caroline." He introduced a tall auburn-haired woman with brown eyes and a slightly startled expression. "You've already met her sister, and our resident potter, Eleanor Standon" – he indicated the woman with the rough hands and monocle, who had followed them into the room. "Two other members of our little family" – he inhaled with a loud sniff, gesturing at the eccentrically dressed man who had pestered Georgy Barker outside the garden wall – "Mr Ronald Wadsworth – who has an interest in blowing glass. And Miss Virginia Lauderman, who changes her mind so often with regard to her talents that I'm never sure in which direction she is at present projecting herself."

Virginia Lauderman was in her mid-forties. She was sitting on the arm of the chair from which Mrs Martin had half risen during her introduction. In many ways she contrasted sharply with Mrs Martin, with her prematurely white hair, pale-hazel eyes, and man's shirt tucked into faded corduroys.

Before leaving the room in Simon Martin's wake, Sandy stole a second glance at Mrs Martin. She was maturely attractive, with a longish, but delicately oval face in which a fleshy lower lip pouted in curiosity as she stared after him, fully meeting his gaze. Once again he detected that same sense of fright, of something vulnerable, in her dark-brown eyes.

Without asking, Martin poured him a whisky when they were sitting in what was furnished as both office and study. Hundreds of books on art lined the walls and there was room for three large mahogany desks, on which, partly hidden by mountains of computer paper, were scattered two electronic typewriters, several different makes of expensive computer together with colour monitors and at least two equally expensive dot matrix printers. A closer look at the computer paper revealed strange patterns in bright colours. If these were works of art, then Virginia Lauderman – he assumed they must be hers – must be very prolific, because the paper was everywhere in extraordinary abundance, over desks, chairs, and in piles everywhere on the floor.

"Ice in the fridge there." Simon Martin pointed in the vague direction. "Water in the tap." He sat with his legs crossed and leaned his chair back against the wall, examining Sandy Woodings, as if appraising this person he had once known, and thought he had understood, in this new-found light. He seemed more amused than worried or unnerved by the detective role.

"Would you mind telling me first the reason for your earlier awkwardness?"

"I am known to be an awkward man. It wasn't out of character." He didn't actually smile – Sandy remembered him as a man who never did – but his eyes performed what could be taken as an equivalent, as he took an affable swig from his glass.

"You were drunk and deliberately provocative. Belligerent, according to Inspector Andrews's report."

"Who's denying it? So – fine me and be done with it!"

Sandy ignored the whisky, noticing how carelessly Martin dumped his glass on one of the works of computer art.

"Would you care to tell me what your relationship was with Angela Hawksworth?"

"Certainly. Our relationship was the time-honoured and hallowed one of artist and model."

"And what kind of relationship is that?"

"Let's put it in a simpler way then – businessman and his most cherished asset."

"Here in the village the generally held notion is more of lovers."

"Lovers! Nice kind of word, isn't it! You're a man of the world. Artists and their models have been known to share a carnal relationship."

"Are you admitting such a relationship existed between you?"

"I'm admitting nothing, my dear Detective Chief Inspector Woodings."

"Inspector – or Mr Woodings – would be a reasonable

enough way for you to address me for the purposes of this interview."

"And you can play by my rules or you can sod off in the same direction as your monstrous superintendent."

Sandy touched his forehead with a thoughtful index finger. For the moment, Martin was perfectly right. They were in his house. Taking him into headquarters had achieved absolutely nothing. His posture, the mischievous look in those dark-blue eyes, the strongly bowed shoulders and hard muscular triangle of neck now tensed to balance his heavy broad-browed head made it a matter of common sense to play ball with him, at least for the moment. Simon Martin merely balanced his large glass of whisky in one powerful labourer's hand and regarded him.

"How long had she been your model?"

"About two years."

"How often did she come here to model for you?"

"When I was in the mood, about every second day. If I was really flowing, daily."

"Did she come here on Monday May 7th?"

"No. She last modelled for me the day before."

"On a Sunday?"

"The days of the week mean nothing to me. She did a couple of hours' modelling. An ideas session only."

Sandy gazed at Martin evenly, eye to eye. "The obvious question then. Where were you for the whole of the evening of Monday May 7th?"

"As you very well know, I was here. My own home and Englishman's castle!"

"With every single other resident to prove it?"

"Not quite! Eleanor was in London – trying to flog dishes to Harrods."

"That's very convenient for all concerned, isn't it?"

Martin actually chuckled. "Bloody convenient – yes!"

Sandy hesitated, observing Martin even closer. "When you last saw her, on the Sunday, did she seem different in any way? Did she say anything that struck you as odd? Did she seem unduly nervous? Anything at all that might not have made sense at the time but which might have meant something in the light of her subsequent murder?"

"Not a thing!"

"I take it that her death and the manner of her death came as a shock to you?"

"A great shock – naturally!"

"Because you had lost your most cherished asset? Or because you were fond of her?"

"For both of those reasons." He allowed his chair to fall noisily on to its front legs. "And for another very good reason, which might sound more plausible to the prosaic minds down at your central headquarters – money! The death of Angela will cost me a great deal of money. You wouldn't have the slightest conception of how much money."

"I'm willing to be educated."

"I'll do better than explain. I'll show you. My workshop is only through the back door." He downed his second glass of whisky, deposited the cut-glass tumbler on the floor, jumped with a lithe nervous energy to his feet and led the way through the rear hallway into the back yard, which was a mason's workshop. They had to wind their way between blocks of recently quarried pale-cream marble. Sandy noticed a label, "Firenze", stuck on one side of a massive cube. Martin had his own mounted diamond-edged cutting wheel, trolleys, a winch cantilevered out from the gable end of a large shed, which, judging by the door and windows, had once been a labourer's cottage older than the main house. Once inside, Sandy could see that the upper floor had been completely removed, exposing the massive oak purlins and rafters supporting pegged roof-stones. Underneath this high roof were pieces of sculpture in varying degrees of completion – Martin obviously worked on many different subjects at the same time.

How distorting the high-arched room was, how much smaller Simon Martin looked in here, an effect which was accentuated by his slightly stooped build and the massive sloping shoulders. In fact he was a little taller than average; it was the gnome-like build and the slightly tensed crouch that gave the impression.

"In your lessons on art, did you come across a Victorian oil painter called William Etty?"

"I'm not interested in William Etty or Victorian art right now."

"Believe me, you should be very interested."

Sandy looked thoughtful, but allowed Martin to talk on.

"Etty was a native of York, as I am myself. Do you know what he was famous for? My home city's most illustrious son and artist? He painted naked young women. It was a thing he did well. He didn't seem to paint anything else, so he had plenty of practice. Naturally I was acquainted with the work of William Etty long before I started as a student at the Slade. We had no money. There were no oil paintings on the walls of my parents' two-up two-down terrace cottage. But I saw them in the galleries, the museums. That shrewd Victorian – how I hated him. Loathed his work with every artistic fibre of my being. Black-haired young women with those rounded pink Victorian bums and tits. He found every excuse to squeeze as many different poses, in all degrees of erotic appeal, on to his canvases."

"Exactly how is this relevant to Angela Hawksworth's murder?"

"Do you want to understand my relationship with Angela or not?"

"Painting naked females – that can't surely have been very unusual among artists, even in Victorian England?"

"I think you're deliberately playing the Philistine, just to draw me. Of course the study of the nude has always been quite basic. What my younger self objected to was the hypocrisy – the sheer massive volume of titillating masculine hypocrisy. Etty's pictures were bought to be hung behind discreet curtains by day and leered at under gaslight by night."

"I think I have been very patient with you, Mr Martin."

"For God's sake – it was a betrayal of the very notion of art. Can you understand that?"

Sandy Woodings sighed. "So – I understand."

"Piffle! So much of what the young Simon Martin thought about such things was simply that. I was so pissed off with the nude, I went through an abstract phase. I was successful at it, too. It made me a reputation and quite a lot of money. But I was being false to myself. Some stupid kind of reaction – rich Victorians in their white beards, concealing the truth about themselves behind velvet curtains."

"So what's the point?"

"The point is that I allowed an emotional reaction to cloud my judgement. I was wrong. It took me until middle age to realise it. I found that I had learnt more from the despised canvass of that Victorian goat than all I had picked up from teachers and contemporaries at the Slade or elsewhere. A rediscovery of sexuality – that's the honest truth! I had rediscovered just how important balls are to the art of sculpture at a time when straight life had become unfashionable. That was what Angela Hawksworth meant to me!"

"You seem to have gone a very roundabout way just to tell me that you fancied her."

"I give up. Why don't you just believe in your own eyes!"

Martin pulled a sheet back, which had been covering a life-size representation of Eve. The figure was sculpted with the fluency and detail of a previous age from a large block of the creamy Florentine marble Sandy had seen outside. Angela Hawksworth had been a beautiful young woman. She stood, half leaning against the stem of a giant fern, her head demurely inclined downwards at an angle. Her long hair was swept back over her forward-projecting right shoulder and was held in place by a wide band – very similar to the ribbon found on her dead body – which circled her high forehead. Apart from the band, she was completely naked, and it wasn't that kind of prurient nakedness with hands in contrived poses or cunningly placed pieces of foliage. The small mounds of her girlish breasts were highlighted by the pose, as was her full hip, pushed outwards as if she had been lost in some exotic sexual fantasy, her right hand held down with palm outstretched, parallel to the ground, in some play at resistance.

"Come on then, Woodings – immediate impressions?"

"She certainly was beautiful."

"What you man is erotic. Voluptuous, for God's sake! Why are you so stubborn you won't honestly admit it?"

Sandy knew very well that Martin was right, but he said nothing.

"Can you honestly refuse to understand my point?"

"Honesty is an ideal close to any detective's heart, Mr Martin. While we're concerned with honesty, will you answer me honestly? Did you kill Angela Hawksworth?"

As they had been talking, a light had been gathering in Martin's eyes. There was an extraordinary aggression now in his voice and he stared at Sandy like a madman. "You wound me. You really do. You and everybody like you. Damn you, Woodings, for the stupid man you are! Damn your stupidity. Damn you all!"

7

Friday, May 18th: he was beginning to understand just what the assistant chief constable, Meadows, had been worried about. The case shouldn't have been over-complex. But Martin made it complex.

The conversation with Martin was still on his mind the following morning, when he arrived at headquarters at 8:30, parking his black Capri in the spot specifically reserved for him, ignoring the lift and taking the stairs two at a time.

"What have you done to your hair, Mrs Parks?" he demanded, in genuine surprise.

"Never mind my hair," she retorted, pushing her glasses back up her nose. "I've brought all of those peculiar books I managed to find in the central library – which, I might add, cost me three-quarters of my lunch hour yesterday."

He took the five books, spreading the pile out on the desk surface, and opening each at the introductory pages: all except one were modern, printed in the last ten years, with photographs of assistant professors of botany or knowledgeable young women in ethnic dresses. Two of these were fine, exactly what he wanted from the botanical point of view, but only one had the kind of herbal information he was after and this was the most unlikely of them, an old volume with a soft grey cover, which had been so much handled that he couldn't even read the author's name on the cover, but found it inside, on the page facing a photograph of an elderly gentleman with a white beard

52

and a thinning high forehead, capped by white curls. Richard Lawrence Hool, Fellow of the National Association of Medical Herbalists. The book had been published by the Lancashire branch of the association to which this august old gentleman belonged, through "subscriptions of its members, together with those of a few friends" and printed at the *Visiter*'s Works, Tulketh Street, Southport.

Now he knew the reason Mrs Parks was hovering over him: she was delighted with herself and this particular find. "You said you wanted one of the older volumes – the librarian dug this one out from the basement of the reference section."

"Wonderful, Mrs Parks. Just the job. Precisely what I was looking for."

"Go ahead. Have a good look! I guarantee it will make you laugh."

He continued to browse through it, glancing through the section headings. Section one was labelled, *RAMBLES OF A BOTANIST, FROM JANUARY TO OCTOBER: What He May Find.* He scanned the next page or two, found the month he was looking for.

In May we find the oak trees in full bloom and a large number of the speedwells, the bird's eye primrose, the dwarf valerian and the hawthorn, and our common chickweed with its beautiful star-like flowers.

Confirming Mrs Parks's prediction, he laughed heartily. With some pride, Mrs Parks added, "The illustrations in it are very basic – that's the reason I collected some of the more modern ones. So you could look up whatever you wanted in glorious Technicolor."

"Let me give you a big kiss, Mrs Parks. As soon as you have made me an appointment with Dr Atkins."

"When do you want to see him and where?" Mrs Parks made a play of hovering within easy distance of the door, watching him over the spectacles which had once more slid down her nose.

"At the mortuary. Sometime – any reasonable time – this afternoon. Tell him I'd like to inspect the body with him. And could you please remind him about the analysis of the salad."

"The analysis of the salad," she repeated in a slow monotone, scribbling in the pad with the gold-plated ball-point he had given her on her silver wedding anniversary two years ago.

"And where do I get hold of you later on this morning when I need to let you know his reply?"

"The murder headquarters at the old school in Dossage." This time he chased her successfully through the door, laughing to find himself outside and unexpectedly wet from a sudden light May shower.

By the time he arrived in the village the rain had stopped and the sun was out again, glistening in the cut grass and in the new leaves hanging down, like gloved fingers, from the sycamores.

He took the road south of the old school, at right angles to the path which led to the Martins' house, and entered a much more modern part of the village, where the recent fall of rain still shone on the tarmacdam and the dug-over gardens had the dark wet richness of Christmas pudding. Before going home the previous evening he had carefully read through the statements of the Hawksworth family, and this was his first opportunity to talk with them personally. He parked his car in front of their small semi-detached house, shook hands with them as he entered the front door and was invited to sit with them in a lounge which occupied all of the ground floor. A door at the back led into a small kitchen extension.

"I'm puzzled by the fact that you never reported Angela missing when she failed to return that evening." He addressed himself particularly to the girl's father, a man who couldn't have been much older than forty, with an even more youthful profile. Though balding, there was enough of his once fair hair to show from whom Angela had inherited her colouring.

"I've been kicking myself about that ever since, sir," he said quietly, in that apologetic tone that people so often adopted under these circumstances.

"Please, Mr and Mrs Hawksworth – believe me when I tell you that we're not in the least interested in moralising. Nothing like that. It doesn't matter. What matters above all now is the truth. Just the simple truth – that's what we owe to your daughter. Now tell me – perhaps you, Mrs Hawksworth – why you didn't call the police when she failed to come home that evening? Was it because it had happened several times before?"

She nodded, with her lower lip turned inwards and tears in her eyes.

"Did you think you knew where she was then?"

"We weren't sure. We talked about it. If she hadn't contacted us by lunchtime the next day. . ."

"Did you think she was with Paul Thorpe?"

"That's what we weren't sure about," Mr Hawksworth interrupted. "She was going through one of those very difficult phases lately. She always seemed to be going through some kind of phase, did Angela. Our other daughter, Monica, has always been much easier to manage."

He had seen the younger sister, a slightly built teenager, with the same fair hair as her sister, but not nearly as attractive, who had rushed upstairs as he had entered the hallway. Now he looked directly into Mrs Hawksworth's eyes for a moment, and then away, noticing that she had the same slight build as the younger daughter. Angela Hawksworth, with her extraordinary good looks, must have seemed both unusual and awkward in this household. As awkward as a gifted child among uneducated parents. He nodded sympathetically.

55

"I'm sorry to have to ask this kind of question. But did Angela have any enemies? Any reason why somebody should dislike her to this extent?"

"We've asked ourselves who could do that! We've asked ourselves over and over. But we could think of nobody."

"Her relationship with Paul Thorpe – tell me a little more about that, Mrs Hawksworth."

"It's been something between them on and off for years. At first we thought it was a very good thing. Angela seemed to settle for a little while. She had pictures of him up in her bedroom. Just a minute!" The mother dashed out of the room and upstairs, with tears close to her eyes. While she was away, he asked Mr Hawksworth how fit Angela had been, had she been an athletic girl at school.

"We're all that kind of family, sir." He nodded proudly. "Both of my girls did well at running and sports generally. Angela was the captain of the hockey team all the way through from the juniors."

Mrs Hawksworth reappeared with a photograph. It showed Angela and Paul Thorpe as youngsters – they couldn't have been more then fourteen or fifteen years old, with the boy's arm, heavy even then, round the girl's shoulders. They wore punk clothes and had the fashionable surly expressions, Angela with her head inclined to the side, her eyes slanted towards the camera with calculated disdain.

"Posing even then!" remarked her mother.

"What do you mean by that, Mrs Hawksworth?"

"That notion she developed. She thought she was going to become a famous model. That's the reason that horrible man encouraged her!"

"Simon Martin – is that who you mean, Mrs Hawksworth?"

She nodded.

"Would you mind if I took the picture with me – I'll let you have it back safe and sound within a couple of days?"

She nodded, overcome by emotion.

"I'm still far from clear about what happened – between Angela and Paul Thorpe. When did they break up and why?"

It was Mr Hawksworth who replied. "They often had rows. We were never sure it wasn't just another of them, maybe lasting a bit longer."

"When did the present one happen then?"

"Months ago."

"How many months – I'm sorry to have to press you, but it might be important."

"I couldn't be sure. Months. What would you think, Marion?"

Mrs Hawksworth agreed with him, shaking her head. "I know they still saw each other now and then. I think they just met so they could argue."

"An important question, so please think carefully about it. When did she last go out with Paul?"

"Not for many weeks. She rarely mentioned him at all lately."

"She didn't mention meeting him – or his approaching her at any time, say in the week prior to her death?"

"No, sir."

"When did she first meet Mr Martin?"

"I don't know that for sure, either, Chief Inspector, because she went very quiet and secretive about it. But it was at least two years ago."

"I don't want you to go away with the wrong idea about our Angela, sir!" Mrs Hawksworth interrupted. "But girls can be difficult. I think she wanted to talk to us about it. I often thought that. But she knew that we wouldn't take to it, nothing between her and Martin. There were rows enough about it at first, when she did talk, so she had reason to become secretive."

"You knew that she was modelling for him – that she was modelling for sculptures?"

"Yes. The whole village knew."

The man added, "And we're heartily ashamed of that."

"There's nothing to be ashamed of in that. Modelling is a perfectly respectably profession. She might even have been right. She might well have become famous in time too." Sandy realised he was saying too much and blinked, then nodded before changing the subject.

"This is another very important question, so please take your time and think about it. To your knowledge, when did she last go over to the Martins' house?"

"It was the day before. On the Sunday."

"How long did she stay there on the Sunday?"

"Just the morning. She came home for lunch."

"Are you absolutely certain she didn't go there, even briefly, on the Monday?"

"She stayed in all day Monday until after tea. It wasn't like her. We suspected something was up."

Once again, Sandy made a careful note in his book. He looked sympathetically towards the mother. "My next question may surprise you. You see, I don't know if you had some kind of knowledge, maybe an inkling at least – only I must be frank with you both and I have to ask it." He paused, weighing his words carefully. "Were you aware, Mr and Mrs Hawksworth, that Angela was three months pregnant?"

"Oh, no! Oh, Brian!"

"Then you didn't know. I am sorry, Mrs Hawksworth."

"Oh, come on, Marion, love. We both know she'd become very excitable. You noticed she was off her food in the morning and she was sick for days."

"Then you suspected?"

"I tried to ask her. I tried very hard with Angela." Mrs Hawksworth was weeping now, just weeping and shaking her head.

"You see, sir," said Mr Hawksworth earnestly, with his arm about his wife's shoulders, "Angela was such a lovely little girl. So beautiful. She was as pretty as an angel. But all it ever brought was heartbreak."

"I understand, Mr Hawksworth. Please don't distress yourself any further. In particular I see no reason why we should broadcast the fact that she was pregnant. If you wouldn't mind, I particularly have my reasons for wanting to keep that a secret among ourselves for the moment."

8

Sandy drove from the Hawksworths' home back to the old school, parked his car, walked back to the small semi-detached house again and then noted the time on his watch. As he had done in the company of Jock four days earlier, he then walked the distance from the semi-detached to the murder scene and timed it – thirty-five minutes.

Her mother had been very certain that Angela had left home between 7:00 and 7:10 in a determined frame of mind.

"Determined?" he had asked. "Yes," Mrs Hawksworth had replied with certainty. It was as if, she said, Angela had plucked up the courage to do something important. Whether pleasant or distasteful, Mrs Hawksworth simply did not know. There had been a single telephone call quite late the same afternoon, at about 5:15, which Angela had made a point of taking herself and about which she had seemed particularly vague. Mrs Hawksworth, who had been present in the living-room when Angela had taken the call, did not know who had been on the telephone, but she thought it had probably been a man's voice, judging from what little she could hear from five or six feet away. A man's voice on the telephone – had he been arranging a meeting then?

Was it as a result of that call that Angela had set out into the wood later in the evening? Had that call had something to do with the apparent resolve in her face noticed by her mother when she had left home?

The timing of the meal was a lot easier. She had sat down to eat at about 6:40, and had finished just before leaving the house. Taken with what Doctor Atkins had noted about the stomach contents, this pointed to her having been killed about an hour later – say 8:15 p.m. at the latest. Which fitted in nicely with his timing of the walk from her home to the wood. And it was somewhat earlier than they might have assumed from initial impressions. Parts of the picture were definitely coming together. Not some tramp chancing on an attractive young victim by accident. No sexual assault at all. Somebody who knew she was pregnant – therefore somebody who knew Angela very intimately, and hence somebody from this village. Which in its turn created two prime suspects, Thorpe and Martin.

He gazed at the two teenagers in the photograph, two youngsters who had met at school, liked one another, fallen in love. Something terrible had happened. But he didn't know exactly what. Something that had eventually resulted in murder?

Replacing the photograph in his wallet, he climbed out of his car and entered the medico-legal centre. Passing the woman on the desk with a wave, he walked unannounced into the room with its banks of the dead all tidily placed away in their stainless-steel-fronted drawers. Doctor Atkins hailed him from an adjoining door, told him immediately that there had been no news as yet from the botanists, and then took him through to the mortuary proper with its steel drain in the centre of the floor, where he had arranged for the body of Angela Hawksworth to be put out, covered only by a large green sheet.

"Something in your report, Doctor," Sandy remarked, inspecting the naked and crudely stitched up remains. "Since Mrs Pendle – the old girl who found the body – didn't touch her at all, yet you made a point of remarking that somebody, presumably her killer, turned her to face

61

away from him. I'm intrigued by that little performance at the end of all that carnage. What do you make of it?"

"Possibly because he wanted to look at her dead body and yet not have to face her, as it were?"

"I think the same, but it's strange, don't you think, Doctor?"

"I've come across stranger."

Sandy elevated his eyebrows, with a perplexed look in his blue eyes. "Perhaps you could explain something else to me. The wounds on her back – you have gone on record as declaring that these were the first to be inflicted. Can you be sure? Or to put it another way, why are you so sure on that point, doctor?"

"If ever you have the misfortune to have a knife thrust into you, Chief Inspector, then you may be certain that you will bleed. If you are alive at the time the blade cuts your flesh, not only will you bleed externally, but also internally. Into the wound itself. We can see this quite easily under the microscope if we take a tissue section of the margins of the wound. In the wounds on her back there is undoubtedly a surrounding tissue reaction. Ipso facto – she was alive when these were inflicted."

Sandy ignored the mildly sarcastic humour of the doctor. "Is that all you've got?"

"No. Those wounds also showed evidence of tearing at their edges. The unfortunate girl was still alive when they were inflicted. My guess would be that she attempted to move even as the weapon was inserted."

"I see." He went back to the body and studied it carefully once more, before replacing the green sheet. "Yet her face is entirely unmarked."

"Yes, Chief Inspector!"

"Which is also interesting, Doctor?"

"Not particularly unusual in a stabbing."

"How big is a three-month pregnancy?"

"How high in the abdomen? Not very. Perhaps just

showing above the pubic bone – and then only to an expert."

"Yet her attacker managed to perforate it."

"With so many wounds about the lower abdomen, it would have been surprising if it hadn't been perforated."

"And all these wounds – the wounds over the abdomen – showed no evidence of what you call a tissue reaction?"

"I won't pretend that I have searched the margins of every individual wound. But not in any I tested – which was about one in five of the wounds, taking representative samples."

Sandy's enquiring eyes met those of Doctor Atkins for a moment. "Sorry to be so persistent – but one final question, while we're still in the presence of the body – those wounds on her back, the first wounds to be inflicted, could they have been inflicted by someone who actually stood to the front of her? Let's say a man were embracing her, the weapon concealed in his hand somehow. They embrace . . ."

"I've already given that some thought. Not outside the bounds of possibility – the wounds have come from above and to the girl's right-hand side. In an embrace, such as you suggest, one wouldn't even have to suppose a left-handed killer. The right hand, in such a close proximity, could be brought above and to her right – provided the blade of the weapon was adjacent to the little finger, when the thumb of the attacker's right hand could be used for additional force curled over the end of the handle."

He was still thinking about that, trying to imagine it, as he walked through the doors of the old school, where he was accosted by a highly excited Mrs Pendle, who had been waiting there for him.

Her expression was jubilant. When he invited her into one of the interview cubicles, she refused even to sit down, taking hold of him by the sleeve and tugging at him as if he were a dull-witted pet dog.

"Haven't you solved it yet? Don't you know who killed her yet?"

"What are you trying to tell me, Mrs Pendle?"

"I know who did it. I know who killed Angela!"

Sandy's eyes narrowed. He must have been touched by the same nervous energy as Mrs Pendle because he was standing too, each of them inclined towards the other across the surface of the small flimsy desk.

"Satan!" she announced triumphantly.

"Lord almighty!" He sat down, exhaling loudly through his nose.

"Oh, no! Not what you think. This is a different kettle of fish entirely. Satan is only what he calls himself. I've met him several times in the last few months. I wouldn't know what else to call him. A total stranger otherwise. But the only place I've ever met him is in that wood. Never seen anyone who looked more wicked than him in my life. He's the one all right. He did it, Chief Inspector!"

9

"He's tall, very tall, and scraggy – horrible black hair! It's rather long, like one of those hippies, but only over one half of his head, which I suppose is more like a Red Indian. Oh, and I shouldn't think he has known soap for weeks! Yes, over this half." Mrs Pendle indicated the region of her left temple.

"He's shaved the other side of his head?" Sandy asked mildly.

"No! The left side is the hairless side – I think. His hair is on the right side. The other side is revoltingly pink. Bald, yes, but not shaven." She shuddered. "He wears a long black coat down to his calves. And when he looks at you, his eyes look through you. Shall I tell you the one strange thing about him? Yes, the one thing that is the strangest thing about him is his voice. To hear him talk, you'd say he was quite well educated."

"No horns, Mrs Pendle?"

"You don't believe he even exists, do you?"

"I know a lot about you already, Mrs Pendle. Your husband came from Lancashire, with a name like Pendle. But your surname was Sedge before marriage. Sedge, an old village name. Linked with herbalism for generations."

"Yes, Mr Tricky-the-Loop! My family have lived in Dossage at least since the seventeenth century."

"A village girl is murdered. It couldn't possibly be a

village man who murdered her. So you put the blame on someone alien. Some ridiculous outsider."

"It's you who are being ridiculous. Do you know what your presence in this village is doing to people? You make everybody suspicious of everybody else, reporting all the old skeletons to your door-to-door inquisitors."

"Good day, Mrs Pendle!"

"Do you realise it will take years for all the dirt to settle?"

Angela Hawksworth's body was buried the day after he had inspected it at the mortuary. Sandy attended the funeral service in the village church just behind the centre in the old school. He noticed that Paul Thorpe was in attendance with a woman who must have been his mother. The absence of Simon Martin, or anyone else from his artistic household, was noticeable. After the service, which was followed by burial in the village cemetery, Sandy walked back to the old school and thought very hard over the latest unhelpful pile of statements taken in their continuing door-to-door enquiries.

He should bring Paul Thorpe into headquarters and personally question him. The timing, in relation to this morning's funeral, might be unfortunate, but it could equally serve a useful, if somewhat harsh, purpose. Thorpe had looked very emotional in the church. Sandy thought about it hard and long, feeling just a little emotional about things himself, then decided he first needed another look at the video tape of the doctor's examination of the scene of crime. When he found they didn't have it at the old school, he told them to get hold of it immediately and left the incident centre in a very impatient temper. He drove into his office at police headquarters in the city centre and tried hard to take an interest in the body of a tramp which had been discovered after two whole weeks, hidden under a pile of newspapers in a back yard only two hundred yards from the town hall. But he put the file to one side, idly opening the desk drawer containing the books on herbalism, and lifting the old herbalist's manual with its sea-grey cover on to the desk surface. He stared at it curiously once more: *Common Plants and Their Uses in Medicine.*

It had been a lovely morning for a funeral: a clear blue sky, the fourth in a row. He toyed with a white sealed envelope that had been in his possession for a full twenty-four hours, thought about Tom Williams, his sergeant and friend, who was recovering from a serious wound in his shoulder and who would be found from first light on his allotment.

On sudden impulse, he tossed his car keys into the air, caught them, strode briskly downstairs, got into his car and then drove, in that same restless mood, out of the city into the Rivelin valley.

"When can we expect you back in work, you idle bugger?" he groaned, physically exhausted from the very steep climb from the valley road to a high point on the allotment-blanketed slope.

"When the cows come home," said Tom, who was looking very relaxed in a short-sleeved cotton shirt with red and white stripes, his injured right arm nestling uselessly in one trouser pocket.

They sat out in the light, drinking tea that tasted all the better from having been brewed in the open air and poured into a couple of ex-army enamelled mugs.

"I could do with an old hand to figure out Georgy right now. He's been acting out of character ever since I came back from the holiday."

"You put his nose out of joint with the kidnappings case, that's what's the matter with Georgy."

"I'm not so sure. He's too thick-skinned to worry about it for six months. No! It's something more recent. Something relevant to right now. And Meadows calling me on the blower, even when I was on holiday!"

67

"It isn't my problem any more. Just look at that! I mean it – isn't it damned beautiful."

Sandy stared with wide-open eyes at the well-tended early growth on the allotment. It was beautiful all right. He could see that.

"You and me, Tom. How long have we been together? Right from when you took me under your wing as a raw inspector."

"Yeah! And then you moved above federation level and I stayed one of the boys," said Tom, cigarette hanging from his Hapsburg lower lip as he poured himself a generous top-up of tea.

Sandy knew that he felt good with Tom. That was all there was to it. The five years' difference in their ages, the difference in ranks, simply didn't matter. He nodded, because he could appreciate Tom's point of view: it was there in the blue sky and cabbage white butterflies looking for some nice green leaves.

"How long do you think you can keep this up, Tom?"

"Until the resurrection," replied Tom with conviction.

Watching Tom happy with his eighth of an acre, there was a sudden intense memory. A glimpse of a figure at the top of a darkened staircase. A cry of pain. Tom's pain. Tom who had probably saved Sandy's life by putting himself between him and a madman with a twelve-bore shotgun.

"And what about the eight months when the sun isn't shining?"

"You're wasting your time."

"I had to ask. You understand that." He grinned a little shyly, took an envelope from his inside pocket and held it out to Tom.

"What the hell – !"

"Go ahead – open it."

"Not until you tell me what it contains first!"

"It's from the top, Tom. The chief constable himself."

"What interest has he got in me?"

"Your six months on the sick is up. You have the choice, Tom. Retire – with a commendation – on a sergeant's pension. Or – "

"Or what?"

"Detective inspector!" Sandy nodded at the still unopened letter.

"Who the hell woud want an inspector with one arm?"

"I would, Tom."

Tom held the envelope tight in his closed fist and looked uncertainly at the rows of seedlings in front of the ramshackle greenhouse. "So – when and where do I start?"

"Straight away, if you wouldn't mind. There's a video sequence I need to see and I'd like you to see it too."

In a small room with drawn curtains they watched the recording of Chief Superintendent Georgy Barker and the tiny figure of Doctor Atkins arriving at the spot under the holly tree. The camera followed the doctor as he put on his gloves, then lifted the clothing to inspect the wounds over the back and, together with Georgy, turned the body over.

"Stop it there. Play it back thirty seconds," Sandy said urgently to the technician operating the machine.

"Look at that, Tom! What do you see?"

"A dead body," retorted Tom. "Blood-stains on the ground. Blood-stained clothes."

"That's just it. Blood-stains, Tom. Her dress is blood-stained low down at the front!"

"What does that mean?"

"It means that when some of those abdominal wounds were inflicted, there was enough of a heartbeat to make her bleed! She was alive. Alive, when she was stabbed low down in the abdomen."

"How do you mean? You mean – the pregnancy!"

"That's exactly what I mean. That whoever killed Angela Hawksworth not only knew she was pregnant, but also hated that fact enough to kill her."

*

Caroline Martin was just setting fragrant rosemary about the tulips that were already flowering in the old stone sink, when she saw the two detectives come in through the open gates. One of them she did not recognise, an older man of about fifty, with brushed-back grey curling hair and one arm in a sling inside his jacket, but she recognised Chief Inspector Woodings. Immediately their eyes met, she sensed danger in him and her heart immediately beat in a desperate and weakening palpitation and her mind went uselessly blank.

"Simon is in London," she managed to stammer, although she realised he must know already since permission had been required of the sergeant up at the school.

"Yes – we know about that, Mrs Martin! Let me introduce Sergeant Williams. It's you I want a word with – if you wouldn't mind?"

"Please come in," she murmured politely.

She ignored the presence of the sergeant, who appeared to be dumb anyway, and watched the chief inspector closely. His eyes wandered about her lounge. She noticed him glance towards the two tall windows. Perhaps it was because he knew what effect his presence had on her that he remained silent for so long just looking about the place, until she couldn't bear it any longer. She sat down in an armchair and spoke:

"You want to know where I was at the time poor Angela was killed?"

"We know where you were. You were here all evening, with everybody else except your sister, Miss Standon." He had terrifying eyes. Calm and blue. She wondered if they had checked up on Eleanor's alibi with the woman from Harrods, but he said nothing about that, simply watched her reaction.

"You think that's suspiciously simple, don't you, Mr Woodings?" She could feel the tremble in her voice.

"It's my job to suspect things," he replied, without attempting to alleviate her anxiety.

"I did not kill Angela. Nor can I believe that anybody in this household killed her."

His gaze was not so much belligerent as persistent. There was such a powerful concentration in his eyes that she was certain he could detect any lie instantly.

He said, "She came here very often over a period of two years – you must have got to know her quite well?"

"I'm afraid not. We hardly spoke. We didn't really hit it off – such a difference in our ages, of course."

"And she was just Simon's model?"

"Yes. That's what she was."

"Did you see her the last time she came here? I'm referring to the Sunday, the sixth of May."

"I can't remember if I saw her or not."

"Please try to remember, Mrs Martin."

"You see, she would simply walk round the house to the studio at the back if Simon had already arranged it. It would have been so ordinary."

"Let's try going through everything you did on that Sunday morning."

"There's no need. I do believe that I remember. I did see her. Yes, I saw her arrive. She looked in at one of the windows for Simon and when she failed to see him in the drawing-room, she walked straight round the back."

"At precisely what time, Mrs Martin?"

"I should say – yes, about ten in the morning."

"And what time did she leave?"

"I'm not certain – "

"A whole day? Part of a day?"

"Simon had a meal with us at 1:30. She must have left before then."

"And she did not come here on the Monday – Monday the seventh?"

"Not to my knowledge, no."

71

"But you couldn't be sure, since she could have come here and walked round to the studio at the back of the house without your seeing her?"

"I am sure."

"Why are you so sure?"

"I – I usually knew when she was here."

"I see."

Her brown eyes regarded him, but she made no comment.

"I'm interested in the fact that you all manage to live here as a sort of family."

"Yes, we do."

"And it comes off – it works?"

"Is there any reason why it shouldn't?" Caroline Martin thanked God for this upsurge of anger in her.

"I could think of many potential reasons."

"No doubt you could."

"Your husband is an unusual man."

"Simon is gifted."

"It isn't always easy living with the gifted, is it, Mrs Martin?"

"No – it isn't!" How did he know everything? Everything!

"Mr Martin's relationship with the murdered girl – "

"Relationship?"

"I'm sorry, but I must ask for the simple truth. Did he love her?"

"Love is a strong word for it. I simply don't know if he loved her."

"I don't believe you're being truthful with me, Mrs Martin."

She couldn't bring herself to answer. How could she explain to this policeman that he had touched on the one subject that mattered to her? That she felt so strongly about the meaning of that simple word.

"He is your husband."

"Yes." She nodded. "Yes! But I've forgotten my manners. Perhaps you would both like a cup of tea?"

She had taken him by surprise. He would have liked a simple cup of tea. In that instant she realised, incredibly – no! Surely not! Yet the only alternative explanation was that it actually pained him to say no to a cup of tea.

"What exactly do you do in the household, Mrs Martin?"

"I did train at the Slade, like my husband. But I'm not in his class, of course. I help my sister, Eleanor, with the pottery side and generally enjoy performing all of those menial duties covered by the term housewife." She shrugged her shoulders, with a slightly bruised smile.

"How long have you been married to Simon?"

"Seventeen years next month."

"No children?"

"I often tell myself that it's a step further than Van Gogh managed to achieve."

"Van Gogh?"

"Just a personal thing, Chief Inspector. Of all the artists who have ever lived, I admire him the most. You asked about love. No human being has known more of love at its most vulnerable. You only have to look at a single picture by him."

Was she imagining it, or had his voice become a little gentler? "If I remember my art correctly, it cost him his life?"

"Yes."

"You're very clear about what you mean by love? Do you love your husband in this simple way?"

The respite had been a trick, a temporary thing. She couldn't conceal the shock at this brazenly bare question. Her fingers were trembling. She had to answer. There was no point whatsoever in trying to bluff it out.

"I – I don't love Simon – not love, not any more, but that isn't to say I don't care for him very deeply. No doubt you

73

will jump to extraordinary conclusions as a result of this confession?"

"It isn't in my nature to jump to conclusions, Mrs Martin. I appreciate the truthfulness, but I must ask you to expand a little."

"Because I'm married to him, you mean? I did love him when we married, of course. But that was seventeen years ago. I don't know how to explain it – how you never want it to happen and yet it does so in spite of you, dying little by little."

With a sense of dreadful shame more than panic, she watched him raise his eyebrows. How could he be expected to understand? No human being should be expected to understand another.

The wood held all the secrets. It also assuaged Sandy Woodings's discomfort after questioning Caroline Martin so savagely. The conversation had astonished him. He couldn't believe her when she said she didn't love her husband. It might have been a simple ploy to distract suspicion from Simon Martin – or from anyone else in the Martin household.

The restlessness had subsided into questions. So many questions. Why had Angela's parents not reported her missing when she hadn't returned all night? Why had her murderer chosen this place for murder? What would cause a girl of twenty to go into a wood in the evening, when the dangers were drummed into every little girl from childhood?

At 7:45 p.m., having returned to Dossage alone after his evening meal, he asked himself these questions, standing ankle-deep in bluebells on the path where the girl had probably come face to face with her murderer. Was it the man she had arranged to meet, whose voice had been overheard by her mother as they made some arrangement over the telephone on that fateful afternoon? She had arranged to meet someone – of that much they were certain. If that person were innocent, then why had he not come forward and volunteered the information? Somebody familiar to her must therefore know something. Sandy had the infuriating feeling that a great many people knew more than they were telling him.

Walking on now, through soft evening shade, with the shadows of movement from the overhead foliage, underfoot the crunch of beech-nut cases and dead leaves – he considered the fact that her mother had described Angela as looking determined. Determined that something should be settled. Angela's mother had not noticed fear. Sandy did not think that a daughter could hide fear from her mother.

No – it could only have been for romance that Angela Hawksworth had come here. Why else choose such a venue? A conversation could be held in a car, a pub, even a sculptor's studio. You met with somebody in a wood at twilight because what you had to say to one another was suited to that mood.

So the answer had to lie with one or other of the two men, Thorpe and Martin. He was staring fixedly at the twenty-foot holly tree when he heard a faint sound, turned and shook his head. He recognised the voice. As it came nearer, he started to frown. Then he saw her, dressed all in black, running faster than he would have thought possible.

"Oh, merciful heavens! Chief Inspector – oh, thank God! Thank God it's you!"

"Whatever is the matter, Mrs Pendle?" He took hold of her, steadied her, while she panted for breath and stared all about in a circle, wide-eyed.

"I've found him. You wouldn't believe me, but now will you believe me!"

"In plain English, Mrs Pendle – who have you found? What on earth is the matter with you?"

"Satan! Oh, God! Oh, Lord! Murdered! Just like Angela. Somebody – they've – murdered him. If only you had believed me and gone and found him first. They've murdered him – oh, dear me! Blood everywhere! I've never seen so much blood."

10

It was no good pretending otherwise. He had made a mistake, a serious one at that, in not listening to Mrs Pendle. In his bones he knew that he had missed a golden opportunity in failing to follow up her observations about the stranger in the wood. Now here he was, just as she had described him – tall, black coat, disfigured to start with, with half his face and head bald and the other half covered in long unkempt dark hair – and murdered! His body showed multiple stab wounds. Worse even than that, slash wounds. This had not been such a one-sided struggle as that with the twenty-year-old girl. This victim's fingers were shredded to the bone in an effort to ward off the stabbing and slashing blade. The undergrowth was flattened in a ten-yard radius from the desperate struggle between murderer and victim. Sandy would have put his age at perhaps thirty and, despite his lean build, the signs of the struggle bore testimony to his state of physical fitness. It had happened no more than two hours before Mrs Pendle had found the body, according to the calculations of Doctor Atkins, who seemed quite capable of working steadily at his task, despite the attentions of detectives, the ever-present video cameraman and the distant sirens of police cars blocking off the roads that ran about the perimeter of the woods.

"Mirror image of the last, wouldn't you say, Doctor?"

"Not quite." Doctor Atkins straightened from a close examination of the wounds about the man's back and neck. "There was something more careless about this one. Messy! And the victim is hardly as pretty." He stretched his back, which must have ached from bending. "Would you care to give me a hand to turn him over, Chief Inspector?"

Sandy remarked the weight of the body as he helped the doctor. "It would take some strength and physical fitness to do all that," he added emphatically.

"Indeed!"

"Could a woman have done it?"

"Perhaps an Amazon," the doctor chuckled. "Or a woman who was extremely fit and one hundred per cent out of her mind."

He was examining the extensive pink scar that covered most of the upper left side of his face. "Now isn't this interesting – ?"

"What do you make of it? Some kind of burn?"

"Give me a hand – here, let's have a look at his arms. Aha!" He indicated a striped effect, bands of red extending up the inner surface of both forearms and upper arms.

"Plastic surgery?"

"Right first time. The site where the surgeon took his skin grafts. But look here! There's more!" He indicated the folds of the elbows, where the creases were knotted and scarred along the courses of the veins.

"He was a drug addict?"

"Yes – and I think I might be able to guess how he became so pretty. I've only seen it once before in my life. They inject themselves anywhere they can find a vein. Run out of them in the arms and legs eventually. What's the odds he injected what he took to be a vein in his left temple – only what he was injecting was his left superficial temporal artery. With the result he cut off half his scalp from its arterial blood supply. The skin would simply go gangrenous and fall off."

"So he was an addict. Living rough from the looks of it.

He must have been here and we missed him in our searches."

"Probably knew the woods like the back of his hand. Reasonably warm this time of year."

Sandy had begun to empty the man's pockets in a search for identity. No wallet. No name. No money. He thought there was going to be nothing at all until he found an inside pocket in a place he hadn't expected it in the black great-coat and from this he extricated a delicate little lady's watch.

"Damn!" he murmured.

"Mean something?"

He didn't appear to hear the doctor. He just stared down at the rather surprising object found in the dead man's pocket and repeated his exclamation.

"Damn! I've been very stupid."

Josie was pampering herself in the five-foot circular jacuzzi with gold-plated fittings when he arrived at her flat. He had to let himself in with his own key and poured himself a double whisky and then a couple of Martinis, which he carried into the bathroom.

"Look at me!" she exclaimed pathetically.

"I'm looking." He lifted his glass in genuine admiration for that magnificent woman's body emerging here and there from a richly-scented creamy white foam.

"I feel like a revolutionary," she purred, directing his fingers to the triangle of her neck, undulating so he would get the message. Since meeting Josie he had discovered a skill at massaging the back of her neck, a skill he had never realised he had. "I look at myself," she said, directing her eyes fleetingly at the circular mirror on the ceiling over the bath, "and I declare war. War against fat."

"I don't want you to start disappearing in the wrong places."

"You can't even lie convincingly," she whispered mood-ily. "Whatever is the matter with you?"

"Nothing you couldn't cure – if you really tried."

She finished her glass, then commandeered his. "And I suppose you're going to want some supper and you'll have the nerve to eat it all in front of me?"

"I can make do with a couple of those cream doughnuts you hide in the fridge." He massaged away, as she polished off the second glass.

"That's downright wicked – can't I have any secrets from you?"

He moved his fingers, following some telepathic direction. "I want your advice as a woman, Josie."

"Oh, yeah!"

"I mean, what would take you into a wood at dusk? Would you go there to meet someone? And what kind of a meeting would that be and with what kind of a someone?"

"You must be joking!" She took both his hands and crossed them over her voluptuously slippery breasts.

"If you were in love?"

"I'd have to be mightily in love."

"Would you do it for privacy? Not for romance but to have some argument out with someone in privacy?"

"With a man? You must be out of your mind!"

"That's what I thought."

Damn! he thought once more. A visit to Mrs Hawksworth had confirmed his moment of enlightenment at the scene of the most recent murder. The watch had belonged to Angela. It had never been missed in the first place because she rarely wore it. Her mother had not noticed her taking it on her last walk – and now Sandy knew very well the reason she had felt the need for it. Timing! A meeting so precisely times she had needed a watch.

"I don't know, though." Josie was having second thoughts. "I suppose there would only be two exceptions – teenage love or middle-aged lust."

"Do you lust, Josie?"

"Oh, brother!" She umm'd and ah'd, inclining her head

back so he could kiss her. She was still umm'ing and ah'ing as he carried her, wearing nothing but her scented lather, back into the baroquely decorated bedroom, with the pink sheets opened like pouting lips in a skin of inviting black satin.

11

The four assistant chief constables, along with the chief constable, had their offices on the first floor of the head-quarters building, with large plate-glass windows facing south.

On Wednesday, May 23rd, Assistant Chief Constable Meadows hesitated, with Sandy Woodings's typed report on the drug addict's murder under his splayed hand. "Richard Belton, eh? It really is similar to the Hawksworth girl's murder, isn't it?" He interrupted his reading of the report to ask a question. "No problem identifying him?"

"He was well known to the casualty staff in all of the city's main hospitals." Sandy didn't mention the fact that they had only to mention the nickname, Satan.

"Nasty business! Looks as if it must be the same killer."

"It must be related, at the very least. But Doctor Atkins thinks the feel is different – whatever that means. Clumsier somehow." He searched his mind for the right word. "Messier."

"But in the same wood. Multiple knife wounds."

"Different blades. Belton was killed by an even longer blade. The deepest wounds indicate more than twelve inches. The Hawksworth girl was killed by an eleven-inch blade – and in her case the blade had an unusual design, curved in section, where this latest one was of conventional section."

Meadows's well-groomed white-haired head nodded contemplatively. "Carry on then. Keep me posted. Anything at all significant – "

Sandy Woodings made no attempt to leave.

"What is worrying you, Woodings?"

"There has been a paring down of the investigation. I presume you agreed to it, sir?"

Meadows was either a poor actor or he wasn't interested in acting; there was an unmistakable expression of wariness on his face. "Barker says there's nobody moving. So why not indulge in a little trout fishing?"

"While we were fishing, a second person was murdered."

A finger brushed invisible sweat from Assistant Chief Constable Meadows's pink forehead: it was already hot outside. After a fortnight of sun, the weathermen on the television were predicting a heatwave. "Do you disagree with Barker's view that the killer is still in the village?"

"No – I don't disagree."

"Very well. Let's hear what's bothering you then."

"We're playing at gentlemen and time is running through our fingers."

"And people are thinking we've gone soft in the head? That it's some kind of softly softly approach because we don't want to upset Martin, the international celebrity?"

"We have two main suspects and as yet neither has been questioned in depth, as far as I can determine."

"Martin was brought into headquarters – against my better judgement."

"Not a scrap of useful information was obtained."

"You make my point for me."

"Why, sir?"

"Why are we playing gentlemen? That's what's sticking in your craw? Well, let me try to explain. I was once involved with a very similar case, one velvety snake of an actor. He killed his ladylove in a premeditated and a brutal way. His motive was purely mercenary. I was the arresting officer and the bugger got off. He got off and promptly skipped the country. The reason he got off was because I let my hurry to convict him get the better of me. I had to watch him laugh in my face in the courtroom knowing that if I had taken more time, gathered better evidence . . . And the evidence was there. Believe me, the evidence was lying on the ground waiting to be picked up."

"Then you think Martin is our man – that's the conclusion arrived at in my absence?"

"Martin – or Thorpe! One or other of them. I'm not in a hurry. But I want whichever of them killed her – and the drug addict. I want it strong enough to get a conviction twice over. For a start, there's the question of motive, which is easy to see perhaps with Thorpe, but what motive could Martin possibly have?"

"She could have been pregnant by him."

"So what?"

"She could have insisted he marry her."

"Using the pregnancy as a lever? You've met him – can you honestly believe that?"

"Martin is complex. His motive could be equally complex."

"Then give me your complex theory."

"There's a violent streak in him and it's very close to the surface. He's difficult, hard to fathom. He's the head of a very strange household in which there are complex inter-personal relationships and undercurrents."

"You mean you can't give me any hard reason."

"No – not yet."

"Then play the gentleman."

Sandy returned to his own office two floors higher and facing north and had a cup of Mrs Parks's excellent caffeine-loaded coffee. He had another browse through the book by R. L. Hool, F.N.A.M.H..

Lecturing on "Chickweed and Its Uses", on May 15th, 1897, to 300 members of the Wigan and District Amalga-

mated Association of Botanists – they thought I was speaking from imagination or romancing about the benefits derived from the use of it!

He thought about Mrs Pendle, who had just happened to be on the spot to find both bodies. Telephoning the old school, he asked the sergeant to get a message to Mrs Thorpe to the effect that he would see her at home later that same morning. Then he depressed the rest and telephoned the medico-legal centre. Doctor Atkins wasn't in but he spoke to the doctor's secretary, who brightened his morning. The report was through from the botanists and he made an appointment to call in and discuss it with Doctor Atkins later that afternoon. By the time he replaced the receiver, ex-Sergeant, now Inspector Tom Williams had taken up a chair uninvited, and was sitting comfortably opposite him with an expression of considerable satisfaction. Tom had listened with ears cocked to the tail end of Sandy's telephone conversation, looking disgustingly tanned under his back-brushed grey curling hair and with an outrageous tie, a full-colour reproduction of Seurat's bathers, sprouting from a brazen orange shirt.

"Feeling a bit liberated, are we?" Sandy grinned.

"Feeling great!" Tom laughed his familiar old cackle. "I spent all of yesterday getting myself further acquainted with the details – so here I am, raring to go!"

"Congratulations!" Sandy leaned over the desk to take Tom's hand warmly. "Right then – here's what we do. I'll take Paul Thorpe's mother and you have a look at the lad's statement to Georgy. See what are the main holes in it and then take it through, word by word, with his pal, Jacky Arber." How could you credit the look of sheer happiness on Tom's face – when the clown had done nothing but wish for early retirement before it had been forced under his nose.

"Where do we meet up and when?"

"Lunch time – the old school!" Sandy had to call back to

85

Tom over his shoulder, since he was already through the door and into the corridor, walking fast in the direction of the staircase.

The Thorpes lived in a cottage that was obviously constrained to fit the shape of the land available to it. The living-room was wedge-shaped, following its cheese-slice share of village centre. There was no garden, just a back yard paved with broken and oil-stained stones. A single sorry-looking apple tree sprouted from a tiny patch of soil immediately adjacent to the living-room window, reducing the light squeezing through an already too small casement, but compensating prettily with a cascade of pink blossom.

Mrs Thorpe herself was surprisingly small, a mouse-like woman in her late forties, with hazel eyes set deep in a lined face, and straggly hair combed without a trace of fashion and parted on the right.

"Would you like a cup of tea, Mr Woodings?" she asked him, as he followed her tiny spare frame through the hall and into the unusually-shaped room.

"Not for me, thanks – but feel free yourself, if you like."

"I can wait," she replied, sitting, without attempt at comfort, on the edge of one of the black vinyl armchairs opposite him.

As he pulled his notebook from his pocket, he registered the brown carpet, with yellow-black flowers, which must have been chosen so it wouldn't show stains. There was an overpowering smell of cat in the room, emanating from a cushioned basket in the corner.

"Would you care to tell me a little about Paul, Mrs Thorpe?"

"What is there to tell? He's my son. I lost my husband when I was thirty-eight and he was thirteen."

She watched his eyes move to the twenty-three-inch colour television. It looked new and as expensive as the stereo deck and video recorder. She read his mind and answered his question before he asked it.

"Yes. Paul bought the television and the other fancy stuff. He bought it all with his own money. He bought the television for me. I watch it a lot these days."

"Paul is a good son to you, is he, Mrs Thorpe?"

"I couldn't have asked for better. Maybe that isn't the impression they'd give you hereabouts, but it was never easy for him. Children are very conscious of things. Like at school, never having any money. That was the reason they picked on him. He had to be tougher than the others, it was a question of being able to take care of himself. But not bad. Not wicked!"

"And this business at the well-dressing?"

"Of course he was blamed for that too. And he was foolish enough to let them think it was him, when he knew very well who it was – "

"You know who it really was then?"

"Yes, I know who it was."

"You don't mean Angela Hawksworth?"

"Who else? Oh, it wasn't anything new. She was always daring him to do something, as if she didn't dare to do anything herself. She was a wild case all right, wilder than my Paul. She led him on, you know. She encouraged that side in him."

"You didn't like her, did you, Mrs Thorpe?"

"I didn't hate her, Mr Woodings. The Lord teaches forgiveness and hate is not a welcome visitor to my heart. But she abused my son and I can't easily forget that."

"Abused Paul?"

"It's a hard word, but I mean it. I wish he had never met her."

"Paul was in love with Angela, wasn't he, Mrs Thorpe?"

"Oh, yes! Like a fool."

"Right up to the bitter end – I'm right, am I not?"

"He loves her still."

"I must ask you this. It's obviously a very difficult question for you. But will you please tell me truthfully if you have ever seen Paul with a knife? A knife with a long blade, much longer than just an ordinary pen-knife. A blade as long as a carving-knife, but with a very odd shape, curved in its section?" He traced the curve of the blade in the air for her and she shook her head, widening her eyes for a moment at the sunshine coming in through the pink display on her one apple tree.

He had noticed the change in her – she had began slowly to wring her hands. "You never saw him with such a knife – or something like a knife, that could be used as a knife?"

"Paul doesn't need knives, he's good enough with his fists."

Sandy studied this put-upon little woman, who liked cats. He had met many such little women, seemingly incapable of anything. How far would a mother, even an honest plain Methodist mother, go to protect her only son? He didn't need to think too hard to come up with an answer. Also the fact that since it was she who gave Paul his alibi, then Paul gave her the same in return. She had hated Angela Hawksworth – he was certain of it. There was deep-felt passion in that lined face, those small brown eyes tucked back into her own small but vital world. Was Mrs Thorpe herself capable of that impulsive act of violence that perhaps all of us are capable of, given sufficient desperation?

"Paul says he went out riding on his motorcycle on the day Angela was killed. What time did he get back home?"

"About eight. Before half past."

"Did he leave the house at any time in the evening or night?"

"Not to my knowledge."

"How did he seem when he came in? Can you remember, Mrs Thorpe – a little after eight o'clock – he must have come in from riding many times just like that. On this occasion was there anything about him that struck you as unusual? His mood? His manner?"

"I didn't notice anything unusual at all."

"Were there any stains on his clothing? Blood-stains?"

"Nothing like that."

"Did he mention Angela that evening? Did he say anything about her at all?"

"He didn't mention her. He wouldn't have mentioned her to me anyway, since I didn't like him to talk about her in my presence."

"And he stayed in all night after that?"

"Neither Paul nor Jacky left the house. Neither of them left the house until Jacky went, and that was after midnight."

"Exactly what did he do here, the rest of that evening?"

"He watched television and talked with Jacky."

"Here in this room?"

"Yes."

"I couldn't help but notice that you have a telephone, Mrs Thorpe. Did Paul have that installed, along with the television, the hi-fi deck and the video recorder?"

"Yes," she said simply.

"But he's unemployed and these things cost money. Even on hire purchase, the weekly payments would be astronomical."

"He bought them cash. We're not a family that has ever depended on owing anything to anybody."

"Can you tell me where the cash came from, Mrs Thorpe?"

"You'll have to ask him that. Because I don't know where he gets his money from. He doesn't tell me and when he doesn't want to tell you, there's no way of making him if he doesn't want to. Which is a thing you'll find out for yourself, Mr Woodings."

He made straight for the Drunken Duck, only to find

Georgy had got to the pub in the village centre before him. Sandy was ordering a half-pint of bitter and two cheese sandwiches when Tom joined them. He looked disgustingly cheerful, slapping a pound coin on the bar and sucking between his teeth as the half-pint he had ordered frothed out of the pumps into his glass. He was actually humming "Return to Sorrento", which seemed to be the only tune he knew, as he joined the two senior officers and carried his beer and sandwiches to a table under the wide Georgian bow window.

"Guess who's been spending a good deal of money then?"

"Paul Thorpe?" asked Sandy phlegmatically, sinking his teeth into a thick slice of crumbly Lancashire cheese.

"You've been looking into the crystal ball again," Tom wheezed, not the least put out and savouring the first mouthful of beer through the froth.

"Now that you've wet your whistle, tell us what's making you look so pleased with yourself."

"Closer than brothers, our Paul and our Jacky. Bikes! Boy, I used to like bikes myself, but these are some bikes. Do you know what kind of bikes our two young pals tear about the Derbyshire countryside on? Brand spanking new BMW -K's! 100 RS's! From the looks on your faces, it doesn't mean much. But let me tell you they're the latest – only came on the market a few months ago. One-litre four-cylinder engines. Approximate cost apiece, four and a half thousand quid."

"Bought cash?"

"Right on the nail."

"A round ten thousand – if we add to that one colour TV, video recorder, expensive hi-fi deck. So, where the hell would two unemployed twenty-three-year-old lads get hold of ten thousand pounds cash?"

"Arber told me to mind my own business," crackled Tom.

"Interesting! But what about the weapon? Did he volunteer anything on that?"

"Are you referring to our knife with the fancy blade – or the phallic artwork in pink and white carnations that caused such a stir at the well-dressing?" Tom cackled again. "He claimed he hadn't seen any knife of that description. He knew all about the artwork, though."

Sandy was now staring fixedly at Georgy – Georgy, who seemed more interested in Tom's tie than what they had been discussing. Georgy, returning his gaze, grinned and then took an almighty swig which finished his beer.

"What have you got to suggest then, Georgy?"

"I suggest that you have a little word with the headmaster of the village comprehensive. He's called Canute, honest to God!"

"A little word about what?"

"An addict murdered! Two kids trundling on 140-mile-an-hour bikes!"

"Drugs?"

"Now did I mention drugs?" Georgy undulated as one spade-like hand searched his bulk and came up with a small black diary. "Now let's see – a half-pint of beer, that's ninety calories – " He was performing some kind of intricate calculation of the calories in beer and weighing them against units of insulin.

"Can you make a start on the headmaster right away, Tom? I'll join you after I've been into headquarters and forensics."

"Right then – grill the headmaster!" said Tom, who was watching Sandy, who in his turn was noticing how Georgy had arrived at a definite conclusion from his deliberations.

"Before you go – " said Georgy, all of a sudden illuminated by a handsome grin. "Old custom – when a man has been elevated from the ranks!" He pushed his empty glass in their direction and laughed his great cackle, like a gigantic old hyena.

As Chief Superintendent Barker enjoyed his own private joke – a joke Assistant Chief Constable Meadows would most certainly not have approved of – Mrs Margaret Thorpe made her mind up about something that had been on her mind since the detective had left.

She climbed the stairs of her cottage, with her heart pounding. Outside the door to Paul's bedroom, she paused to take courage, then she crossed the room and looked down to where the cheap rug finished about a foot under the edge of her son's bed. With her heart ever beating faster and sickeningly harder in her chest, she peeled back the rug, found the short length of loose floorboard. She clawed at its edges with her fingernails, lifting it a fraction, getting a better hold, tearing it up out of the floor and staring with widened eyes into the hiding-place in the grey dust between two oak joists, enormously thick and infested with wood-worm.

Reaching down into the void, with her hands violently shaking, she lifted it out and dropped it as if it were white-hot on top of the bedclothes. Something that had been brought back from the first war by her father, Paul's grandfather. With eyes that did not look sane, she stared at the German bayonet – the razor-sharp and carefully polished blade with the deep trough along its length that her father used to say was put there to hold some vicious poison.

12

Angela Hawksworth, May queen, aged twenty, had been brutally murdered. Yet the sun continued to shine down on the Rivelin Valley as Sandy drove back into the city, with his car window down and the roof flap open. The soft warm air moved sluggishly in the blue distance, like a very fine wood-smoke, and people were hanging wall-baskets on the front walls of their cottages as he cruised by.

Maybe the sun didn't care, but somebody cared. It was a different kind of caring perhaps, but it was care, worry, fear, that had resulted in the murder of Richard Belton, alias Satan, educated – Mrs Pendle had been right again – as a teacher of the English language, but finally ending his life as a drug addict. Sandy Woodings knew a good deal more than he had known yesterday. He knew that Assistant Chief Constable Meadows had, if not directly lied, spun a cock-and-bull story about some actor murdering his mistress in order to conceal the real reason for the restraint he had ordered over the whole enquiry. From this he surmised that Georgy must have been saying something important. Georgy had felt he had earned that pint of beer!

Sandy changed his mind about going into headquarters first, and headed for the medico-legal centre. He arrived at 2:15 to find a curious Doctor Atkins waiting in his office to receive him.

"It's quite an interesting little shopping-list," commented

the doctor, pushing the typed sheet over the desk surface, the generic names followed by the common names in brackets.

"I took the liberty of striking out the lettuce, cucumber, cabbage, radish and tomato," said Doctor Atkins, with a smile.

"Thanks!" Sandy said automatically, nodding his head as he read through what remained on the botanist's analysis of the contents of Angela Hawksworth's stomach.

> *Spiraea ulmaria (Meadowsweet)*
> *Ballota nigra (Black Horehound)*
> *Gentiana pneumonanthe (Marsh or, more likely,*
>   *English Gentian)*

"Unusual ingredients in an otherwise commonplace vegetable salad. What does it mean, Chief Inspector?"

"I have my suspicions, Doctor. But I need to get back to my office to confirm them." He folded the typed sheet up so that it fitted neatly into the inside pocket of his lightweight pearl-grey suit. "Anything else come of the detailed post-mortem on Richard Belton?"

"Only that he was positive for the Australia antigen."

"What does that mean?" He was already on his feet, watching in some puzzlement as Doctor Atkins popped momentarily into the small laboratory next door and returned with a kidney bowl containing a disposable hypodermic syringe, one tiny glass ampoule and a swab for skin sterilisation.

"Like most of his fellow-addicts, he was a walking carrier of infectious hepatitis. Dreadful condition – spread by blood or blood products." Sandy winced as his mind went back to how he had helped the doctor to turn over the heavily bloodied body. "A condition much feared, with very good reason, by pathologists. Fortunately, we have just come up with a decent preventative serum. So come on, my

94

friend – roll up your sleeve." His grin looked too gleeful to be interpreted as apologetic.

Mrs Parks had the strong mug of coffee ready within one minute of his storming through the door, placing it down with infinite caution next to the cloth-covered manual of R. L. Hool. He drank it scalding, in an almighty draught, as he read: *Queen of the meadows, or Meadowsweet. It is one of the common plants indigenous to Great Britain and Ireland. Meadowsweet is a wild plant found growing in ditches, around the sides of ponds, by roadsides, riversides, in woods.* There followed a description of the plant's anatomy, its roots, leaves and flowers. *It acts as a tonic when employed in cases of dyspepsia, dropsy, rheumatism, fevers, cramps and all sorts of bilious attacks, sour belchings and stomach affections of every kind.* He read a further description of how to prepare its leaves, or make a tea-like concoction, possibly combined with Wood Betony, Agrimony etc. *Being an anti-acid, it allays and corrects the acids accumulating in the stomach far better than carbonate or bicarbonate of soda, magnesia, cream of tartar, tartaric acid, saleratus and bicarbonate of potass. Meadowsweet not only allays the symptoms but prevents the recurrence.*

Another draught of the powerful coffee and he moved on to Black Horehound in the book's index. *In Black Horehound we have one of the most efficacious remedies that we can use for the cure of biliousness, bilious colic, and sour belchings.*

He hardly felt the need to look up English Gentian, but he did, and read, *The diseases in which its employment is indicated are as follows: Stomach disorders.*

"Mrs Pendle!" he exclaimed determinedly, before suddenly finishing what was left of his coffee, grabbing his jacket from the back of his chair and dashing past the bemused Mrs Parks, taking the stairs two at a time.

*

95

Even as he climbed out of his car, parked opposite the gable end of the old cottage, he could hear that unmistakable voice:

"Clumsy boy! Oh, for goodness sake, watch my petunias –"

"Take it easy, Auntie Emily," said another voice, male and with a local village accent.

Rounding the corner on to the flagged path, he caught sight of Mrs Pendle, together with a young man in his early twenties dressed in jeans and summer shirt. They were performing a balancing-act, the young man on top of a paint-splattered and tottering stepladder, with Mrs Pendle in the act of handing him a very large wall-basket which he was expected to attach to the stone wall of her cottage.

"I must speak to you, Mrs Pendle."

"Not just at the moment, Chief Inspector. Oh, Lord!" she squealed in alarm as a piece of trailing lobelia some-how managed to detach itself and fall on the path at her feet.

"It's too urgent. I can't wait," he murmured impatiently. It was already 3:45 and he had still to go and talk to the headmaster at the local school. "Here!" he said, taking the basket out of her hands and lifting himself with the basket in both his hands above his head several tentative steps up the ladders. He was showered in peat compost as the lad struggled to align the securing-holes with the plugs he had fixed into the wall, using a hopelessly small screwdriver for the large round-headed brass securing-screws.

"I just hope between the two of you that there's a single geranium left alive in there." Mrs Pendle hurled encour-agement with her jangling wrists making a frenetic music and her hands holding fistfuls of her hair.

Climbing down, Sandy Woodings took her by the arm, dragging her reluctantly from contemplation of the basket into her quaintly furnished living-room.

"Thank you, Jack!" she shouted from the hallway back to

the young man, who was putting the stepladder away. "I'll see you tomorrow, maybe."

Even in his hurry he couldn't help but notice the light-switches, which were of the old white pottery sort, with a little flat piece in the middle which you turned round to work them; on this she'd stuck a piece of red adhesive tape to tell her which way to turn them on and off. He was, however, too busy to take Jock's earlier precautions and sat down heavily in one of the offensively repellent armchairs, under the art nouveau mirror, with an eccentrically placed hole through which protruded a small hand holding a dessicated collection of wild grasses.

"Now then – what's so vitally important?" she asked, stroking the remains of plumage on the green parrot that had somehow appeared on her lap as soon as she had sat down.

"Meadowsweet, Horehound and English Gentian, Mrs Pendle."

"Ah!" she murmured, with a visible indrawing of both cheeks. "There!" she said distractedly. "There – off you trot, Coddles!" She pushed away the resisting parrot. "Too old to fly." She looked pleadingly at him, with her face cocked at an angle. "Poor love can only walk or hop."

"I shouldn't need to remind you that this is a murder enquiry, Mrs Pendle."

"My goodness! Have I become the prime suspect all of a sudden?"

"I believe you know more than you've told us. It's absolutely essential that you tell me all you know – right here and now."

"I most certainly had nothing to do with it."

"If you know something and the real killer is aware of that, then surely you must realise that you yourself might be in danger."

"I really have told you everything I know."

"You gave Angela a herbal mixture for an upset stomach, didn't you?"

"These doctors – they invent their own universities and they conduct them by their own rules. It's a crime for the ordinary citizen just to wish to help her neighbour."

"Angela Hawksworth was suffering from morning sickness. Morning sickness because she was three months pregnant. Are you trying to tell me you didn't guess the reason she came to you for that prescription, Mrs Pendle?"

"I did ask the poor girl if she was in any kind of trouble. We're rather like a big family here. I didn't press her – if I had she wouldn't have come back for help ever again. I mean, I never imagined for one moment . . ."

Outside he heard the young man walking away down the path. Suddenly he jumped to his feet and dashed after him, catching up with him by the two carved stone gateposts.

"Just a moment – did I hear Mrs Pendle call you Jack? What's your full name?"

"Jack Arber," he said, gazing back evenly.

"Paul Thorpe's pal?"

"One and the same!" he replied cockily. "Can I go now, Mr Policeman?"

Sandy nodded, staring after him, then turned back on Mrs Pendle who had been watching this with what might have been an imitation of astonishment from her open doorway.

"Are you two related then? He called you Auntie."

"They all do. It's only a kind of pet name the villagers have for me."

"There are many more questions, Mrs Pendle, but they'll have to keep until I have more time. But I'll be back and I'll want the truth from you next time. And take notice of my warning – if you're hiding something then you're placing yourself in serious danger."

Once again, before climbing into his car, he stared at the figure now just vanishing round the slight bend. He had never met Jacky Arber, just read reports of other detectives' interrogations of him. So that was Jacky Arber, who claimed to know so little about where Paul Thorpe got his money from!

He drove the two hundred yards from Mrs Pendle's cottage to the old school, parked in a hurry and strode into the building searching for Georgy Barker. Georgy wasn't there. He was told that he had gone to join Tom in questioning the staff at the comprehensive school. Moving with even greater haste, Sandy climbed back into the car again, another short journey, four hundred yards to the school entrance, then a hundred yards of slow progress through six hundred children pouring out of the main doors – he could do nothing else except wave them aside and move in fits and starts, with the children deliberately obstructing him, waving cheekily in front of the windscreen – so that he arrived at the main doors feeling irritable and frustrated.

Pulling Georgy to one side, he told him about the developments with Mrs Pendle.

"We have enough to take her into headquarters right now," he argued.

"Enough for questioning but nothing at all we could arrest her on," said Georgy, thoughtfully toying with his unlit briar.

"I know she knows something."

"I'm beginning to think that everybody in this village knows something. Why don't we take the whole village in for questioning?"

"Be serious, Georgy."

"Wait until you hear what the headmaster has reluctantly admitted – "

"The headmaster?" He stared at Georgy – he had almost forgotten the headmaster.

"That's right. Williams will fill you in and Mr Canute is waiting for you to have your little chat with him in his office."

"Where are you off to now, Georgy?"

Frank Ryan

"Back to the incident centre in the school. What else do you propose to do?"

"At the very minimum we should put someone on Mrs Pendle's tail. I think we should have her watched twenty-four hours a day from now on."

"That's three men completely tied up."

"Six. I want a tail on Martin as well. Either we do that or I'm taking them all in, Thorpe, Martin, Mrs Pendle – the whole caboodle!"

"As you wish. Your case, Chief Inspector!" Georgy had a mischievous glint in his eye. As if Sandy were doing exactly what Georgy wanted him to do.

Sandy joined Tom, who was still interviewing Mr Canute. After they had been introduced and everybody had sat down, Tom addressed the teacher, a sheepish-looking man in his late fifties. "Would you mind just telling the chief exactly what you told me earlier?"

The man sighed, ran a green ball-point along the parting of his thinning straight grey hair, and declared:

"Pot, cannabis – whatever you want to call it. There was a single occasion. Something I thought relatively minor – "

"With Paul Thorpe?"

"Yes, Thorpe and at least half a dozen others. They were caught in the toilets at lunch time, passing a cigarette from one to the other."

"You should have reported it immediately."

"It was difficult to be sure because when discovered they immediately flushed the remains down the loo. But their behaviour was suspicious and the master who discovered them, Mr Simpson, who taught history, quite properly reported the incident to me."

"How long ago was this?"

"Oh, donkeys' years ago. Thorpe was in his final year, so he would have been fifteen years old. What is he now – twenty-two, twenty-three? That would make it seven or eight years."

"Would it be possible to speak to Mr Simpson?"

"No good," Tom interrupted. "Mr Simpson is deceased."

"So you performed a little enquiry of your own, Mr Canute?"

"Oh, yes. They all denied it of course, but I suspected it was cannabis. I called all of the teachers in the school together and had a strong word. We kept our eyes and ears open but nothing else was heard or discovered."

"You behaved foolishly."

"That's easy for you to say now. But it was all so vague. It might have been a false alarm, and several of the boys involved – well, some of our brightest – at least three went on to take A-levels and then to university."

"You've given Inspector Williams a list of their names?"

"Not until I first try to have a private word with their parents – I'm afraid I must adamantly refuse."

"Mr Canute! This is a murder enquiry. We haven't the time or the intention of playing games of etiquette. I want those other five names and I want them now. This minute. I think you understand the gravity of what we are dealing with."

"Very well. But I must express my disapproval and I want it recorded that I did it on order and with the greatest reluctance."

He left Tom collecting the list of names, addresses and photographs where possible, then returned to the old school and sat thinking with a mug of coffee. He was still undecided whether to take Mrs Pendle in for intensive questioning. Sooner or later he would have to do it, but as always it was a question of timing.

So they were making some connection with drugs. And Georgy was behaving as if it were all the more important. As if Georgy were only reluctantly in league with Meadows. Sandy filed all of this in a closed compartment of his mind just for the present.

He had his evening snack in the old school, calling all of the murder team together for discussion. They copied out the list of names, distributing them to everyone concerned. It would be a long night, searching through the statements they had already collected to see if any name cropped up twice, looking for connections. Sandy took the floor with the old-fashioned blackboard, listing what they now knew about Mrs Pendle, the herbal salad taken by Angle Hawksworth on the evening of her murder. He also itemised Paul Thorpe's plentiful and inexplicable supply of money, plus the fact that there was a connection, as yet to be properly evaluated, with drugs. Mrs Pendle! He drew a circle round Mrs Pendle's name, some kind of connection with Jack Arber, therefore some possible connection with Thorpe. A tenuous cobweb was appearing on the board, linking Angela Hawksworth, Paul Thorpe, Jack Arber, Simon Martin – and Mrs Pendle. What did Mrs Pendle know? What could possibly be her reason for refusing to tell them?

At 9:15 in the evening Constable Brown, the man tailing Mrs Pendle, called in on his handset to say that she had just left her cottage. Sandy Woodings felt instinctively that this was important. He must have upset her, caused her to think. Wherever she was going, he wanted to know.

Brown gave them a progress report at intervals, the top of Vicarage Lane – she actually walked directly past them all in the schoolroom but they made very certain that nobody showed a face at a single window – then on into the village centre, up the Northhead Road, walking very briskly, with Brown attempting to keep a good fifty yards behind her.

"She's gone right, into the playing-fields," Brown's voice muttered in some irritation over the receiver.

"Keep on her, Brown," said Sandy urgently.

"It's almost pitch-dark. There's no moon. I'd need to

shine my torch on her to follow her in there," said Brown fretfully. "What do you want me to do, sir?"

"Close up on her if you can. Whatever you do, don't lose her."

13

Mrs Pendle had been aware of the policeman ever since he had slipped over her wall and set Bunter, her donkey, braying; just as she had known without needing to look round that he had followed her when she had left the house with its door secure and the garden carefully shut so the animals would be safe. Now, once within the playing-fields, she ran as fast as her feet would carry her to the darkest part, the gulley under the willows, where she threw herself flat on the ground and lay there without moving for a long time. The policeman walked by her twice, once at a distance of about thirty yards, and the second time, on his way back to the entrance, no more than ten yards away. Even after he had gone she lay there without moving a muscle, because the slightest movement set all of her bracelets tinkling – and because she needed all the luck she could get, she hadn't dared to leave them behind her tonight.

When at last she did move again, it was cautiously, with her arms crossed, each hand silencing the bracelets on the opposite wrist, across the fields in a diagonal direction, emerging on to a main road, then finding a small lane that was virtually invisible, but which took her round the periphery of the village in a south-westerly direction. She walked a good mile and a half before emerging on quite a different road, a very winding one, only poorly illuminated, and which took her in a direction from which she could clearly hear running water. Finally she seemed, in this roundabout fashion, to have reached her destination. She paused outside the house, almost instantly heard something which alarmed her, and caused her to scuttle quickly and with only the faintest tinkling across the narrow and very steep road, into dense undergrowth on the opposite side.

Something was happening – something which puzzled her, quite distracted her from her original intention.

A figure had emerged from the house.

When it was closer to her, Mrs Pendle could just make out the pale shape, something large: the figure was carrying something large and white across the road exactly where she had crossed and then plunged into the undergrowth where she was hiding. There was a strange ringing in Mrs Pendle's ears and a shiver came over her. She stared after the figure, feeling like someone in a terribly realistic yet ghastly nightmare. And that peculiar quality of a nightmare, the inability to resist, was there as well: that was the reason she followed the figure, keeping to a poorly demarcated path, which took her deep into the hilly coppice standing on the site of the old village quarry. All of a sudden she started physically. Immediately in front of her, erupting – oh, Lord! – so unexpectedly, she had very nearly been caught in the bright blaze of light.

A fire! The figure had lit a small fire, well away from the house and out of sight and probably out of hearing of the road. In the densely wooded surroundings, Mrs Pendle had no difficulty in drawing closer, close enough to see the legs wearing jeans and the heavy blackish jacket as the figure bent over the small flame, throwing things on the fire. Each time something was thrown the flames crackled into renewed savagery. Mrs Pendle was close enough, no more than twenty yards away now, to hear the strange sobbing sounds emanating from the figure, to make out the large white cardboard box on the ground from which pieces of paper were lifted, inspected, ripped violently into quarters before being case on to the fire.

There was a familiarity about those pieces of paper, as one by one they were condemned to destruction.

Photographs! That's what they are – photographs!

She could make out the surface sheen on the pieces in that slight pause before the fire took hold. She would have loved to get even closer and she wondered if she dared, perhaps a step or two. She'd have given the bracelets from both wrists to have seen just one of those photographs before it was rent asunder and destroyed.

A step, a second step – she found herself held back by a low bush of prickly berberis – but now she could see things even more clearly.

Definitely photographs. A great many of them. Hundreds of photographs, torn one by one, precisely, and with a sobbing and sighing which became more terrifying the closer she came. It was as if the heart were being torn from the figure with each act of destruction, that was why the nightmare was at once so curious and strangely appealing. Then suddenly, with a last and terrible action, from the box was lifted something magnificent and billowing white.

Extraordinary!

The noise of the sobbing had reached terror proportions. The hands held the thing, which so resembled a human soul, the hands tried to tear at the thing as if this was the last judgement, tried to rip this human soul to shreds, but either the thing was unrippable or the fingers had not strength for the task so that, with a cry of anguish, it was thrown on to the flames intact, lifting the furnace into an inferno, the very flames of hell itself, it seemed to Mrs Pendle. A private hellish torment. The realisation was so awesome that her throat just made the noise in spite of her – she just couldn't stop her throat from crying out. The figure jerked, turned in her direction. Throwing caution to the wind, Mrs Pendle broke her cover and ran back in the direction of the road, certain that the figure was running after her. *Running.* She was too old and her chest developed a stitch after only a hundred yards. As the figure closed on her, she felt the hackles on her neck rise – as something reached out and touched her and she felt a piece of her shirt tear along the stitching, but she just swung herself away from that clutching hand, round a tree and continued to run. The road. Oh, thank God, the road! She had reached it. She tripped, fell flat on the palms of her hands. Her hands hurt her as if she had been crucified, but she just gulped a mouthful of air and ran along the road, dodging out of the light over a low stone wall into a field that smelled of cowdung, where she lay gasping for breath and her head spinning with all sorts of considerations. Had the figure got a good look at her? Had the tinkling of her bracelets been heard? She lay flat on her face in the shade of the wall just as she had earlier with the policeman and tried to control the noise of her breathing, listening hard, certain she could hear that same breathing, that terrifying sobbing breathing all about her; her ears were filled with it.

Waiting, waiting. Nothing happening. When would it happen? How long should she wait? She was capable of waiting in the shelter of that wall for all eternity, rather than face that figure with its sobbing breathing.

14

"Mrs Pendle!"

She was still so terrified that her heart stopped when she heard the shout. Then it thudded sickeningly as she made out a figure climbing out of a car on the opposite side of the lane. She wasn't waiting to see who it was, she made one last panic-stricken run for her front door.

"You've given us all rather an anxious time of it. Three hours since you gave our man the slip."

Mr Tricky-the-Loop detective! Now she recognised the voice, even as her hand shook all over the place attempting to fit her key in the lock.

"I must ask you to come back for questioning to the old school, Mrs Pendle."

"What for? Oh, for goodness sake!" She was putting every fibre of her being into trying to get the door open. Suddenly it gave way and she was inside. She even tried to slam it on him but he was too quick for her, following her into the hall where she had left the light on deliberately.

"For questioning, Mrs Pendle."

His eyes on her now, how he could read her with those eyes! He could see at a glance how upset she was and she didn't even have a story to tell him that he would believe. There had been no time for thinking up stories.

"Oh, dear!" she murmured, with the idea of putting a hand to her head – she had been ill. She had fainted on the playing-fields. That was the first idea now to come into her head. She had been sick and she had fainted and only now come round. But would he believe it? With her hand to her head, she managed somehow to stagger through the living-room into the tiny room at the back with the sloping ceiling, the buttery, where, from under the cooling-cupboard with its zinc grill door, she pulled a bottle of Martell's cognac. Because she was still feeling faint, it occurred to her. Oh, why wouldn't her mind work! Because she was feeling so drained – which was in fact a gross understatement of the truth. Cognac – she now poured it into her upended mouth from the neck of the bottle before he could get to her and take the bottle form her.

"That's enough of that." He was more than a little late in wresting it from her resisting grasp, screwing the cap back on and putting it back with a gesture of impatience in its hiding-place. "I want you in a fit state to answer my questions, Mrs Pendle."

"Never mind your questions." She heard her own voice come out as a high-pitched fisher-woman's shriek. "Give me back my property and clear off out of my home. You are trespassing, in case you didn't know. It's rest I need and not some further round of questioning. I'm not in a fit condition to come back with you for one of your third degrees after I've just had a blackout."

Sheer terror of that sobbing figure now oddly lent her boldness: she jerked her head up to face him eye to eye. Oh, Lord – the way he was staring back at her, such a disconcertingly calm assessment in those altogether too clever blue eyes.

Half an hour later, sitting with her tremulous elbows either side of a mug of coffee on the table top in the murder headquarters, she found his eyes had not changed, that same disbelieving knowing look in his eyes, but without the half-smile she had come to associate with Mr Tricky-the-Loop. There was only one other man present, an older man with grey hair and a gaudy tie, who sat on a chair close to the wall and listened attentively without taking his left hand out of his pocket.

"You blacked out on the recreation ground and you remember nothing until you came round five or ten minutes before I met you at the gate to your cottage?"

"That's right."

"Precisely where in the recreation ground did you black out?"

"I'm not sure."

"On the path?"

"It might have been."

"Constable Brown searched the path for you and he didn't find you."

"Do you mean to tell me that I was being followed? And this is a democracy."

"So – if it wasn't on the path, where was it?"

"I'm not sure. Maybe close to the trees."

"Which trees, Mrs Pendle?"

"Trees. The birches. There's a little coppice running right through the recreation ground. I remember now. I wanted to cross it more diagonally. The path went in the wrong direction."

"And you thought you knew the way from past experience – even in the dark?"

"I have lived here all my life."

"The way across diagonally – from the entrance on Lowedge Road, to the opposite corner?"

"That's it."

"Tomorrow I shall ask you to show Inspector Williams exactly where you blacked out. And tonight, when you get home, I shall expect you to let us have your trousers and pullover for forensic examination. We can find out a great deal these days from so very little."

"I most certainly will not allow you to examine my clothes."

"Then I shall have you taken into headquarters and put into a cell where you will be undressed."

"This is a free country. I know the law."

"This is a murder enquiry. You were the first person to find the body. The dead girl's last meal contained herbal remedies for nausea. She was three months pregnant. You have already admitted to me that you supplied her with these herbs."

"What do you think I prescribe for my patients? Hemlock? Or deadly nightshade?"

"It would certainly make my day if you did, Mrs Pendle."

"Just because I was the one who found the bodies."

"It has been known."

"I go into the woods. I do no harm, collecting a few simple plants for the good of my neighbours. You're all the same – city people. Did you know that thirty years ago this village wasn't even in Yorkshire? It was Derbyshire. We're Derbyshire folk. Ordinary country folk! People who know and trust one another."

"Angela Hawksworth trusted you. She came to you, Aunt Emily! Why to you and not to her doctor?"

"Herbs were medicines long before doctors and their pills. They try to make out that we're just silly. Dangerous – that's the irony."

"Dangerous?"

"Yes, dangerous! Them! Oh, how they hate all the old things, the old ways. Why do you think the Rare Breeds Trust was founded? Talk to the village people. Talk to Mrs Sheridan – "

"Thank you. Who is this Mrs Sheridan?"

Oh, how stupidly she was behaving. Mentioning old Sheridan like that! She must be out of her mind. "Take no notice of me, Chief Inspector. I'm ill. Talking through my hat."

"You must have a soft spot for Paul Thorpe. Because he's village?"

"I prefer him to the outsiders, who only change and destroy and respect nothing."

"After I spoke to you, you left your cottage and animals unattended and set out for some unknown destination on some unknown mission. You deliberately gave my man the slip and back you came, hours later, with a fabricated story of a blackout."

"I'm telling you the truth. I did black out." She held her head with her two hands. "This has never happened to me before – never!"

How could his eyes stay so hard and ungiving? Had he no heart whatsoever?

"I'm asking you again, Mrs Pendle – where did you go tonight? Where? Whom did you meet? To what purpose?"

"I walked out of the cottage for a quick breath of fresh air. I might have had some vague idea of calling in on Angela's parents."

"The recreation ground is nowhere near her parents' home."

"No! I hadn't decided in my own mind. I wanted to walk around for a while to decide what was best. One never knows what to do. I mean, under the circumstances – you can see how I wasn't sure if my calling on them would have been at all welcome."

"I don't believe you, Mrs Pendle."

"What do I have to do to convince you?"

"Tell me the truth. Did you intend to call in on Paul Thorpe or his mother?"

"Why on earth should I call in on the Thorpes?"

"Their cottage is not so far from the recreation ground."

"Then why don't you go and ask them? Go ahead – if you haven't already."

"Rest assured that we will, Mrs Pendle. If not the Thorpes, then the Arbers. I heard you say to young Jacky that you would see him tomorrow. Why should you want to see him tomorrow?"

"To pay him for helping me with the baskets."

"So you decided to pay him tonight?"

"No! Goodness me! Why don't you go and ask the Arbers too!"

"Here." He suddenly lifted her left wrist, where there was a long graze. "You didn't have this when I saw you today. How did you graze your wrist?"

"I must have done it when I fell. There – what did I tell you . I really did fall down, you know."

"You lost a few of your trinkets at the same time then?" He indicated one of the bracelets on the same wrist, where several signs of the zodiac were missing.

"I – I suppose I must have done," she whispered, hardly daring to think where that might have happened.

"Then we shall have a good search for them tomorrow – when you show us the spot where you fell. Don't worry, Mrs Pendle, gold is usually very easy to find. Gold glitters."

That, now, was what she was very much afraid of.

15

On Friday morning, May 25th, Superintendent Hugh Bearder, who was in charge of the city-wide drugs squad, was woken in his bed by a call from the incident centre in the old school in Dossage.

"Who's that? Woodings – Sandy Woodings! For pity's sake, it's – it's only 6:30 in the morning."

"Sorry to wake you so early. But you're an elusive so-and-so during working hours, Hugh, and it's important I have a word with you about something."

"What's so important?"

Sandy allowed Bearder a few seconds' grace to collect himself. "You know we're investigating the Dossage murders? Well, it seems there might be a drugs connection." He listened carefully, caught the momentary pause in Hugh's breathing. "I wondered if I could pop in and have a chat? In your office later this morning?"

"I can't see – I mean, I don't know just how you think I can help."

"Would 9:15 be convenient? In your office? Fine. I'll look forward to seeing you, Hugh." Replacing the phone, Sandy looked thoughtfully at the sheet of paper on which he had been summarising his thoughts.

A little after 8:00, Tom trudged through the school doors, having exhaustively scanned the spot where Mrs Pendle claimed she had fallen, using a metal detector.

"Found anything?"

"Grass and nettles!"

"You took samples?"

"All we did was to take samples."

Sandy grinned at Tom's disaffected expression, thanked the technician as he carted his plastic bags back with him to compare with whatever they could find on the clothes Mrs Pendle had reluctantly parted with at one o'clock this morning.

"You don't seem surprised," declared Tom, nestling his freshly-poured mug of tea in the cradle of his hands.

"I'd have been astonished if you had found something." Sandy stood by the window. Something inside him had changed gear: he had to conceal the inner sense of excitement.

He put a uniformed inspector, Charlie Earnshaw, on the trail of the youngsters who, seven years ago, had smoked reefers in Dossage comprehensive school's toilets. Tom he put on to further investigation of Paul Thorpe and Jacky Arber. He wanted to know where they went, how they spent their day, whom they talked to, what they talked about. The Martins had become his special concern – and it was to the growing dossier on that household that he applied his spare hour. Eleanor Standon, potter. Virginia Lauderman, Jill of all trades. Ronald Wadsworth, glass blower – and the only man in the house, apart from Simon Martin himself.

Bearder's office was identical to Sandy's own, but two floors higher and with its double-glazed window facing north. Sandy sat facing him and the window as he outlined a concise summary of the dead drug addict, the puzzle of two out-of-work men with ten thousand pounds to spend, finally the story of the headmaster.

Bearder lifted his eyebrows, shaking his head. "The names Paul Thorpe and Jack Arber don't ring any bells."

"What would you think, then? Just a series of coincidences?" Sandy watched Bearder purse his lips, leaning back in his chair, with his hands flat on his desk.

"The headmaster was a little bit naughty. He should have called us in there and then. We could have been discreet. Nip these things in the bud. But there you are. Some slight suspicion and all of it donkeys' years ago. There might have been something to do with cannabis. But it would be impossible to do anything about it now, of course."

Sandy merely nodded, still watching Bearder.

Bearder shifted his hands a fraction of an inch. "Was that all you wanted to talk about?"

Shrugging, Sandy seemed reasonably satisfied. "Just one other thing – nothing concrete, mind you – "

"Well – let's hear what's on your mind."

"It's this cocaine business – "

Bearder's hands lifted several inches before coming to rest again. "What cocaine business?"

"I mean, when I did my stint in drugs – in the late seventies – cocaine was popular then too. After that it appeared to go completely out of fashion. And now it's the in-thing with the artistic set."

"I thought it was cannabis we were talking about," said Bearder, running plump puzzled fingers over his shiny seborrhoeic scalp.

"Well, yes! Cannabis! But there can't be the same money in it as cocaine. You know, it's interesting, Hugh – " Sandy prodded distractedly at his pocket before remembering he no longer smoked. Then, shaking his head, he added, in baffled appeal, "Not enough of a kick to it! Flash! That was the term, wasn't it? They used to inject it then, mixed in a cocktail with heroin. Now they snort it through their mouth or up their noses. They must have something in common, pop singers and artists."

"You're very interested in the drug scene, all of a sudden."

116

"Oh, just an idea. I ask myself, what would an artist do when he's run out of ideas of his own?"

"Cannabis lasts longer."

"No – not cannabis, Hugh. And not heroin neither – I've been thinking about that too. No, the big H is the loner's escape. But cocaine is what you find at the centre of the party. Along with the charm and wit – and the ideas."

"The problem is the effects don't last very long. The heavy punter has to keep taking more and more at very short intervals. Ten – or even twenty grams in one session."

"I've thought about that too," said Sandy. "Put the short duration of the flash together with the initial cost – what do you have?"

"You tell me."

"A very expensive habit, Hugh. Big money! Ipso facto, big fat profits for the pushers."

"So big money might be the motive behind the murders?"

"Cocaine is a multi-million-pound industry."

Bearder made no reply, just watched Sandy with an increasingly blank expression.

"Just out of interest – what's the street price these days?"

"Sixty quid."

"Sixty pounds a gram. At that rate, ten thousand pounds would buy how much – about a mugful?"

"So you have been wondering if somebody took too much – went a little crazy?" Bearder attempted to read his mind.

"That is one of the questions I asked myself, yes."

"I think it unlikely – not just with cocaine alone. Maybe if they had taken a cocktail – LSD perhaps?"

Sandy sighed affably, so that his next question took Bearder completely by surprise. "What on earth is going on, Hugh?"

"I'm beginning to wish I knew."

"You know – you're not a convincing liar."

"Now look here, Sandy!"

"Shall I tell you something else? You're not even as convincing as Meadows. And you can pass the message on, if you like."

The sense of excitement had never left him since yesterday. There was still a good two hours before lunch, and he left headquarters, driving east through the city centre, into the quarter that had seen rather too much demolition in the last twenty years. Ronald Wadsworth worked six mornings a week in a ramshackle shed that must once have been a mechanic's little hideaway for tax evasion.

That was the first surprise. The second was the sight of Wadsworth himself, out of his foppish clothes and stripped to the waist, against the heat of the smelting-furnace. His torso was that of a very fit man, with a hairless powerful chest, oily with sweat, and arms that would have done justice to a horizontal-bars gymnast.

"We met once – when I was questioning Simon Martin. Detective Chief Inspector Woodings." Sandy's glance took in the youngster, who was obviously Wadsworth's assistant.

"I could hardly have forgotten," said Wadsworth, who made no pretence of pleasure in seeing him. "I'll say one thing for you people. You certainly know how to pick the most awkward moments."

"Why don't you just carry on doing what you're doing. I can wait for a natural break."

Wadsworth turned his back on him in an overt display of hostility. In the meantime Sandy made himself comfortable on a swivel chair which had padding coming out through the splits in the leather seat, while this middle-aged glass blower treated him to an astonishing display of manual dexterity. Lifting an orange-hot glass creation on the end of a long iron tube, he blew down the tube, spun it round a few times, blew again, while his assistant pulled here and there with tongs or stuck bits on to the surface that resembled strings of rosary beads. The effect was to cover the original orange with a hundred-odd eyes and to extend what might have been antennae or legs here and there. This was followed by a few seconds' reheating, then some further refashioning by swinging the whole round in a wide circle, like a very delicate and heavy-tipped majorette's baton. There was a moment's expert hesitation before, with an expression of only partial satisfaction, Wadsworth placed the results, which resembled a hundred-eyed hedgehog with wings of multi-coloured glass, on his workbench and chopped off the still dependent blowing-tube. With a sigh of reluctance, he waved "time for a break" to his assistant, and joined Sandy Woodings on one of the dilapidated swivel chairs.

"Can we talk without the music?"

"Turn it down but not off, David." Wadsworth lifted his eyebrows at the young man. "My nerves are bad, you understand and it helps me to relax."

Sandy looked Wadsworth in the eye, much as he had stared last night at Mrs Pendle. He would have preferred it if Wadsworth hadn't been too relaxed, but given the circumstances, he could only try to ignore the music, a kind of symphony of zither-like oriental twanging and cymbalist percussion.

"Neither of us has the time to waste, Mr Wadsworth, so I'll come directly to the point. How open was the relationship between Simon Martin and Angela Hawksworth? Did they make any attempt to conceal the fact that they were lovers from Mrs Martin?"

"That's some question. Have you seen the sculptures he did of her?"

"I've seen some of them."

"Yes, of course, everybody knew they were, as you delicately put it, lovers."

"But that wasn't so very unusual, was it – Simon Martin taking a young woman as a lover?"

"No. That wasn't at all unusual."

Frank Ryan

"So why was Angela Hawksworth different?"

"You've met him. Do you think you could read his mind?"

"You haven't answered my question."

"The truthful answer is I don't know. I don't even want to know."

"What was your relationship with Angela Hawksworth?"

"There was no relationship."

"She came to the house very frequently over a period of two years. I can't believe you when you say there was no relationship."

Wadsworth inhaled noisily through his nose. "Should you be questioning me like this on your own? Doesn't the law demand that there should be at least one other to hold your hand?"

"The law directs me to question you any way I like. When I am ready to ask you for a formal statement, then, and only then do I need a witness. So let me repeat the question."

"There's no need. Let's just say that Angela and I made no pretences of how we felt about each other. Each of us pretended the other did not exist. Does that fully answer your question?"

"You seem determined you won't help. You don't care who murdered her and why – is that it?"

"That's about the size of it. My – have I actually shocked you?"

"I don't shock easily, Mr Wadsworth. Does Simon Martin or anyone else in his house take drugs?"

"Drugs?" Was he mistaken or did Wadsworth have a sly little smile to himself?

"Cannabis? Cocaine? Heroin?"

"Not recently. At least to my knowledge. We all went to the Slade together. That's how we first became acquainted. I couldn't speak for those few early years. I mean, hash is as common as cigarette smoking at a certain stage in one's life."

120

"But leads naturally into the temptation of harder drugs?"

"The weak-minded will eventually discover their crutch."

"What about you yourself, Mr Wadsworth? Do you take drugs?"

"Dangerous in my art – wouldn't you think? Get my shaky fingers burnt."

"Well – let's say it is just possible that Simon Martin does or did take drugs. Cocaine for instance. Under those hypothetical circumstances, where do you think he would obtain his supply?"

"Those circumstances are too hypothetical for my liking, Chief Inspector."

"Does the name Thorpe – or Arber – mean anything to you? Jog the memory?"

"No! Should they?"

Of course he might be completely wrong. For instance if Thorpe had supplied Martin, through Angela, then the animosity between Thorpe and Martin wasn't all it seemed to be. And it pointed to new subtleties. He would somehow have to get to Martin's bank statements. If large, unexplained sums of money had been taken out – !

"Maybe I don't see it right, but I can't help feeling it's an odd situation, one man living under another man's roof."

"Maybe you're not seeing it right."

"No one man of the house?"

"How quaint! I suppose what you're getting at is asking if I'm some kind of parasite? Let me tell you, I pay my share. I always have paid my share."

"Simon Martin can't be so easy to live with. Hardly the sort of man most people would choose to live with."

"Simon is a very successful artist. That kind of company is stimulating. Even the friction stimulates. A thing you probably wouldn't understand."

"I'm very interested in the change in Simon Martin's art.

121

I believe he was very successful at abstract sculpture – then, suddenly, a big change."

"Not big. Galactic, I'd say."

"What explanation would you give for the change?"

"Reason?"

"Artistic reason."

"Good grief! Please don't ask me for reasons. I know nothing about reasons. The whole artistic world is mad and utterly unreasonable. Bedevilled by artificiality, false values. The piece of dross that Gauguin would have wiped his arse on will sell for a hundred times more than the best and most sincere product of a man every bit as good, but less well known. Simon understands the artificiality better than most."

"You seem to imply it wasn't artistic reasons at all?"

"Believe me, even Simon himself wouldn't know a reason if it jumped out of the block of marble and bit him."

Sandy wondered if Wadsworth thought of himself as one of those unappreciated lesser artists. "Economic necessity?" he enquired evenly.

"You don't understand at all, do you? I doubt if you really have a clue."

"Maybe his abstracts weren't in demand any more?" Sandy picked up a perfectly spherical ball of glass, too big for a paperweight, of almost opaque black colour, and finely balanced on three eighteen-inch blood-red legs.

Wadsworth took it out of his hands and placed it back on the bench. "You couldn't be more wrong. It had nothing to do with that mercenary rubbish of supply and demand. Let me tell you, I don't like Simon. Not *like*, but I damn well respect him. Why do geniuses always have to be bastards?" Wadsworth sighed as if he regretted allowing his feelings to get the better of him.

"What then – he had lost the knack?"

"Oh, the divine inspiration!"

"What was so special about his abstract work?"

"You might try the Tate. Nearer to home, the Walker art gallery in Liverpool."

"I'm asking you to tell me, Mr Wadsworth."

"Can you imagine an art devoted to the sinister side of man? An art of violence, mass destruction, torture – the whole thing, the horror of our twentieth century on a megalomaniac scale. Not just the carnage and the pain, but somehow the good in it too, the good aware of the bad, one unable to dissociate itself from the other – that great conflicting gory soup that is the heart of man. How else could you express something that big except in the abstract? Oh, I admit the bastard's genius. Homo sapiens – sadist and poet – mass exterminator, while at the same time getting his knickers in a twist about environmental pollution."

"Simon Martin could put all that into an abstract sculpture?"

"Let me tell you, Chief Inspector, that he could hit that nail on the head, not just once but again and again. Right from the first time I met him in his first year as a student. I can't explain it. It's just in him. I don't believe he knows how to miss."

"To preserve wayward genius – was that the reason you all gave him an alibi for the evening of the murder, Mr Wadsworth?"

"A simple village girl, with pubertal tits and a decent head of hair! To tell you the truth, it broke my heart. I could have killed her myself. Just as any one of Simon's friends and admirers. Because of what she somehow did to him. She finished him, you know. Have you any idea what it's like to know genius – to live under the same roof with genius? Then she came along and he's churning out William Ettys in Florentine marble! She finished him. That bitch finished *everything*."

16

He met up with Josie for an early lunch in an Italian
restaurant which specialised in "slimmers'" vegetarian
pastas. Leaning across the table in a confidential manner
in her white cotton flying-suit with purple belt to match her
purple ear-rings and purple shoes, she whispered intently,
"All I had yesterday was my high-fibre breakfast cereal, an
apple at three o'clock and my tea."

He blew her a kiss because of the earnest light in her
widely spaced saucer-innocent blue eyes.

"And do you know what I had for tea? Grilled plaice and
five chips! And cauliflower cheese, with low-calorie cheese
sauce – followed by a low-calorie yoghurt. And I cycled two
and a half miles at resistance-factor twelve on my exercise
bike."

"And have you lost weight?"

"Have I Nelly!"

They were sitting next to the window and Sandy felt light-
headed, gazing on to the sunlit city centre, busy with the
lunch-hour shoppers. The town hall was looking splendid in
light-caramel sandstone, on one of its pinnacles the figure of
a steelworker, slim-waisted and muscular arm raised, wield-
ing a hammer. Wadsworth – the figure had reminded him –
had declared himself capable of murder. How extraordinary! A powerfully built man, much more animal than initial
impressions had recorded, a woman hater – the way he had
talked about Angela bore no relation at all to the beautiful

young girl Martin had sculpted in Florentine marble. With the exception of Eleanor Standon, whose London alibi had been corroborated, every one of the occupants of Martin's home was capable of murder and had had the opportunity, given that their mutual alibis were lies.

The waiter arrived, a jovial teenager, who seemed quite happy to talk calories with Josie. The music had also changed, a long-playing record or cassette of the Supremes, and Sandy sat back and half listened to the nostalgic sounds of his own courting years. A line caught his attention and he listened more closely. How apt! When his problem lay not with the scarcity of clues, but with their multiplicity.

Josie ordered for both of them, and the waiter shouted their order to the spotlessly clean open-plan kitchen, where an equally young and good-natured chef tossed pizza bases into the air like pancakes. A bottle of sparkling sweet Lambrusco made its appearance before them. They touched glasses, Josie's eyes in a happy daze with the sunshine. He had moved in his thoughts to Paul Thorpe, his mother, Jacky Arber, Mrs Pendle. All of them, he was certain, knew a great deal more than they were telling him. All of them just as capable as the Martins' household of murder.

The lasagne seemed to arrive within minutes and Josie allowed him the honour of first taste. Bowing old-fashionedly, he tested a mouthful. "Almost as delicious as you!" he whispered. And although she looked as if she wasn't to be taken in by his obvious flattery, it was true that he felt like taking Josie in his arms and rushing her back to her sumptuous apartment and making love to her. The song had changed and he listened to another record of a similar vintage. Love – that was the message of course, but this time a forbidden physical love with its tender but disastrous physical consequences. It was like a momentary revelation: a new thought hit him, or more accurately a new interpretation of what they already knew to be important. Something! It wasn't so much a thought as a depth of feeling. God in heaven! He waited, with heart pounding, for the verse to repeat itself. The pregnancy had always been vital. He had always known that. But he hadn't realised just how vital. Yet sitting here, facing Josie, who looked more dangerously gorgeous with each additional sip of sweet Lambrusco, he couldn't take the feeling further. It wasn't the right time for absolute concentration.

Chief Superintendent Georgy Barker was the last person he wanted to meet just now, but Georgy was waiting for him just inside the door to the old school, wanting to know exactly what had been discovered in his conversation with Hugh Bearder.

"Bearder is lying through his teeth – just like Meadows."

Georgy grinned hugely, as they moved in a disorderly tandem into the main interview area, where Inspector Earnshaw stood up to greet them.

"You look pleased with yourself, Charlie." Sandy eyed the hands clasped behind the man's back, the widely spaced, firmly entrenched legs.

"Found three out of the four we wanted," he said, passing a summary sheet over for Sandy to read. "Amazing how the mention of murder can loosen muscle-bound tongues!"

"So they did share a couple of reefers?"

"Supplied by either Thorpe or Arber."

"Who were present at the time – two of the original six?"

"That's right."

"So now we have a definite connection to drugs. Enough, if we want, to bring those two sparks in for questioning."

"Do you want me to arrange it?"

"No. Not yet. Even if they admitted it, it would be nothing – a misdemeanour. I want to know where it fits in, if it does fit in, with our murder enquiry. Which reminds me – no sign of Tom Williams?"

"He hasn't arrived back yet. Arber seems to be giving him the slip."

"What do you mean?"

"He radioed in – as soon as Arber spotted him coming, he took off on his motorbike. But Williams jumped into his car and has gone after him."

"Really? Exactly where has Arber led him?"

"Last heard from him on Abbey Lane."

Arber! He reflected on Arber, then moved rapidly to the two sergeants who were filing the reports into the computer in the adjacent room. He wanted a specific file extracting – the report Tom had prepared after he had visited Arber last time. The details of the bike. Within thirty seconds one of the sergeants had put the appropriate disc into the drive and Tom's report flashed on to the screen. BMW 100RS. An extremely powerful machine, fitted with citizen-band radio. That was what he had been looking for. It meant that Arber and Thorpe could almost certainly keep in touch even when separated.

Constable Brown was in the incident room when he returned. Brown had visited Mrs Pendle to tell her they had found no gold trinkets with their metal detectors at the spot she had indicated.

"How did Mrs Pendle take that?"

"I'd say she looked worried, sir."

Sandy considered this with interest. "What about her clothes?"

"There were traces of grass and soil on trousers and top – but plenty of clay too. Of a sort not found on the playing-fields. And flakes of carbon."

"Carbon – you mean soot? Something from a fire?"

"Nobody would be burning a fire in this weather."

"Unless they were burning rubbish – or something they wanted to get rid of." He was thinking that Mrs Pendle's cottage had open grates in every room.

"She didn't change her story? Still claimed adamantly she hadn't left hat spot?"

"That's it, sir!"

Sandy Woodings gazed at Georgy, who had taken up Earnshaw's stance, the pair of them regarding him curiously, hands clasped behind backs, against the furnace of light streaming through the square-paned windows.

"I'm going into the village. I'll take Brown's handset with me. Brown – you get hold of another for yourself. Get back to watching Mrs Pendle and for God's sake, this time, don't lose her. I have a certain feeling about Mrs Pendle."

"Yes, sir," said Brown, handing him the leather-wrapped walkie-talkie.

He returned to the sergeant on the information desk and gave him very careful instructions. "I won't leave the village. Call me immediately you hear more about Arber and his location. Or anything else that strikes you as seeming unusual. There's something going on – and I want to know what it is."

"Right, sir!"

He left the half-smiling Georgy in that same watchful position in front of the window and drove down the lane until he came to Mrs Pendle's cottage. At the cottage he stopped momentarily, climbed out to look into the garden, remarked with satisfaction that his man was nowhere visible. From there, back in his car again, he turned left on to the main road towards the picnic area, following the route taken by Mrs Pendle and her pig on the morning she had discovered the body, cruising about a hundred and fifty yards, turning sharp right, along a street that was lined by much more modern houses. He checked the address in his book, climbed out, and then knocked smartly on the brightly-varnished front door. It was the house in front of which Mrs Pendle had made such a loud banging on that fateful morning, in response to which the window had been promptly and firmly slammed shut.

"Mrs Sheridan?" He extended his hand to grasp the fingertips she offered him. "I'm Chief Inspector Woodings.

Would you mind if I came in and had a few words with you?"

For the first time in half an hour, Tom Williams picked up the car microphone and called the incident centre to tell them that his location was the same as before and that he was parked a hundred yards from where he had seen Jack Arber park his motorbike, off Abbey Lane, close to some big trees. In all of that half-hour the bike had remained in view, and he had simply waited for Arber to reappear. Now it was impatience as much as anything that caused Tom to engage the drive on his automatic gear-box, holding the steering steady by means of the swivel ball especially fitted to the wheel to accommodate his one good arm, and inch towards the parked bike. When almost abreast of it, he noticed the presence of the second bike. He radioed back again, reporting that Arber must have arranged to meet Thorpe and that they had both left their bikes and gone into the wood. Although Tom did not know Dossage well, he was familiar enough with the woods that surrounded it to realise that this was an eastern entrance to the wood in which Angela Hawksworth had been killed. He radioed in yet again to say he was getting out of the car and following Thorpe and Arber on foot.

The entrance led to two gateposts without a gate. A gate would have been a waste of time anyway, since the wood could have been entered at any point along the road, as there was neither a fence nor wall along its perimeter. The ornamental gateposts were of rough-hewn redwood tree-trunks and had probably been erected by bored foresters, because he could see now that what he had entered was a small foresters' base workshop. Giant cylinders of oak, elm, beech and sycamore were scattered all about him. There was a small red brick hut with a blue slate roof and several buildings of corrugated iron with interiors open to the air. This must be where they cut up fallen and otherwise culled trees. A large open-air furnace was evidently used to burn off the smaller wood and branches, while the trunks were sawn down to manageable size using the larger bench-mounted circular saw in one of the open sheds. Approaching the red brick hut, he looked in at the one window, saw a simple arrangement of table, chairs, workbench and a litter of woodman's tools, but it was otherwise empty. He walked on a dozen yards beyond the furthermost shed and looked around him.

He was already deep enough into the wood to notice the silence.

He could just glimpse his car parked in front of the bikes, the road, and on the opposite side of the road a continuation of the same wood which ran all the way east as far as the city boundary. The route branched where he stood into a main bridle path running directly west, and two smaller paths running north-west and south-west. There was no indication which direction Thorpe and Arber had taken. Deciding on the main path, he moved quickly along the dry level ground for about half a mile, doing some thinking as he walked. Ever since he had left his car he had had the feeling that he had been watched from some hiding-place and even now was possibly being followed. No doubt a knight in shining armour would not have allowed himself to be put off by such a feeling, but as far as Tom Williams was concerned the object of the exercise was to gain information while practising self-preservation. He called the murder centre on his handset, telling them once more his precise position, adding, "Tell the chief I'll hold my position here, but I see little point in searching deeper. And you can tell him for nothing that I don't like the feel of it."

Sandy Woodings had politely accepted the tea proffered in a Derby cup and saucer and had learned over a somewhat trying fifteen minutes from the humourless Mrs Sheridan that she had indeed seen Mrs Pendle taking her pig for a walk at about 6:15 on the morning she had found the body, that she knew Thorpe, Arber and Mr and Mrs Martin by sight, but knew absolutely nothing more about any of them.

"This animal-welfare group – ?"

"The Rare Breeds Survivors Trust?"

"Yes. What is it exactly?"

"As its name suggests, it was founded to preserve rare breeds among domestic animals and livestock."

"I believe Mrs Pendle was a founder member."

"She most certainly was not. Emily Pendle takes a great deal too much upon her shoulders. I predict, Chief Inspector, that she will get herself into hot water one of these days with these delusions of grandeur."

"What exactly do you mean by that, Mrs Sheridan?"

"Well – I'm sure you already know a great deal. Herbalism! I ask you. I mean, there are some who would criticise me because I dabble a little in astrology. But it's a case of knowing where to draw the line, isn't it?"

So – he was looking at the village astrologer! Sandy concealed his amusement. "Rare breeds of animals. Herbalism! What else does Mrs Pendle dabble in then, Mrs Sheridan?"

"You name it. Anything she can make money from. Fortune telling. Whatever they call it – biorhythms! That fanciful hotch-potch of scientific mumbo-jumbo and superstition that people refer to as the occult."

"Which is very different from orthodox astrology?"

"Astrology is a respectable profession."

"Yes. I am sorry. I didn't mean to offend you. I think I am beginning to see – "

"I doubt it, with all due respect, chief inspector."

He would have liked to have discussed this topic in more detail, but his handset bleeped. In the presence of such a suspicious and inquisitive character, he made an excuse and took himself upstairs to the bathroom, where he listened to the message from the switchboard sergeant about Tom and his predicament.

"What's happening with Martin?"

"I'll have to find out and call you back."

"Make it quick, will you," he said, idling away the few minutes of waiting by opening the window and inspecting the view to the front of the house, nodding at the clear view of the road all the way to the entrance to the picnic area. When the sergeant came on again, he told him that Martin had been followed to the northernmost perimeter of the wood, where he had entered it, apparently intent on having a solitary stroll.

So Martin, Thorpe and Arber were all within a section of wood roughly five by five miles in area! Sandy Woodings gave an immediate order.

"Tell our man on Martin to get close to him. I don't care if Martin sees him. And tell Inspector Williams to hold his position. I'm on my way right now."

Tom Williams had predicted the chief's reaction, which he received none the less with a reluctant sigh. He had just switched off the handset, when he heard a mechanical roaring, which could have been the circular saw being switched on. But he didn't really think that was so on reflection and, running back along the bridle path, found that his misgivings were justified. Thorpe and Arber were astride their machines. They had misled him, made a fool of him. He started to run in the direction of the road, but had only got to within three hundred yards of the foresters' hut when he realised that they were not, as he had assumed, making their escape.

"Hey, you clowns!" he shouted, at the same time speaking urgently into his handset. "Those two buggers are coming back up the path after me."

There wasn't time to run, it took all of his concentration just to wait, balanced on his legs like a matador facing two charging bulls, and to jump aside at just the right moment to allow a quarter-ton of rapidly accelerating steel to brush past him. Thorpe came first and then he had to dive with equal dexterity when Arber followed.

"You're crazy!" He climbed to his feet and shook his fist after them, until they turned and he could see that they intended to come right back.

Blazing with anger, he couldn't do a thing about it. He ran into the trees to his right, diagonally, so that he was in effect heading back towards the road. Within seconds they were abreast of him, riding across each other, entwining their paths round him as he continued to run. His ears were deafened by the roaring of their engines. They were so close to him he could read the letters BMW on the shining aluminium engines. Every second he expected the flash of silvered chrome and steel to veer just those few inches and turn him into mincemeat.

"Bloody lunatics!" He thumped at Thorpe's shoulder and received a kick in the back from Arber, who was on the opposite side of him.

"Didn't you want to talk to us, Mr Policeman?" Arber's voice taunted him, as he deliberately checked with his front wheel inches away. "Well, you've found us. Here we are. Let's hear what you've got to say to us."

A kick from Thorpe caught him behind his left knee and knocked him sidelong into a tree. He tried to kick out in his own defence, and narrowly avoided having his foot taken off at the ankle by a spinning back wheel. Using the tree as a fulcrum, he swung round with all of his weight and he managed to push with one foot at the region of the saddle on Arber's machine, causing the bike to wobble and then Arber to go sprawling. He started to run again. Thorpe was coming after him. He could hear the machine screaming in high revs close behind him. Twisting and turning round trees, he made it as difficult as he could. He jumped over a small stream that had cut its bed a good two feet down into the peaty soil and continued to run, listening as he did so. The stream had delayed Thorpe. The bikes' engines moved away for a minute or so during which he made good progress; he could actually see the road through the trees in front of him. But then, as if out of nowhere, Arber arrived directly in front of him, blocking his path, and Thorpe's roaring sounded once more behind him.

Sweating, he found a heavy sawn branch in his hand. He had run as far as he was going to and now he weighed in his mind his chances of cracking Thorpe over his helmet-less skull. Tom Williams was as close to killing a man as he had ever been in his life when there was a screech of brakes and Woodings, followed by four uniformed officers, ran through the fringe of trees and grabbed hold of the unresisting and still maliciously grinning Thorpe and Arber.

"I'm arresting you – both of you." He spoke with icy anger. Turning to the four officers from the patrol car, he said, "Take them down to headquarters and book them for assault. Don't let them share so much as a word with each other. Lock them away separately. We'll find out how perky they feel after a night in the cells."

Then he used his handset to check on Martin's position. Martin was still strolling at his ease, completely unaware of what had happened no more than three miles away.

It was a deeply thoughtful Sandy Woodings who watched the two roughnecks, now restrained with handcuffs, being bundled into the back of the patrol car.

17

"How are you – any damage?" Sandy put his hand on Tom's shoulder, as they walked towards the parked cars.

"I'm not hurt. I'm more livid than shaken."

"Are you up to driving – or do you want me to give you a lift back to the school?"

"I can drive myself, thanks! And I'm coming back with you. There isn't a power on earth that would stop me now."

With a smile of approval, Sandy watched Tom get into his white Ford Escort, start it up and pull away. How damned glad he was to have Tom back at work with him.

Back at the school, with a very interested Georgy and Inspector Earnshaw present – Georgy sitting astride a chair, with elbows on the backrail – Sandy tried to think through exactly what had been behind the incident. It was Tom's theory that Arber had deliberately led him there, where Thorpe had been waiting, in order to play games with him. The motive had been simply to make a fool of him and what he represented, the city's police force.

"What do you think?" Sandy turned to Georgy and Earnshaw.

"Could be. Seems in character," said Earnshaw, while Georgy just stared at Tom curiously, his attention focused on the latest of his outrageous ties – a scarlet stripe, which looked like a stick of Blackpool rock with a picture of a Ferrari just below the outsize knot.

"You think that Arber knew you were looking for him – maybe saw you following him earlier?"

"It's funny, but I'd have never thought so up to when I saw the parked bike. But he knew I'd come to talk to him at home. Maybe he just put two and two together?"

"And he could have made the arrangement to meet up with Thorpe using the CB radio while Tom was chasing him," said Earnshaw.

Sandy's eyes met Georgy's: that quaint and derisory smile. Georgy didn't believe Tom's simple explanation any more than he did. He tapped Tom in a friendly fashion. "There's work ahead of us – off we go then down to headquarters."

Baiting Tom had been incredibly stupid. Just as stupid as Simon Martin, artist and intellectual, giving a policeman a bloody nose and having to be carried bodily into the back of a police car! Thorpe was the real suspect where the murder was concerned, but Arber was assuming such significance in Sandy's mind that he picked him first for interrogation.

A silent Tom sat with him in the interview room and Georgy watched through the one-way mirror.

"Assault on a policeman is a serious offence – a mug's mistake." He spoke slowly and calmly, so that his words would stick. "Not the sort of thing I'd have expected from a smart would-be entrepreneur."

"What's one of them when he's at home?"

"That's the information I want from you, Jacky."

"We never touched him. Never so much as laid a finger on him – in spite of him knocking me off me machine and doing a good hundred quid's worth of damage."

"You thought you were tough. Two young men on bikes trying to run down a man close to retirement age with only one good arm. Go down well in court – maybe we could make that an attempted murder."

"If we had wanted to run him down he wouldn't be in the shape he is right now."

"So – I'm listening. What *was* the game then?"

"You people always giving us a hard time – following us everywhere we go. You think we're stupid! You think we don't know."

"Know what?"

"Some geezer always there. Different geezers. Different cars. But it sticks out in the village. It only makes folk laugh."

If Sandy Woodings was surprised to hear this – especially so since the murder team had not put Thorpe and Arber under surveillance until yesterday, and then it was only Tom – his face showed nothing.

"So you saw Inspector Williams today – ?"

"We only came back up t'bridle path to see who it were like – then the bugger made a spectacle of himself dodging about and waving his arms. Just a bit of fun. We couldn't resist it."

Tom shifted his stance against the wall, but managed to keep his mouth shut.

"So – what were you and Thorpe doing there, hanging about in the wood?"

"That's our business."

"Thorpe is a psychopath and you're smart, Jacky."

"Your stupid inspector called us both little shits. Psychopath – I like that. That sounds like a promotion."

"You're too smart not to realise that Thorpe is heading for serious trouble. This is a murder enquiry. Somebody who knows something about a murder and conceals it from us is aiding and abetting – and that's almost as serious as the murder charge itself."

Time for a slight pause: if Sandy had still smoked, he would have opened the packet and offered one.

"You knew that Martin was in the wood, didn't you?"

"You've got your knickers in a twist, that's all I'm going to tell you."

"How did you know he was in the wood? Did one of you

137

follow him, then drive round to the other side and call the other over his radio?"

Jacky Arber unflinchingly took the full force of Sandy Woodings's stare, sitting quite happy with himself in his laceless trainers, blue jeans and sleeveless white tee-shirt, with tattooed arms much slimmer than Thorpe's, but sinewy and wiry, resting on the table surface between them. How could a couple of kids brought up in the pleasant rural surroundings of Dossage have turned into such hardened criminals?

"All right, Jacky! So Thorpe is your friend. He's important. He's done things that make you important too. You're not a couple of nobodies. Learning some stupid little trade and taking orders from some brainwashed loser. Instead of that, you take your orders from Thorpe – that's right, isn't it?"

"We're mates. I don't take orders from nobody."

"Not even when it came to Angela, Jacky? Some looker, wasn't she? And a mind of her own. She was going places too. Like you and Paul."

"What's Angela got to do with it?"

"Took a fancy to her, did you?"

"Angela was Paul's girl."

"There was no law against you fancying her too. Village beauty queen. The one girl who could see further than the village boundary. Nobody could blame you for fancying her."

"Jesus! Oh – no!"

"No, what, Jacky?"

"I don't know what you're on about."

"Maybe she had too much spirit? Things happen. It wasn't your fault. Then Paul got jealous – ?"

"You're not pinning Angela on me. Oh, no you don't!"

"You know we'll keep ferreting until we come up with something. Think about it. You've got a good brain – use it. Murder – aiding and abetting. Concealing information. You pick any of those charges – let me tell you they're big ones. Millstones, Jacky! One of them round your neck and you'll sink behind grey walls all the way down to your old age."

"And if you can't find no evidence – then you'll trump some up?"

"There is a way out for you, Jacky. One option Thorpe doesn't have. You're going to have all night to think about it. Think what he would do if the situation were reversed. I think I know how he'd play it, I know him that well already."

"And I know him a whole lot better than you," said Arber aggressively.

But that was an understandable immediate response. Give him twelve hours on a hard bed with only his thoughts for company.

It was 9:10 p.m. when Sandy arrived back at his flat, where he poured himself a glass of whisky, neat. Drinking alone was unusual for him but then he had given up cigarettes. He caught the tail end of the nine o'clock news on the television – striking miners whistling the Laurel and Hardy theme tune as squads of riot police marched in to confront them on the picket lines. He was still laughing when the weatherman with his new computerised maps talked about the continuing heatwave. The coastal town of Oban in Scotland had recorded the highest ever temperature for the 25th of May. But something was going wrong with the isobars over the Atlantic and for a while it seemed the heatwave was to be interrupted. There was even the possibility of freak storms.

Thoughtful a moment, he finished the glass, then picked up his telephone and called the children. It was his ex-wife, Julie, who answered.

"Oh, hello, love! How's things?"

"Things are fine, Sandy." She hesitated. "They enjoyed Devon. I – well – thanks, Sandy!"

"That's fine." He understood why she was feeling so

uncomfortable: Julie and Jack were now living in the house that she had once shared with him. But then he couldn't complain, because it had been his idea, so that the kids could stay where they had grown up, and Jack's family could remain with his ex-wife, Mary. Before either had the chance to say anything more, a childish voice broke into their thoughts.

"Is that you, Dad?" asked Marty, his youngest daughter. "I've picked up the extension," she said, in a husky low-pitched sing-song.

"You sound as if you've just woken up."

"You know that toothpaste Mum bought? Well, I've cleaned my teeth with it tonight and it tastes like Germolene."

"I'll have to buy you some nicer toothpaste."

There was a commotion and then Gerry's slightly older voice came over the telephone, accompanied by abuse from Marty because he had taken the telephone from her. "We were watching a programme tonight on the television about Mozart, Dad. Guess what? There was a lady who said she had the great thrill of taking part in his wind compositions." Gerry gave him a verbal impression.

Sandy laughed. "Good night, two little monsters!"

18

The meteorologists were accurate in their forecasts. That night saw a terrific change in the weather, with high winds and driving rain. The sound of the wind kept waking Sandy Woodings and he passed the time by continuing to turn things over in his mind. The wall of silence from Arber had genuinely surprised him: all too often the leather-jacketed thugs became little boys as soon as they realised that the game was up. There had to be something important afoot to explain the cool brand of hostility he had sensed throughout the interview in Arber's plain brown eyes. Something of the young man with a purpose. This sense of purpose, whatever that purpose turned out to be, was what enabled him to stand up to the questioning. But what kind of purpose could make him resistant even to the threat of being charged as an accomplice to murder?

Confused thoughts came into Sandy's mind as he drifted in and out of sleep. Macabre notions and meanings. The two-foot phallus embroidered in flowers on the well-dressing. The possible link between Arber and therefore Thorpe, Angela Hawksworth and Mrs Pendle. Mrs Sheridan talking of Mrs Pendle being too ambitious for her own good – was she referring to just the penchant for mysticism or something deeper and more sinister?

One thing he was certain of: there was more going on in the village than he had even begun to realise.

After driving into headquarters at first light through the

appalling unseasonal weather, he first had another go at the unchanged Arber, before spending two hours questioning, even more intensively, Paul Thorpe. It was extraordinary, but he just couldn't get a thing out of either of them. He made no progress whatsoever. It was as if he were questioning religious or political fanatics rather than village louts. In their truculent and hardened faces some deep sense of destiny hung – a real light of purpose, that gave each his desperate determination.

They had to be charged and were, two days later, on Monday, May 28th, with assault on a police officer. The magistrates, impressed by the fact that Inspector Williams had not been seriously hurt, took the view that it was a malicious prank and fined them a hundred pounds each, which meant that by lunch time Thorpe and Arber were once again free to go about their secret conspiracy.

Yes, conspiracy was the feeling that best described the unease Sandy had felt ever since he had tossed and turned in his bed on the Friday night. Something was planned and he felt powerless to stop it. It was bad luck, this change in the weather – it would make fieldwork just about impossible.

After lunch on the Monday he returned to his office at headquarters, and made a determined sortie at the pile of paper-work if for no better reason than to keep Mrs Parks happy. Tom arrived, having spent longer than Sandy at the magistrates' court, and in his presence, Sandy telephoned the school headquarters and asked about Mrs Pendle. But it was all useless. The man watching her had reported in thirty minutes before: Mrs Pendle was behaving herself, spending all of her time with her animals or tending her garden.

"I'll frankly admit to you, Tom, that the whole thing has me baffled."

"If you ask me, we should have thrown more at Thorpe and Arber. Held them for a lot longer. In time that pair would have talked."

"I had the impression they would never have talked, Tom." Sandy shook his head, staring out of his window at the rain that was battering itself against the double-glazed panes.

"You never made anything at all of the drugs angle."

"I had my reasons. I assure you I don't underestimate it."

"I don't understand what the hell is happening," Tom grumbled and, as if to make life even more difficult, pulled out a cigarette from his silver case – the one with the collector's postcard of Marilyn Monroe sitting half turned with her back to the camera and her cute bottom cuddled by a white ermine stole – and lit it.

"I deliberately don't want to make too much noise about the drugs connection just yet. That goes for here at headquarters and in the centre at Dossage too. So watch what you're saying."

"You're the boss."

Even the smell of the cigarette was driving him to distraction. "I have the feeling that things are coming to the boil. Have you ever had that feeling, Tom? Right down to your very bones – that all you have to do is to let the maximum number of ingredients work on each other in the pot."

Tom's expression was dubious but the casual way he smoked his cigarette said he was easy. True to form, he was wearing a different tie, a broad grey silk creation, with a harlequin's mask under the knot that might have been the two faces of Janus. Sandy was beginning to wonder if Tom, the age-old confirmed bachelor, had found himself a woman.

Mrs Parks must have read their mood because she appeared unbidden with two mugs of decent coffee and half a dozen shortbread biscuits. Sandy winked at her as she raised her eyebrows on pulling the door to after her.

"Tell me, Tom – where would you go from here?"

"Me? I'd have another crack at that Martin character."

Sandy watched Tom down his coffee in huge indecent draughts. "How? Just exactly how would you go about it?"

"If you ask me, there's been too much talk about all of this art business."

Sandy had another thoughtful sip at his coffee. "All right then – let's have some action. How about a nice little trip across the Pennines?"

He picked up the intercom and asked Mrs Parks to put him through to the Walker art gallery in Liverpool.

On the two-hour drive, Tom surprised Sandy with another of the interests he had acquired in his six-month flirtation with retirement. He mentioned an entirely new ambition, which was to own a string of greyhounds. As they crawled along the M1 motorway north into the dense rain-mists around Leeds and then took the M62 all the way west, through a virtual thunderstorm and hurricane at more than two thousand feet above sea-level, Tom made himself comfortable in Sandy's passenger seat and enlightened him on the depth of a good dog's chest and the length of a winner's toes, so that before they knew it they had passed through a wet and windy Lancashire, arriving out at the part that had been renamed Merseyside in the county shuffle, but which had never really regarded itself as part of Lancashire anyway. Liverpool, whose boast was that it was made up of a third Irish, a third Welsh and a final third which didn't know where it had come from except that it wasn't English. An amazing if depressed city, which out of this pot-pourri had produced an abundance of talent together with an impressive art gallery to complement it.

Before setting out, Sandy had, in a telephone call to the gallery, made certain that somebody who knew something about sculpture would be available to give them advice and that the exhibits he wanted to see would be on display. A wise precaution as it turned out, since the four sculptures by

Simon Martin were not on public display but had only recently been returned by the Tate, which had borrowed them for an exhibition. The art director was Vanessa Short, a thirty-five-year-old Liverpudlian, who met them at the reception desk and led them down a green marble staircase into the basement.

"Do you know Simon Martin personally?" he asked her during the descent.

"I've never been introduced to him personally – I've seen him at various exhibitions." She stopped a moment, looked at Sandy Woodings curiously. "You said over the telephone that you needed to see the sculptures to help you in your enquiries. What kind of enquiries, might I ask – or is that some big secret?"

"We are investigating a murder, Miss Short."

"Mrs!" she laughed. "A woman doesn't have to wear a ring to be married. But that's astonishing. A murder! What possible link could a murder have with a work of art?"

"That's what we're here to find out," he smiled back in his turn, following her spare healthy figure through a door into a vast storage room.

Giant racks full of framed oil paintings were stacked in apparent random order behind crates presumably full of others, either in the process of being sent elsewhere or recently acquired. They moved from here into a small room where racks of watercolours, out of their frames and stacked in their window-mounts dozen by dozen, were set out in rows, like a gardener's vegetable beds. The policeman in Sandy caused him to search for windows only to find none. They were in the basement, hence no windows, and from the watercolour room they entered a final storage area, at least as large as that for oil paintings, with only two entrances, the door they had come in through and another in what he had to presume was an outside wall.

He had a good look round this room. Fragments of

145

classical stone and marble clashed with Georgian and Victorian figures. Two men she called John and Arthur were busy moving four monstrosities, or at least so they looked as they were being wheeled into a display area on forklift trucks. They had to wait for the men to finish and leave them in order to study the works of the younger Simon Martin with what Mrs Short obviously considered the proper appreciation.

"Just what are we supposed to be looking at?" Tom gaped without any pretence at understanding.

"A hundred thousand pounds' worth of high imagination!" she replied succinctly.

"These are all bronze?" asked Sandy, walking from one to another, until he had satisfied himself that he had had a proper look at all four of them.

"Indeed! And quite old ones for Martin, twelve years at least. Done perhaps five or six years after he had taken the gold medal at the Slade. Art is a very tricky living, Mr Woodings. Martin is one of the very few fortunate ones who found themselves in demand more or less straight from school."

"I find them fascinating."

"Glad you don't feel your journey was wasted."

"Oh, no! Not at all. Tell me a little more about them. For instance, how would someone go about manufacturing – creating – such a work of art?"

"Oh – the usual would probably involve a trial miniature. Something in clay, as a child moulds plasticine. When he, or she, gets the model right, then there are various techniques for putting the conception into shape. Knock it out of a block of stone or marble. Or for instance mould it in wax, which is then blocked with clay, the wax heated to vapour and the bronze poured in to precisely fill the vacated gap. What has been known for two thousand years and hasn't really been bettered – the lost-wax method. But I should add that Martin has always been different. I am told – and I suspect it is true – that he doesn't need to see any preliminary work-up. He has sufficient powers of imagination – and believe me, that means *some imagination* – to see the finished thing in its massive three dimensions."

"Something like Michelangelo seeing the Pieta when it was still in its block of marble?"

"So he claimed – oh, but there I go! It's almost instinctive in us to call it all nonsense."

"I think I can see why his art was so sought after."

"Each piece might take him six months to complete. So there wouldn't be all that many, even in a lifetime."

"Hence such works as these – your gallery congratulates itself that it bought them for a song even at twenty-five thousand pounds each?"

She smiled at him. "Today they would fetch ten times as much."

"Really?"

"Extraordinary – you see what I mean."

"Yes, they are, aren't they? Do you feel an influence when you look at them, Mrs Short?"

"An influence? Yes. Yes, I suppose I do."

Sandy Woodings was glad she felt it too. There was an extraordinary, to use her word, power, about the four sculptures. Massive, gnarled, green-bronze, twisted and turned into a distortion of what was nevertheless an exercise on the human form. In his course on the philosophy of art, he had never come across any modern artist who even remotely approached these brooding explosions of energy.

"Please tell me what it is you see in them." He looked urgently at this tiny knowledgeable woman.

"Aggression! We have a nickname for them – the four furies! They were really intended for out-of-doors. Can you imagine their effect, say massed together in front of the United Nations?"

"Yes. I could imagine it, Mrs Short."

147

"Well – if you've seen what you came to see . . ."

"Thank you very much! You've been most helpful."

Sandy had to apply a tug of the sleeve to Tom, who could hardly tear himself away from the sight of a hundred thousand pounds multiplied by ten for a ton of brass coated with copper sulphate.

"Did you realise anything, back there?" Sandy asked Tom, when they were back in the car again and just turning off the slip road on to the M62.

"I realised that there's a lot more ways to have a flutter than just the dogs and the gee-gees. And there's some flutters that must be more certain than others, if you only have the right inside knowledge."

"And that's all you realised?"

"I realised one or two things about the helpful Mrs Short, quite apart from her attitude to the gold ring on the third finger, if that's what you mean?"

"You haven't seen his latest stuff, have you? Martin's sculpture, I mean? If you had, you'd have noticed all right. You'd have noticed that all four of the furies were male."

"What else would you expect?"

"What else indeed?" He nodded mildly. For a moment then – ! But he could see that Tom was probably right. Yet, at that moment, as he was looking up at those eight-foot figures, he had felt an inkling of that same intuition as when sitting in the Italian restaurant with Josie. For a long while he drove and he thought no more about it. He was more concerned with this weather, which would take days to blow itself away. But then, just as he was almost home, he felt a sudden new surge of interest in those four sculptures. Of course they were nothing other than fantastic nightmares. They reminded him of his recent night spent struggling with similar images of terror. Terror: pain: incomprehension in the face of a perplexingly ambiguous world. It was hard to

148

believe that the mind that had created them had not also been insane as well as brilliant.

And then that change! That extraordinarily delicate and beautiful figure of Eve, with her hand held out.

19

On Wednesday the wind disappeared as suddenly as it had
appeared. The sun shone again from a clear blue sky and it
felt several degrees hotter. At 8:30 a.m. when Sandy first
arrived in the village, the heat spiralled in visible currents
over the earth, the trees and cottages, a transparent but
tangible soft cushion that brushed his skin and glowed a
thick pastel blue over the hills of Derbyshire no more than
two miles distant. He could see the attraction of Dossage to
Martin and his coterie: the village still had so many of the old
Derbyshire characters living in it, people who had been born
here and whose families had lived here for generations.

Suddenly he felt like kicking himself. How stupid they
had been! Angela's pregnancy had always been the most
important clue! He parked the car at the old school and
made his way on foot to the odd-shaped cottage, shaped like
a wedge of cheese, radiating from the green.

"So you knew – ?"

"By now," replied Paul Thorpe, "Auntie Emily will have
told the whole village that Angela was pregnant."

Of course. Sandy nodded, noticing how Thorpe was
sweating. This was something he hadn't realised before, just
listening to Georgy's tape. Yet it wasn't fear – he had been
sweating even before Sandy had arrived, so it wasn't just his
presence making him nervous. So why was he so nervous?

"Martin was the father, wasn't he? So naturally you felt

jealous. She was about to leave you for him. She was finally going to leave you for good. This time there could be no changing her mind about it.''

"You couldn't have got it more wrong. The baby would have been mine!"

"I don't believe you."

"Believe what you like. The baby would have been mine – it was that crazy man who was jealous.''

"In your signed statement, made to Chief Superintendent Barker, you said you had broken off with Angela for months before she was killed."

"That wasn't the whole truth."

"Let's hear the whole truth now, then."

"We met now and then. We talked."

"You don't conceive a baby from talking."

"Sometimes we did more than talk."

Sandy studied that perspiring face, the dark straggly curls hanging down, wet from sweat, over the two big bosses of forehead.

"How can you be sure that Martin was not the father?"

Thorpe blurted in pained anger. "Because Angie told me."

"And you believed her?"

"It was the truth. She did it deliberately. She wanted to get pregnant. That was the time we talked about getting engaged."

"That's easily said – but how can you prove it to me?"

"You prove it different."

"I know she had finished with you. Her parents told me so."

"We made it up. But they didn't tell you that, did they. Only the day before she was killed. We were going to go back together. That was the reason we made it up – the baby!"

"You told Mr Barker you just passed without speaking in the street."

151

"I lied. It had only just happened. Angie killed! I didn't care if I lied or not."

"Why should she want you back again?"

"The baby! It was going to be my baby."

"That baby she told you was yours?"

"Mine! Mine! Why do you think that bastard, Martin killed her!"

"I'm utterly convinced of it," said Sandy to the gathered team of Tom, Georgy, Brown and Earnshaw. "The pregnancy was the motive. I've felt it in my bones from the beginning. Whoever killed her made a point of stabbing her in the right place. That points to some degree of hate. Hate like that – it should be obvious."

"If only we could be sure whose baby she was expecting, said Tom earnestly.

"That's just it – I think we can. Not Thorpe's, as he tried to convince me. It just had to be Martin's. Let's say it had been Thorpe's, then why on earth should anybody kill her? Martin?" He shook his head vehemently. "Even so, I can't believe that. I can't believe that just because she had got pregnant – ! For God's sake, it wouldn't have mattered that much to him, not enough for him to have killed her. Wrong man!" He shook his head again.

"No man is the wrong kind of man," said Georgy. He had started the heaving and rolling, searching his pockets.

"With his money and his attitudes. Come on, the solution would have been a therapeutic abortion – if he bothered at all."

"You like her, don't you?" said Georgy quietly.

"Like who?"

"I think you know who I mean." Georgy wore the trace of a smile, putting his pipe between his teeth.

Was it that obvious? Sandy watched Georgy light his pipe. Suddenly he felt terribly restless.

*

He waited two days before calling on her, to find her kneeling on a flat stone at the edge of the big rockery which bordered the fish-pond on three sides. She could be forgiven for the shock at seeing him, because they hadn't been near the house for a week. She looked up with that startled look, which he was coming to believe must never leave her eyes.

"If you want Simon, he's out until tonight."

"I know he's gone to Edinburgh. It's you I came to see."

He didn't want a repetition of the last interview. He wanted to make it easier on her – but already her face was visibly paling, and she had to draw her knees together so as to conceal her jitteriness.

"Shall we go into the house then?"

"I'm sure that's not necessary – unless you want it," he said kindly.

"The rockery is my responsibility." She concentrated for a moment on digging out some dandelions and a resisting dock with her long bare fingers.

"Your relationship with your husband – "

"We discussed that last time, didn't we." Her eyes closed.

He almost put out a hand as if to steady her. "Are you all right?"

"Yes, it's nothing. Thank you, chief inspector!" With a sigh, she eased her back straight – a back that couldn't have been more perfect even at the tender age of twenty. "You didn't believe me – I knew you didn't, you know."

"It isn't that I don't believe you. But I must ask you – did you know that Angela was pregnant?"

She didn't even try to hide the pain in those brown eyes. "Yes – I think I guessed."

"She modelled for your husband. Surely he must have noticed?"

"I'm sure he did notice."

"Then he must have mentioned it to you. You must have discussed it?"

153

"Oh, I had guessed long before Simon told me."

"You knew well before her murder?"

"For about a month, I should say." She carried on weeding among the boulders. Thoughtfully, he watched this simple dexterity – the most ordinary of artists in this household of more ambitious colleagues – as she stepped awkwardly from stone to stone, rooting among the big exotic buds of peonies and the rich old blue of cottage geraniums.

His voice dropped; it was calm, reasonable but insistent. "Was Simon the prospective father?"

"I simply do not know. That's the honest truth." From the bigger clumps at the back, to the blaze of colour closer to his firmly entrenched feet, her long fingers weeded among the gypsophila, the aubretia, the delicate wedding-lace of alyssum.

"But you discussed the pregnancy with Simon?"

"Only in the sense it would interfere with her modelling."

"If you'll forgive me, that's a little hard to credit, isn't it?"

"Is it, Chief Inspector?"

He paused again. There was an interesting severity in his eyes. "Did you hate Angela Hawksworth, Mrs Martin?"

"Good Lord, no!" What a lovely change it made when she smiled. Such a gentle warmth emanated from her eyes. In spite of himself, in spite of the nature of his position and the almighty restlessness which burned away in the hidden depths of his consciousness, Sandy Woodings almost smiled back at her.

Her eyes, that fleeting disarming smile, hovered disconcertingly in his mind even after he had returned to the old school, after he had picked up Tom and they had driven to the spot where he had been chased by Thorpe and Arber. Sandy felt the need to be alone so he sent Tom round by car to the picnic area to wait for him, expecting the walk through the wood to last him at least an hour. With a cursory glance about the woodmen's workshop, which had already been comprehensively searched for every clue as to why Arber and Thorpe had met there, he walked briskly along the main bridle path and was deep among the pines and oaks within a matter of minutes.

Caroline Martin was still there. He shook his head at his own foolish vulnerability. That short-groomed dark hair, the tall but soft and feminine figure, the first signs of age in the soil-stained hands with their drying skin and the strings of tendons showing. At the time of meeting her he could have reached out and – ! It was crazy. How right he had been to send Tom round to wait for him. He couldn't have hidden his feelings from Tom.

How on earth could that madman of a husband of hers fail to cherish her? Only the second time Sandy had spoken to her and yet he couldn't help but feel something of the languid promise of that femaleness in the eyes, the soft and smooth taperings of neck to shoulder, of breasts and hips. She had it all. A pleasant attractive personality. And that vulnerability. No man could have failed to sense that vulnerability.

The question was so obvious, he just had to ask it: was she playing some game just to make a fool of him? Could she possibly imagine that he would allow feelings to influence his judgement? No! He couldn't believe that. He just couldn't believe it.

The wood was beautiful. The quiet silenced all sound from the road even when you first entered. The life within it, birds, butterflies, insects. It was easier in these surroundings to believe in a love that was hopeless and all-giving.

But he had to shake himself out of this. The wood was vitally important to his enquiry. He had more than pleasurable reasons for reacquainting himself with it. Martin walked in it. It had attracted Thorpe and Arber. Mrs Pendle collected herbs here, brought her pig here and discovered bodies. Angela Hawksworth had arranged to meet someone here. She had said, "It's all right, Mum. Everything is going to be all right – for all of us!" and then come into this wood to meet her murderer.

He took a personal bleep with him and drove back in the early evening to Josie's apartment on the Riverdale Road, with his mind still in a ferment. Josie put a Martini in his hand and ignored his mood, lying on the floor in her pink skin-suit and doing her exercises in the middle of the lounge carpet.

"I need your help, Josie. Will you give me your honest advice, as subjective as you like?"

"As one of those peculiar creatures called females?" she grunted, somehow elevating her supine body off the floor, balancing on her heels and the back of her head.

"What I want to know is how or why a woman who is very attractive and would have no difficulty finding someone else, would stick to some absolute shit who treats her without even the most elementary respect? Abuses her loyalty. In every way, seemingly offers nothing but heartbreak."

"A waste of time asking me" – she had turned so that she lay face down, lifting each extended leg backwards into the air – "because I'm that fool."

He shook his head, smiling. "We've never talked about marriage, have we, Josie?"

"Marriage!" She sounded terrified, turning her face, those saucer-like blue eyes, on him at an oblique angle. "What a funny old mood you're in. Marriage! We're what is termed singles, Sandy. Is there something wrong? I thought you and me had a real good thing going for us."

She was right. He toasted the fact she was right. He walked out of the room and used the telephone in the hall to call Brown.

"Nothing happening? Mrs Pendle behaving herself?"

"Nothing at all, sir. Remarkably quiet. Mrs Pendle hasn't stirred out of her place all evening."

"Keep watching her, Brown. I have this feeling in my bones still."

"Yes, I'll do that, sir."

He walked back into the lounge and said to Josie, "You never really answered my question."

She flopped breathlessly onto the deeply upholstered couch next to her, so that he could smell the perfume she must have sprayed over herself while he had been telephoning. "Women in love," she whispered huskily.

"It's important that I understand it, Josie. So will you stop playing games with me."

"Love! Marriage! When you wise up you realise that the whole thing is biological. Teenagers fall in love. That's real love. You never fall like that again. First love. Slow toads and cyclamen leaves."

"Slow toads – ? Will you be just a little more specific, Josie. Explain what you mean."

"Biological. It doesn't stop when the baby comes into the world."

"What doesn't stop? For God's sake, I shall put you over my knee – "

"Love as evolution." Her fingers toyed with the curled black hairs on his chest, tracing the early vestiges of grey.

"Are you being serious?"

"Oh, girly love! With different men it has different meanings."

"This first love thing?"

"Persistent snake!" she cajoled him, snuggling for a more comfortable perch with her body curled and her dyed blonde hair spread fanwise, enmeshed with that of his chest. "Think about nursery rhymes. Beauty and the beast. Nymphs and centaurs."

He laughed, fondling her most ticklish area, her exposed ear and the delicate patch just below her ear on the strap muscle of her neck.

"I'm telling you," she insisted. "Take a class full of

157

sixteen-year-olds to grotty old ancient Greece and put one of those half-man creatures in front of them with his donkey legs and his hairy whatsit. There will be one in the crowd who is sure to fall – ''

It was almost midnight when Mrs Pendle held the tiny figurine of a man against her lips, a man in ancient toga, with the index finger of his right hand raised to the sky. With her other hand she drained the upturned cognac bottle into her mouth, took an enormous breath, before placing the bottle next to the figurine, which in its turn stood reverently next to the telephone on her hall table.

"What's the jolly old thing to be then, Coddles? Time to hoist our skirts, eh? What do you say, my balding little fellow?"

On the table next to the telephone was the piece of white melamine board taken from her kitchen and on which were written those two telephone numbers in felt tip.

Picking up the bottle, she made absolutely sure the last drop had been wrung from it before exchanging it for the receiver. She dialled slowly and carefully, waited for the end to the ringing.

"Mr Palmer – the crime reporter?"

"Who is that speaking?"

"Never mind who, just yet. I know who murdered Angela Hawksworth. Are you interested?"

20

"It's damned hot!" said Hugh Bearder.

"It's hot all right," replied Sandy Woodings, putting his white cup of coffee on its white saucer and nodding acknowledgement in the direction of the window with its venetian blind. It was Saturday, June 2nd: he didn't mind the few minutes of playing the game.

"So you had some urgent reason for seeing me?"

"Richard Belton – you remember Richard Belton? Doctor Atkins found heroin in his blood. Many times the expected levels."

"That was considerate of someone."

"According to Doctor Atkins, he was given, or he injected himself with, quite sufficient to give an ordinary man a general anaesthetic – prior to the vivisection." Sandy drained his cup – a thick piece of pottery with no inconvenient patters that could be erased by the canteen dish-washer. "Add to that the fact that Virginia Lauderman, artist, sniffs a lot. Which could have been put down to hay fever, except that we managed to acquire several of her thrown-away tissues – and you'll never guess what we found."

"Tissues – that she had blown her nose in?" Hugh wrinkled his nose.

"Cocaine!"

"Nasty!"

"You've had a man following Thorpe for a week."

"Damn!" smiled Hugh equably. "The men these days – just no bloody good. He wouldn't have seen you or me at that stage, would he, Sandy?"

"You're running some kind of separate drugs investigation, right in the middle of my murder enquiry."

"We had no intention of spoiling it for you. That stupid man! You know what I mean – either they have the nuance or they haven't. Which is a great pity, really, because we were making progress."

"Progress?"

"The Liverpool connection. A new avenue, as far as we're concerned. Used to be the channel ports. Or London! But cocaine has passed out of the domain of the rich and on to the Saturday nighters. The North of England has become big business."

"So you've got something on Thorpe and Arber?"

"Worth more than its weight in gold – cocaine. You could pack half a million pounds' worth into the back of a motorbike. And what better way to get across the awkward Pennines, without even a decent four-lane road unless you go up the long trek to Leeds."

"So why wasn't I taken into your confidence three weeks ago?"

"Have you any idea how much money is involved in this? It's big business. Half a million is nothing to the organisers! The best organisation this side of the Atlantic and without the disadvantage of the friendly man from the VAT."

"So Thorpe and Arber have a connection with some big organisation?"

"Very big. That's our difficulty. We could pick them up at the right time and take their bikes apart. Or raid their homes when they get back from a moonlight spin – !"

"But that wouldn't get you to the organisation behind it?"

"Believe me, the last thing we wanted was to alert Thorpe. It's a disaster now you say that he's on to us."

"Why the conspiracy?"

"We didn't know there was any real connection. I don't believe even now that there's any really significant connection with the girl's murder. It was merely an unfortunate coincidence, as far as our investigation was concerned, when the girl was killed, drawing attention to our two couriers on their fancy BMW mules. And we know we have a problem, maybe several of them, in the force itself."

"This organisation has penetrated the force?"

"Look here, Sandy – you're human. I'm human. What happens if they hand you a package, two kilos. A hundred-thousand-pound present. They could afford to do it once a week. A divorced man trying to hold together two homes, would you be able to say no?"

"I haven't had it put to me, Hugh."

Hugh smiled. "I'm just trying to make a point. They could test out ten and only one fall. But they'd have that one. You see the worry. A murder investigation – maybe a hundred people involved in that, plain clothes, uniformed, clerks, typists, even the cleaning-women."

"You're a bastard, Hugh."

"That's right. Blame my mother."

He drove out to the old school and searched out Georgy under a cloud of pipe smoke.

"Tell me the truth – did you know what was going on, Georgy?"

"I knew that Meadows had his reasons." Georgy seemed unruffled, hardly surprised. "What do you intend to do about it?"

"I'm going back in to talk to Meadows. Do you want to come along?"

"What for? No, I'll leave it to you. I'm too old for this kind of battle."

But Sandy had something else on his mind, another

avenue which he intended to explore and no better time for it than when he was feeling nice and furious.

Meadows was apologetic at first. He explained that he himself had been sworn to secrecy. It was part of a massive drugs operation, involving police forces in three different countries.

"And meanwhile two people have been cut into strips," Sandy spoke coolly, "but that's a matter of minor importance?"

"Now you listen to me, Woodings. This is something which involves hundreds, perhaps thousands of lives. Either we do something now and do it very quickly and efficiently –"

"Because Martin is an international name! Because he is in danger of skipping the country! I doubt that the entire police force of this country and the mafia together could make Martin do anything he didn't want to do."

"Let me explain just a little to you and then maybe you'll understand. We're talking about the British connection. A billion-pound industry. These people move with infinite care, establish their men and their markets slowly. Think about it. You've been beating your head against a brick wall with two young tearaways. Sophisticated criminals, Woodings, who train their operatives. It's a whole new criminal psychology."

"I don't give a damn about their big operation. I have two murders to solve."

"You're not doing yourself any favours by the tone of this conversation."

"You might do me a favour – I think perhaps I have one owing, sir!"

"What kind of favour?"

"Martin's accounts. I don't believe we couldn't get hold of them from his bank – I suspect the explanation for that is now staring me in the face."

"Demanding Martin's bank accounts are hardly in keeping with the necessary low profile."

"Well, I want to see his accounts. I *have* to see them."

Meadows sighed. "Very well. But I'm now ordering you, Woodings, to secrecy on the drugs side. The information you have just learnt is not to be made known to the rest of your officers on the murder enquiry. Have I made myself clear?"

"Never clearer, sir," said Sandy Woodings curtly.

"Then you'll have them first thing Monday morning."

"I need to see them today, sir."

"Today is Saturday. Are you asking me to get the bank manager out of his home to locate them?"

"I'm afraid I am, sir."

"You're cutting close to the bone, Woodings."

"Thanks! Thanks a lot, sir!"

Under a completely blue sky cut by the vapour trail of a single high-flying jet, he took pleasure in the twenty minutes' drive into the village. Down Vicarage Lane, past Mrs Pendle's extravagant wall-basket, bursting with geraniums and begonias that had survived the hanging.

He had a lunch of cold chicken and salad in the Drunken Duck, a warm half-pint of the city's best bitter, with Tom catching the mood with his floral tie. Well, why not? Sandy was beginning to like Tom's taste in ties. He was fed up with the ordinary, the stiff-upper-lip drabness.

"You look like the punter who has just had a tip from the Queen," said Tom, motioning to see if he fancied another drink.

"No, thanks, Tom. Things to do."

"Aren't you going to tell me what you know and I don't?"

"You tell me. All we've ever needed in this case has been there for the asking. Angela Hawksworth! I mean, what's so obvious, we no longer even think it?"

"That according to all accounts, she looked bloody gorgeous."

Some more pepper on his chicken! Sandy was enjoying himself. "Much too gorgeous to see her future here in Dossage?"

"That's it. If I had been her, I'd have been looking for ways of making it, using my God-given talents to the maximum."

"So she latched on to Paul Thorpe at school. Easy to see him just as a stupid lout. But I think she saw something different."

"Guts," said Tom, who had caught the infectious air of enjoyment, judging from the look on his face as he drained his glass.

"Seen from her vantage, what's the place got to offer? Those who have it – in the main commuters or newcomers, who brought their money in with them and who are either too damned dull or two generations too old!"

"Except for Simon Martin?"

"Yes, Tom. Except for Martin."

"So she latched on to Thorpe, because he was the one with most guts."

"And ambition – and without the brake of scruples."

Sandy sat back a moment and considered how Meadows would view Tom, a cocky ex-sergeant only recently promoted against medical advice to inspector, and whose penchant for razzamatazz ties would surely place him at least as suspect as Sandy himself. It was with considerable pleasure that he took Tom, as it were, into Hugh Bearder's and Meadows's confidence.

"Drugs! So that's it."

"It's certainly a part of it." He nodded. "But it makes Angela's dilemma rather more interesting, perhaps?"

"If we knew how she first came to meet Martin?"

"She was noticed in the village by Virginia Lauderman and brought to his attention as a potential model."

"Virginia Lauderman, who is known to take cocaine!"

"So the question is, just how important is this additional knowledge to us?"

"Let's face it," said Tom with his eyes narrowed, "if one of those lot takes the filthy stuff, then it's a fair bet that all of them do."

"Assumptions are not enough, Tom. What we need is evidence."

"The bank statements – ?"

"Which will be in our hands by this evening, at the very latest."

He looked again at the summary of his interrupted interview with Mrs Sheridan. He was tempted to go back and finish that interview, but he changed his mind and drove instead to the Martins' place. Caroline Martin stood at the window and watched him ring the bell, looking a little less nervous – he noticed the appearance of ruby studs in her ears, the first time he had noticed any jewellery, apart from her wedding-ring. It was her husband however who answered the door. He had obviously been working since his clothes were covered in marble dust and chippings and he had a swollen bruise over the base of his left thumb where he must have hit himself an almighty smack with a hammer.

"Are we to get no peace ever again from you people?" he demanded angrily.

"I need to interview you again, Mr Martin. There are many more questions, I'm afraid."

"Come back in a year. As you can see, I'm busy."

"I don't want to be unreasonable. I could come back, if tomorrow morning is more convenient?"

"I'll be busy all day tomorrow." He stared in a gathering fury.

"Then I'll make it tomorrow evening," Sandy Woodings replied calmly. "Half past seven – I shall expect you to be here!"

Martin slammed the door in his face, while Caroline's face reappeared at the lounge window and watched his reaction. He waved at her, quite cheerfully, expecting nothing. But she must have been so taken by surprise that she waved back, a little flutter of the long fingers. He knew that she must be watching his figure all the way down the gravel path and through the gates in the six-foot wall to his waiting car.

Sitting in his car before driving off, he thought about Angela Hawksworth. He had the urge to go back into the workshop and have another look at the sculpture. Instead he took the picture from its safe keeping between the pages of his notebook and he stared once more into the sparkling brown eyes in that too-beautiful face. He'd have given much to have been able to interview her. To have moved back in time a month, catch her just before her murder. How did her mind work? No good going back to her parents – no more, he suspected, even her younger sister. She had been an enigma to them all her life and she had remained an enigma after her tragic death. Yet he was certain that in her mind she had carried the key to it all. Somehow she had triggered some process. A twenty-year-old exciting by her beauty a murderous jealousy or rage that she had probably never predicted or understood – he wondered if she would have understood even at that moment of revelation, when she first saw the weapon and realised its intention!

21

Something important no longer added up. He had thought
he was on the right lines, he had had a very definite feeling
for what might have led up to that precise moment of the
murder of Angela Hawksworth: but now he was no longer
sure about anything. At 7:30 p.m., sitting at the table in his
flat, with this new evidence – money was the hardest of
evidence – spread in sheets over the entire table surface, he
stared in absolute amazement at the bank statements of not
only Simon Martin, who evidently kept separate accounts
from his wife, but also at those of Caroline Martin, Eleanor
Standon who, in contrast with Martin, did indeed keep a
joint account with Virginia Lauderman, and finally of
Ronald Wadsworth. He read the files avidly, jotting down
important figures on his pad. An annual income in the
previous year of almost a quarter of a million pounds!
Simon Martin was certainly successful beyond Sandy Woodings's estimation. By far the biggest earner in that household, only Wadsworth earned even as much as a tenth of
Martin's income. And yet, no more than three years earlier,
things had been very different. He had grossed less than
thirty thousand, which, to judge from the frequent incur-
sions into the red, wasn't enough to allow him to live within
his means.

"Damn!" Sandy jumped to his feet and dashed across to
his grill where he extricated the smoking remains of a
three-quarter pound of sirloin, threw the mess into his

waste bin and then placed two doorsteps of bread into the vacated grill, standing by it this time, hardly disturbed by the ruin of his evening meal. Reading through the accounts had not quite confirmed what he would have earlier predicted.

There had been regular sums of money taken from every account, but none greater than a few hundred, no large withdrawals in cash – not until six weeks before Angela Hawksworth's murder, when there had been one single withdrawal of ten thousand. Just that one large withdrawal. There was no escaping it. The person who had virtually eliminated her entire deposit account to withdraw the amount was Caroline Martin. Caroline Martin had withdrawn ten thousand pounds in cash no more than a month before Angela Hawksworth had been murdered. Ten thousand – precisely the sum that seemed to have found its way into the pockets of Paul Thorpe and Jack Arber!

"Damn!" he swore again: despite all of his precautions he had burnt the toast.

As Sandy Woodings cut two more slices of bread and placed them under his grill, Constable Brown – who had been sitting in an uncomfortable wooden chair at the darkened window of the vicarage opposite Mrs Pendle's cottage – saw her door open and Mrs Pendle emerge, dressed in a black pullover and light-grey corduroy trousers. Feeding the animals! Brown had no doubt at all about it, since he had been on the evening shift all week and she had performed the ritual every evening at precisely the same time. Nevertheless, in view of the chief inspector's instincts, Constable Brown hurried downstairs through the house and, taking care that she couldn't see him, searched for a closer vantage spot, so he could see what she was up to. Circling the garden, he found an uncomfortable hiding-place behind the four-foot drystone wall that was her boundary, with his long legs precariously bent into a clump of stinging-nettles and the half-moon of his face peering over the broad flat coping-stones, through a straggling lilac.

She had already entered the garden through the small green gate and, passing no more than yards from him, proceeded to visit each of the pens in turn, talking to the animals in a voice that Brown could hear with absolute clarity.

"Good night, my lovelies!" she crooned, perhaps to the geese, since he could hear them gaggling and shifting. "Good night! Auntie Emily is all done in. Sleep well! See you in the morning!"

In the pause, he could see her move about, leave the geese and perform the same ritual with the goats, patting the nanny and holding the kid in her arms, infant-like, a good-night embrace, the placing of a moistened finger on the shiny top of goat-nose, and then on to the donkey.

"Good night, Bunter! Stubborn old man. There, there." She gave the shaggy-coated darling a kiss on the top of his head, between his upstanding ears. "Auntie Emily is off for forty winks in her nice chair. So will you promise to be good and no singing! What do you say? There's a good fellow."

Constable Brown watched her walk back along the path, an unhurried walk, obviously that of a tired, or maybe half-inebriated woman, unto the gate again, close it firmly after her, and yawn in full view as she entered her front door. Brown had been caught out by Mrs Pendle once, so he wasn't going to be fooled by her so easily again. He maintained his position and continued to watch her through her living-room window, patting a cushion into shape in her armchair, then sitting back, her head slightly turned from him but nevertheless clearly visible. She had in fact turned on the light in the living-room, which must have been poorly illuminated even at midday with those tiny stone-framed and leaded windows, so that, given the clear view he had of her, he thought it wise to stay where he was for a while and continue to watch her.

Sandy Woodings, armed at last with two slices of buttered toast, was back at his table again, trying to think of any possible innocent reason for the cash withdrawal of ten thousand pounds. Hardly housekeeping money – the house-keeping was quite easily identifiable; it never varied from month to month. She did not drive a new car – he had seen the communal Landrover, driven by either her or her husband, parked out in the open next to the swimming-pool. No purchase of a work of art, no antique – who would bother to take ten thousand pounds from the bank in cash to purchase anything these days, when a signed cheque would be so much safer and simpler?

There was no getting away from it: *ten thousand pounds cash*. He nodded his head slowly, taking huge bites out of his buttered toast.

Mrs Pendle too was nodding. From the garden wall, the nodding was barely perceptible, the sort of movement a twenty-six-year-old detective constable would not have been surprised to see as a premonitor of sleep in a sixty-year-old woman. If he had been close enough to have seen her eyes, he would have realised differently. The dark eyes in that nodding head were very much alert and wide-open. Focused on the clock on the mantelpiece, a childhood present with enamelled face and each hour illustrated with a character from Lewis Carroll, the poor mechanical thing standing on its head because that was the only posture in which the wheels went round, she followed the slow progression of the minute hand, from Queen of Hearts to March Hare.

"Oh, yes – Auntie Emily must have her forty winks!" she whispered to Coddles, while her stout frame was convulsed with laughter.

22

The heatwave was unrelenting. Even at four in the morning it left its legacy, with open windows and sheets thrown off sticky and perspiring bodies, uncomfortable even in sleep. Back in the city, Sandy Woodings was no exception. He tossed and turned, hopelessly entangled in a recurrent nightmare, wandering on a strange journey through a never-ending maze of village streets, through which the local inhabitants moved in eerie slow motion and subtly harassed him with their silence. In Dossage three people made no pretence at all of sleeping. For Emily Pendle it was excitement – the excitement of anticipation – as much as the heat which kept her awake. For Simon Martin the experience was so unexceptional, he could sit on the edge of his bed and calmly admire the cloudless expanse of starry sky through his wide-open casement window. Paul Thorpe's mood was entirely different. He lay quite still in his sweat-soaked bed and thought about the only thing that mattered to him any more in this world – Angela!

Round and round she swirled inside his head. Angela, as she had looked when he first came to notice her at school. How she had stood out completely from the other girls. Angela so beautiful, he couldn't believe she was an ordinary human – and then, when she had turned to him, when she had picked him out of the crowd and believed in *him*. The sweat rolled down the groove in the centre of his forehead – an ugly forehead, he was well aware, with those two big bumps and the groove in between – and it smarted in his eyes like tears. Tears or sweat, what did it matter. Only Angela! Those bad times, when the beautiful face could be transformed to ugliness by that cruelty inside her. When she didn't get just what she wanted. Angela had always got what she wanted. If she didn't get it straight away, she worked at it until she did. She was clever, extremely clever, as well as just the most beautiful girl he had ever seen. Only for all of that beauty, the loveliness of her, to end up lying there, mutilated, to lie all night long in the cold, alone, to lie in her own blood in the wood where they had gone all those times, their wood, where they had walked together and just talked, and where he, Paul Thorpe, had been the first to take her. *The first!* In the bedroom over the wedge-shaped sitting-room, Paul Thorpe wept silently, with his two fists clenched in uncontrollable rage: at the same moment in time, Simon Martin walked, stark-naked, from his bedroom and out into the galley-style corridor which ran along the upstairs of his house.

He opened the door of his wife's bedroom, closed it silently behind him, and stared at her sleeping form in the full moonlight flooding through the opened window. Her face was turned in repose from him. On the wall over the bed was one of the miniatures she painted – people she knew, always people, in brilliant pre-Raphaelite technique – and which she concealed completely from the outside world. The intimacy of the picture was so like her, the tiny brilliant intimacy and the secretiveness, that he walked soundlessly across to the side she faced. He touched her, touched her cheek with the sides of his fingers. It was a pity that she was genuinely asleep, since the gentleness of the touch, incongruous against the work-callused roughness of his fingers, together with the single word that he spoke, might have helped her. Seventeen years of love, of loyalty! She, more than anyone, might have understood how so much can be said in one simple gesture!

*

172

A beautiful Sunday morning. Sandy woke at eight, a little later than usual, with a roaring appetite. He made himself an old-fashioned English breakfast, then drove into Dossage under a sky as blue as a thrush's egg. Passing the morning joggers as he entered the village, he felt a powerful urge to park the car, strip to the waist and join them.

At the incident centre he brought himself up to date with the reports from his men watching Mrs Pendle and Simon Martin. Nothing! A quiet night. Constable Brown had gone home at midnight with lumbago from crouching in an uncomfortable posture for several hours behind Mrs Pendle's four-foot drystone wall. One thing which did surprise him was the fact that Georgy was there, at the incident headquarters, before him. It caused him to look at his senior more closely than he had for weeks and the scrutiny shocked him. Georgy Barker all of a sudden appeared to be melting away before his very eyes.

Beads of thick sweat hung about Georgy's face, like pearls. In shirt-sleeves, he seemed loose within his skin, he had shrunk down to a mere fifteen stones. When he reached out a hand to take the proffered mug of cocoa from the sergeant, the arm rose in the white balloon of sleeve like a dead limb in a shroud.

"What's the matter with you, Georgy?"

"They're trying to get rid of me early."

"Is that all? I know plenty who'd be delighted, given a reasonable handshake."

"That's what they might like to think!" murmured Georgy, turning a bleary red eye on Sandy, before popping a cascade of sweeteners from a little hand dispenser into the lake of cocoa. "Damn diabetes!"

"I think you're letting hypochondriasis get to you, Georgy."

"And *I* think a man should mind his own business." Georgy worked each sleeve up one additional roll, then tugged Sandy out to where he had his chair placed so as to catch the sun. "So what did you learn from your little conversation with Meadows yesterday?"

"I managed to get hold of Martin's bank accounts – plus the others in his little menagerie."

"So – I'm listening." Georgy wiped his forehead with his fingers and sprinkled sweat on the paving-stones outside the door, like a priest administering holy water.

"Simon Martin is keeping all of the others. He's the only one with any kind of income from his art. The rest are just playing at it. A gross income of quarter of a million a year, Georgy. How would you like that as a retirement annuity?"

"Money doesn't bother me," said Georgy, repeating the sprinkling over the paving-stones. "And who says I'm going to let them do me that easy?"

Sandy grinned: that was more like it, the Georgy he knew and respected. He didn't want to find himself feeling sorry for Georgy. "Ten thousand pounds was taken out of Caroline Martin's account in cash six weeks before Angela Hawksworth was murdered. Otherwise the regular cash withdrawals were small fry."

"You think Mrs Martin bought drugs in large amounts? And that's where Thorpe and Arber come into the picture?" Georgy didn't look at Sandy, but continued to gaze at the sunshine.

"It would certainly explain the jitteriness. I've never seen her other than jittery."

"Only you don't believe it?"

Sandy considered whether he could see Caroline Martin as a hopeless cocaine addict. "It just doesn't make sense," he replied, stiffening.

"So what are you going to do?"

"Use something I've learnt from you, Georgy. Instinct! I know there's something happening. I'm going to use time – wait, although God knows it will be difficult."

"Learnt it from me! I only wish I had a couple of

witnesses!" Georgy inhaled in anticipation, pulling up his trouser legs so that his calves could enjoy the sunshine.

He drove back home and arranged to take his children for an hour's cricket on Endcliffe park. By lunch time the sun was almost overhead and the air had physically thickened. When he spin-bowled the tennis ball to Gerry's bat, with Marty wicket-keeping and the twins fielding, he was aware of the hot air as a solidity he had to force the ball through.

Paul Thorpe had spent the same morning packing clothes, money, soap and razor into a rucksack. Finished, he sat down at the dining-table opposite his mother, and they stared at each other for a moment without speaking.

"I've left you some money – under the floor." He inhaled once, deeply, then walked to the door without a backward glance.

"Paul!" she screamed. She followed him to the door and tried to put her arms round him, to prevent him starting up the motorcycle.

Within seconds he had gone. The bike's engine, as big as that of many cars, could be remarkably quiet when it was needed.

Rushing back into the house, the small dark woman, her face deathly pale, made for the staircase. Her heart was bursting in her chest and she couldn't breathe but she fought through it into his bedroom and lifted the floor-board. There was money there, a lot of money, but the vicious-looking bayonet had gone.

As Mrs Thorpe sat in a bewildered trance on the edge of her son's bed, Sandy Woodings and his four children ate sandwiches and drank lemonade on the grass where they had minutes before played cricket. The day remained idyllic and Sandy would keep a permanent memory of the hot tired limbs sprawled at all angles and decorated with grass-stains and squashed buttercups.

"This is great, isn't it, Dad!"

"It could be worse,' he smiled.

"Running on grass!" said Marty vehemently. "I hate those all-weather tracks. Cinders keep flying up into my eyes."

"Wear goggles then!"

"Will you buy me some?"

"Buy me this! Buy me that!"

"Thanks, Dad. Mum wouldn't. I don't like Mum. I hate her!"

He laughed and tousled his daughter's hair. Marty was at an age when extremes of love and hate came easily.

He carried his handset but still there had been no interruption. No news! He lay back in the burnt grass, the drooping daisies and buttercups, and stared through slitted eyes at the fused green foliage of the perimeter trees. *Extremes of hate and love – was there really just one age?* Here in the park he was a witness to the intimacy of spring maturing to summer. He could smell grass cuttings burning from the neighbouring houses. Girls wearing sandals, more like Greek goddesses each year as he passed further into middle age, young lively arches with nothing more than the flapping cheap plastic sole strung to the space between the first two toes. It seemed inevitable that his thoughts should turn to Caroline Martin. So much so that he hardly heard the bleeping sound.

"What is it?" he sat up suddenly, speaking directly into the handset.

"Thorpe, damn it." Tom was calling him from the old school. "Took off about thirty minutes ago on that bike – we just couldn't keep up with him. We've lost him."

"Then you had better damn well find him again. What about his mother?"

"We're bringing her into the school right now. Don't worry. We'll find him!"

"And pigs might fly." Sandy spoke the words to himself.

The handset was already in his pocket and he was on his feet.

After dropping off the children, he used his emergency light to drive at speed into Dossage. Mrs Thorpe was already there, disclaiming any knowledge of where Paul had gone and why. Sandy murmured tersely to a sheepishly embarrassed Tom. "It's beginning to happen. I was expecting it and now it's beginning to happen!"

Mrs Pendle was also in a highly excited state. All she had managed this morning was a quick round of the animals, with her voice tremulous and her hands shaking.

By 6:15 p.m. she couldn't bear it any longer. She found one of her own best bottles, the blackberry wine she had been so successful with last autumn. Since she had already tried a few bottles from that same batch, she knew it was good, as strong as a good port. With eyes glittering, she sat at her dining-table and poured a generous tumbler.

"To success!" She toasted Harry Tom, who was squatting on the floor next to her, snuffling pleadingly with his naughty schoolboy's ginger-lashed eyes.

"Arber!" exclaimed Sandy Woodings. "Get a car round there and bring him in here."

His mind worked furiously. Thorpe was up to something. If Thorpe was up to something, then maybe his mother might not know – but Arber would know. He thought back to Thorpe and Arber and that business with Tom in the wood. Simon Martin in the wood at the same time! He had almost forgotten his interview with Martin.

He left a message with the desk sergeants. As soon as Tom called in, Sandy was to be informed. He was to be informed, whether Arber had also bolted or whether he had not. If he had not, what he was prepared to say, if anything. "I'm going to the Martins' place." He was already hurrying towards the door. "Call me there. You've got the number."

177

Mrs Pendle, who was now unceremoniously sprawled, with legs apart, on the dining-room floor, helped herself to another generous libation of the deep-red wine, before pouring an equal measure into Harry Tom's saucer. "Cheers!" she laughed delightedly, watching the pleasure on his face as he lapped vigorously with a gusto at least equal to hers.

"Oh, you naughty old boy! You deliciously naughty old man, Harry," she squealed. "Here we are then – plenty left in the old bottle yet!"

Constable Brown, who had unsuccessfully pleaded medical grounds to escape the late-afternoon shift on Mrs Pendle, sat in the boring warmth of the bedroom that overlooked the cottage, and groaned as he watched what appeared to be an exact reproduction of yesterday evening's performance. Mrs Pendle, slightly unsteady, had just opened the gate into her garden, closed it behind her, and was making her way with pockets full of chopped-up apples, popcorn and sugar lumps, to say goodnight to her zoological family.

Brown took the stairs one at a time, with his hand on the small of his back, opened the front door with a sigh, and scurried across Vicarage Lane, to take up his position in the nettles and behind the overshot lilac.

"Good night, sweeties! Auntie Emily *does* love you. Good night, kittikins! A kiss for Auntie Emily! Bunter! Bunter dear! Put that great rude tongue back into your mouth or no sweeties for Percy."

Auntie Emily must go and have forty winks! Constable Brown's head nodded with lips twisted into pained prediction, as he watched the corpulent figure, dressed entirely in black, knitted round-neck pullover, black stretch nylon trousers, and fluffy flowery slippers, close the gate after her, re-enter the cottage. As the bored and hurting Constable Brown watched the light come on in the living-room, as he saw the figure already comfortable in her chair, in a comfort which contrasted markedly with his own discomfort, squatting like an overgrown idiot behind the rough stone wall, Sandy Woodings press the bell on the stonework outside Simon Martin's door, only to encounter a nervous and highly embarrassed Caroline, who had to confess to him that Simon Martin was not there to see him.

"Where is your husband, Mrs Martin?"

"I don't know, Chief Inspector."

He thought she was telling him the truth, but he could not be certain. "Would you mind if I come in anyway?" If she had refused, he would most certainly have waited on her step for a search warrant and her expression signified that she knew it.

"May I use your telephone?" he asked with icy calm, then picked it up and called one of the sergeants he had just left.

"It seems that everybody is doing a bunk. Martin isn't here." Without revealing that Martin was under observation, he managed to discover that their man, in hiding just across the road, had not seen Martin leave the house. "I want the village searched for both Martin and Thorpe. Use arrest warrants if necessary."

He turned again to Caroline Martin, whose face was ashen. "What time today did you last see him?"

"He was here an hour ago. Ten minutes ago I checked the workshop, because I knew you were expected – "

"Did he indicate that he intended to avoid me?"

"He said nothing. He's been uncommunicative all day – for several days!"

"You must tell me the truth, Mrs Martin. Has he been drinking again? Excessively?"

She nodded.

"Who else is here in the house?"

"Everybody – except Ronald – Mr Wadsworth."

"Don't tell me – he's in London?"

"Yes."

179

"Ask everybody into this room, please. I'd be very obliged to have your full co-operation, Mrs Martin."

He asked Virginia Lauderman and Eleanor Standon if either of them knew anything at all about Simon's whereabouts.

They shook their heads.

"I'm going to warn you – all of you – that I know something is in the offing. My instincts tell me that something is about to happen. I'm also very tired of people concealing things from me. Don't try my patience further by behaving stupidly."

"We aren't lying to protect Simon," his wife murmured very softly, with a distressed look. "We all knew he was terribly upset. He's been going out of his mind since Angela was killed. You must believe that is the truth!"

"I don't know what to believe any more, Mrs Martin. But I won't detain you for the present. Only you, Miss Standon. Alone, if you wouldn't mind! Please?" He held the lounge door open for the other two women, adding as they left: "Meanwhile, perhaps you could do something for me, Mrs Martin. Could you ring the police reception desk at the school and tell them I intend to stay here until your husband returns. All night if it proves necessary."

"Must you behave so brutally to her?" her sister asked angrily, as soon as the lounge door had closed.

Sandy Woodings ignored both the question and her anger, turning to the stiffly seated woman who returned his stare without visible trepidation.

"You hate him – Simon, I mean – don't you, Miss Standon?"

"How very perceptive of you, Mr Woodings!"

"Would you care to tell me why?"

"I'm not alone. Ask any of the others – except Caroline."

"I am asking you."

She employed silence: a silence in which Sandy tried to assess this older sister, quite as tall and with potentially much of Caroline's dark attractiveness, but spoilt by some brooding sense of antipathy. Tonight, without the monocle and with her hair down, there was an impression, one he had never noticed about her before, of something injured: a face worn down by care and hard work – which hardly seemed compatible with the role of the artistic parasite, hanging leech-like from Simon's achievements.

"Let me put it another way then – how did you feel about his relationship with Angela Hawksworth?"

"I resented it."

"He was introduced to her by Virginia, I believe?"

"That's one way of putting it."

"You hated Angela Hawksworth – just as you still hate Simon?"

"Hate is too strong a word for it – with Simon, yes – but as far as that silly little bitch was concerned, contempt would put it more accurately."

"You speak your mind."

"You complained people would not tell you the truth."

What a world of difference in two sisters! Eleanor was hard, tough, where her sister was vulnerable. Yet there was something, this need for truthfulness. Sandy had to press this further. He wished he had talked personally to Eleanor sooner.

"I want to talk to you about love, Miss Standon."

"Love!" she smiled, but it seemed partly from horror.

"You'll excuse my bluntness, but I believe we each know exactly what we mean by the expression. I'm not talking about the ordinary kind of devotion. I'm referring to a very special kind of love – a love that is all-consuming, all-giving and all-forgiving."

"I'm astonished that a policeman could be so naive about human nature."

"Don't you believe that such a love exists, then?"

"It would require the same in return to nurture it. That alone would guarantee its extinction."

181

"I believe you know who I'm referring to, don't you?"

She refused to reply: but she knew all right.

"The reason you live in this house, with a man you hate, is that kind of love, isn't it? You love your sister in this way – surely?"

"We've been close since childhood. We had to be to survive. Our parents were artists as well. They weren't unkind. Caring, yes. Have you any idea how hard it is for the vast majority of artists to make a living. They make a joke of the poverty – but they make a sacrifice of their children."

"Until now I thought that Caroline was the vulnerable one. But you're vulnerable too, Miss Standon. I think you know exactly what I mean by an all-giving love."

"Even those nights when he never returned here – she would lie awake all night on the couch, waiting for him. How she could give herself totally to that monster! You must try to understand, Chief Inspector. We weren't even educated in the usual way. We were educated privately by our parents, whenever they thought of it, in between wandering throughout France, Spain, Portugal, Italy. Do you know, we were born in some peasant cottage in southern Ireland, close to the town of Waterford? Irish blood on our mother's side. But we wouldn't recognise the house, or Waterford for that matter, because we never lived anywhere long enough to get to know the name of the main street. We were thrown together. All we learnt, we did so from parents who were themselves half-crazy from poverty and the neglect of the establishment. From them and from books."

He seemed to nod sympathetically, then think before speaking. "I have one more deeply personal question I must ask you. It concerns Caroline – Caroline and her marriage. I could ask her herself, but I suspect you would prefer if I asked you." He hesitated, touching his forehead with his fingers. "Why did she and Simon have no family?"

"Children?" She was genuinely shocked, outraged.

"Is the question so unreasonable?"

"After everything I have just told you?"

"So it was a matter of decision – Caroline would not have a child from choice?"

"I doubt if the notion of having a family was every seriously considered by either of them."

Still watching Mrs Pendle's cottage, Constable Brown was increasingly curious about the behaviour of her parrot. The bird had perched on top of the woman's sleeping head, without waking her. Now –

Leaving his hiding-place and coming round to the paved path in front of the cottage, he peered directly through the window. He had not been mistaken – the bird was actually pecking with unmistakable hunger at the head of which was laid to one side against the back of the chair. Pecking! He could see pieces ripped out by the parrot's beak, torn from the head without waking her. Then suddenly – the detective muttered an exclamation and felt a rush of sweat come over his face – the head fell off and hit the floor with a clump.

"Oh, no!" He clapped his hand to his perspiring brow, then took the handset out of his pocket. "Get hold of the chief – it's urgent!"

Sandy Woodings took the message at the Martins' home: Mrs Pendle had tricked them. She had rigged up a dummy, with a swede carved to shape and covered in a wig for her head.

Mrs Pendle was on the move again! Damn! She had been missing at least half an hour! Mrs Pendle! Paul Thorpe! Simon Martin! Everybody had suddenly taken it into their heads to go missing!

"I'm sorry, Miss Standon – Mrs Martin!" He turned to the two women who had come out into the hallway to watch him take the telephone call. "I'm afraid I have to leave." He turned to Mrs Martin in particular, who was so nervous she

183

was visibly trembling. "If your husband returns perhaps you would be good enough to let us know immediately?"

"My sister is terrified, Chief Inspector. Can't you do anything?"

For the first time this evening, Eleanor Standon appeared to flinch from the intensity of those calm blue eyes.

"Yes – of course. I'll send a man round to keep you company." He turned, as he was leaving, regarding them, moving his gaze from one to the other thoughtfully.

Mrs Pendle had already passed by the playing-fields in that same wide and misleading circle before she noticed the prowling cars. Even without their flashing lights or sirens, she realised what they must mean. They were on to her. But she didn't care. Not now. Not when she was so very close.

At the big dip in the road, and when she was almost there, there was a police car, a clearly marked one this time, containing two uniformed men, and she sat quite blatantly on the wooden seat placed near to the stepover until they were past, confident that they wouldn't see her, in spite of the fact it was still very light. Light enough for her to see, that was after all the whole idea. No scrambling in the dark this time. She could hardly suppress a whimper of delight as, clambering off the road and into the cow field, she wound her way diagonally inwards and away from the road, to approach the old quarry from behind. What with the sun still fifteen minutes above the horizon, there was still the chance that she might even come across the missing charms – naturally she had removed her bracelets tonight! One thing was certain – she would find what she had come for. But even certain as she was, caution made her hesitate when she came to the edge of the small coppice that had grown up over the disused ground. Caution in the memory of that terrible sobbing. And that chase during which she had fallen and lost her charms. Now, although in quite a hurry to get to the actual spot before nightfall, she took great care in looking round her. In particular, her eyes turned towards the house, made certain that there was nothing happening there, nobody entering or leaving, no face at a window. Satisfied, she then bent as low as her old back would permit to reduce any chance of her being seen, moved into the path that led upwards from the road, and found within minutes the circle of ash that had been the fire. Here she went down on hands and knees, combing delicately with her fingers, finding nothing there, before moving her attentions to its perimeter of black cinders. Almost immediately she found what she had been looking for, tiny fragments, which she collected into a tiny mound, before searching even harder, working on the surrounding ground with the fingers of both hands. The movement when she heard it was soft, no more than a twig snapping, but it was enough to cause her heart to clench as tight as a fist, as she froze entirely and probed the bushes round her with all five senses tuned to maximum. Breathing! She knew she had heard breathing.

With a strangulated cry of terror, Mrs Pendle grabbed at the small mound she had scratched together and started to run. *Oh no! Not again!* It was as if somebody a storey above her had thrown a basin of water over her, sweat suddenly erupting on her face, under her arms, a dreadful wet feeling between her breasts and down the small of her back as in running, she heard the sounds of feet following her: feet thumping the ground, so much younger and fitter than her own, an awful thumping of those following feet, a desperate thumping, which left her in no doubt of the intention of her hunter.

23

Sandy drove his black Capri down Vicarage Lane, to pull up with a screech of tyres outside Mrs Pendle's cottage. With Tom on his heels, he ran down the flagged path and stared at the scene through the cottage window. Then he shook his head sadly at Brown.

"You timed her leaving the garden at 7:30 precisely?"

"Just like last night!" Brown couldn't keep the crimson flush out of his face.

"She made quite an elaborate play of it. So it must be something big – important to her. What are we waiting for – break in. Shoulder the front door!" he said urgently.

Once inside they quickly confirmed the elaborate nature of the deception, with a dummy figure made out of cushions and two bolsters, one large swede for a head, partially eaten by the parrot. Accompanied by the grinning Tom, Sandy did a very rapid search of the cottage. The pig's room was discovered without difficulty, announcing itself to their nostrils even before they opened the door. Sandy was less surprised than the others at this, but something in Mrs Pendle's own bedroom did indeed surprise him. This was a curious affair against the side wall, so placed as to be invisible to anyone looking in through the French windows, which was an altar of sorts – he decided that it *was* an altar – with a bronze figurine, presumably a copy of some ancient deity, in the middle of circles with dots in them, cyphers in Chinese, Egyptian hieroglyphs, together with a collection of signs of the zodiac.

"Call reception at the old school. I want to set up a full man-hunt here in the village. In addition to Paul Thorpe and Simon Martin, we're now looking for Emily Pendle! Get them to hurry it up, Tom. I want a start to be made within minutes – and tell Charlie Earnshaw I'm not interested in his protestations of the impossible."

Then, staring after Tom's departing figure and still standing in the tiny hall, which had been created recently by plaster-boarding round the door so that you didn't walk straight into the sitting-room, Sandy picked up the piece of melamine board by the telephone. It had attracted him not so much by the couple of numbers written on it in felt tip, but by the word hand-written next to them, in a barely legible scrawl. It was a word unmistakable to a man who had so often scrawled it unthinkingly on police-station blotting-pads and pieces of scrap-paper throughout a twenty-year career. That word was *evidence*.

From the moment she heard a twig snap, waves of panic had engulfed Mrs Pendle. Running was useless – she told herself that. Her pursuer was younger and fitter than herself. All the same, the notion of standing her ground and trying bluffing, or worse still, fighting for her life, appealed to her a good deal less. She ran.

How on earth could somebody have known she was coming? That was the question, even as she made surprising speed in the direction of the road. Nobody could possibly have known. Unless somebody had found the missing gold charms. Even that would have only given them some clue to her identity – and that a week or more ago – so how on earth could anybody have known she would come back here right at this very time this evening? And yet somebody had been there. Somebody who could only have arrived just as she had. Somebody who had put two and two together. And who was now desperate, with murder once more in that person's heart.

Oh, dear Lord! The road! She had managed to reach it, with only thirty yards between her and those following heavy footsteps. What on earth? Where should she go from here? She just had to keep on running. No time to think. Away from the house – that was the one certain factor that pushed her in the opposite direction. She must run away from the house, down the winding and rapidly climbing road, a road she knew so very well all of her life; Emily Pendle, now sixty years old, playing a very different and more desperate game, running against the pain in her chest, past the bumpy sloping field to her right where she had sledged in the snow as a child, with nothing between herself and mother earth other than an old oilskin. *Run, girl, run!* Bitterly she realised there was nothing in her favour. Not a walker, or a car, and no houses. She couldn't think. She needed every ounce of concentration down in her feet and her aching thighs and calves. Here was the junction where the road continued on into the heart of the village, past big houses with stone walls to their gardens and high hedges. But she would have to run perhaps another two hundred yards to reach the first house, two hundred yards and then batter on the door and – ! Oh, no – she just didn't have two hundred yards in her legs. *Oh, God. Oh, dear God.* To her left, the only alternative. Scragg Wood! Horrible steeply sloping, densely forested Scragg Wood!

"Help! Somebody help me! Help me, please!" Moving more slowly now, with the dragging pain in her chest. "Oh, God! Oh, dear heart," she groaned.

The old legs just wouldn't go. There had to be a rest. The legs and the heart were saying they no longer cared if she lived or died, only there had to be a rest. Yet looking back – strangely, she saw nothing. No figure. She hadn't shaken that figure off – of that much she was certain. So where – ? She screamed again, but it was to give her time. "Help me! Help me, somebody!" But it was to give her time, staring back down the sloping road, to the bend, with the backs of the fluttering fingers against her lips as she put two and two together. The bend. The low wall on the bend. Her pursuer had dodged over the wall. Maybe right now her pursuer was already ahead of her? Right now eyes could be watching her from the wall opposite, waiting for the moment. Why on earth? There could only be one reason – to get ahead of her and yet at the same time, if anybody came, if a car appeared, there would be the escape across the sledging-field. So clever – it caused Mrs Pendle's heart to sicken. *So clever.* And it left her no choice. In Scragg Wood she could at least hide. And she had had a minute's breather, she could make another short run for it, over the low drystone wall, and into the wood before anybody could see precisely where she was going. *Yes.* Yes – in fifteen minutes it would be dark. She ran, swung her legs over the wall – she didn't even have the strength to jump over its two-and-a-half-foot coping – and immediately inside the wood, she crouched and made her way on all fours so she would be invisible from outside the wall. Twenty yards right, then she picked her way carefully down the slope, deliberately missing the obvious large trees, concealing herself behind two closely grouped young oaks, with a four-foot thicket of evergreen Mahonia. Oh! How her heart lurched when she saw the figure arrive at the wall, she could make out blue loose-fitting jeans, a dark formless pullover. But her eyes were smarting with sweat and she couldn't make out the face. Just in the moment of crossing the wall, exactly as she had, by sitting astride it and swinging those blue-covered strong legs over it, Mrs Pendle caught the flash of the long blade. For the first time in thirty years she found a need for the Lord's prayer. *Our Father, who art in heaven.* A terrible nausea had overcome her at the sight of that long blade. The dead body of Angela Hawksworth flashed across her mind and all the hope went out of her. She knew she was a dead woman. But no – not if she could help it. She wasn't going to make it easy for that fiend with the murderous weapon. A full red-blooded rage gave her the strength to crawl further down the slope, from one position of hiding to another. No paths here – she had left the only path right at the top, running parallel to the main road. That gave her the notion that a single blow from a piece of bough or something and her pursuer would fall headlong, down a slope which in places was as steep as forty-five degrees. Only the woodsmen had been remarkably efficient. She hadn't come across anything bigger than a twig lying on the ground and she was already halfway down the slope. *Oh, God.* She knelt on the soft peaty soil and watched the stealthy movements of that figure in jeans and black pullover, moving from tree to tree. There was such a horrid certainty about the movements of the figure. It was hopeless. She knew it must be hopeless. *Oh, God! Oh – Our Father, hallowed be Thy name. Thy kingdom – Oh, Lord – Thy kingdom come –*

Sandy Woodings was sitting in his parked car outside the old school, with the engine idling. He had the piece of melamine board on his lap. Tom was sitting next to him.

"She set up a deliberate ruse to get away. She fooled Brown. She's been gone a good hour or more. On foot! So it has to be here, in the village. The question is why?"

"I think she must have realised that we'd get on to her in a very short time," said Tom.

"I agree. So it was a once-only job. All into that one furtive journey – "

Sandy frowned, seeing Brown come out of the school doors.

"Any news on the manhunt?"

"It will have to be smaller than we had hoped – all the uniformed branch in the city seem to have been put on picket duty. But something will be ready in ten or fifteen minutes at the outside."

"That's too late." His gaze fell from Brown's contrite face to the piece of melamine board. "Give this to the men on reception. Two telephone numbers! Tell them to look them up but not to ring them. Have you got that? Just find out whose they are – let me know straight away."

"Yes, sir." Brown hurried off, glad to have something positive to do instead of keep saying he was sorry.

"What have we done about the Martins?" He turned to Tom.

"We put the man who was watching from outside into the house to keep an eye on them."

"I wish you hadn't done that. We should have brought in somebody else and left the man outside on cover," he said frowning.

"Well – do you want me to put somebody else on to the house?"

"No. Leave it now, Tom." He shook his head, musing thoughtfully. "Mrs Sheridan," he murmured, with his head back against the seat. "Some kind of pagan altar in that cottage. Something she said to me. Something about making money. She needs money. She dabbled in the occult to make money." He saw Mrs Sheridan, that shrewd knowing look on her somewhat prosaic face. *I predict, Chief Inspector, that she will get herself into hot water one of these days – !*

Even as he was still visualising Mrs Sheridan's face, Brown dashed out from the shadowed doorway and wrenched open Woodings's door. "We've just had a report from some old fellow – Honeysuckle Lane. Heard a woman screaming or something!"

"Screaming?"

"Yes. Shouting for help, he claims. Took him by surprise and he took his time calling in, and then the stupid telephone service put him through to headquarters back in the city instead of here."

"Honeysuckle Lane – that's only minutes from Martin's place."

"Martin's house is on a road which is the continuation of Honeysuckle Lane."

"When – what time did he hear the screaming?"

"Eight – maybe ten minutes at the very least – sorry, sir!"

"Hop in, Brown. Get as much information over the radio as you can about what the old man said. We've probably lost too much time already."

Mrs Pendle was stuck, holding on to a tree with both hands, below her a one-in-three slope with no more than twenty yards to the brook at the bottom. "That's it," she gasped in the direction of the figure, which was traversing the slope sideways in her direction. "I can't go on. I've had it."

She could hear the laboured breathing of her pursuer long before the figure came clearly into her sight. It was almost gentle, the figure talking to her, in a husky wheeze, because even her pursuer had been exhausted by the chase.

"You've been very foolish, Emily."

From somewhere, Mrs Pendle discovered a morsel of energy, enough to turn herself round to stumble and career from the tree where she had been standing to another, ten yards further on and parallel to the brook.

"I did it for the animals, you see. Didn't have the money." Gasping, she made it just that little bit further, another ten, maybe twelve feet, another tree to cling to with her battered hands. "You must believe me. That was the only reason."

"I do believe you. It's so easily done. What does it matter now? You made a mistake. We all make mistakes, Emily, don't we?"

That hoarse voice. The last of the light fading. If dark had fallen five minutes earlier, she might have made it. Mrs Pendle flung herself like a weighted sack in the direction of another tree. She sensed the figure catching her up, heard that laboured breathing, closer and closer, she sensed the arm raised, the blade falling. She fell flat on her face – it was the only way she could avoid the blade – turned herself over, dragging at the sloping ground with the fingernails of her right hand. To see! All she could do now was to see.

"It's you! Oh, Lord – I thought – !"

"I told you, Emily. A mistake. You made a mistake. I have nothing against you personally, but you started poking around and who knows what might have turned up. I couldn't be sure what you would turn up. And that chief inspector never gives up, does he?"

"His sort never gives up. He'll catch you. You'll never get away from him."

The breathing was easing now. There was all the time in the world. The figure loomed over Mrs Pendle, who was clinging for all she was worth to the steep slope. "We shall see, won't we?"

"Go ahead – kill me then!"

"First let's have a look at what you've got in your right hand."

With what strength she could muster, Mrs Pendle kicked out at the blue-covered leg that was supporting the figure against the slope and was rewarded with partial success. The figure fell, sprawling, for ten feet before coming to rest against a Scotch fir and clambering back up to her. This time the talking was over. Mrs Pendle screwed up her eyes and gritted her teeth in anticipation of the pain.

"Hey! You down there – drop the knife!"

A man's voice. Distant, from somewhere up the slope.

"You'd better make a run for it while you can," hissed Mrs Pendle at the face that was turned from her and looking up the slope to see just where the voice had come from. The next thing the pain came. A terrible, lancinating pain between her shoulder blades, which spread out to fill every corner of her being, as she felt herself blacking out, as she could no longer see even with her eyes open, and she felt her pain-wracked body tumbling, tumbling down, rolling over and over –

*

Brown was the first to jump the low wall after they had ascertained from their elderly witness where he had seen two figures enter Scragg Wood. A descent at breakneck speed, relying on his twenty-five years, had brought him halfway down the slope before he saw the figure with arm raised – the shout had been his. Now, zig-zagging between trees, swinging monkey-like from one trunk to another, he descended the remainder of the slope in a matter of minutes, finding Mrs Pendle apparently dead and half submerged in the stream at the bottom, which was ten feet wide but fortunately no more than six inches deep.

Then he noticed bubbles coming from the half of her mouth and nose that was submerged.

"Get an ambulance!" he barked into the handset which he had miraculously preserved in his headlong plunge. "Tell them to bring it round to the field down at the bottom."

He had dragged her out of the water with lightning speed, into the field side, and he was now scooping gravel out of her mouth with his index finger. By the time the chief inspector had reached him, he had turned her onto her front, face to the side, and was alternately applying pressure to her chest and lifting the elbows, with her hands folded under her face.

"Stabbed in the back," he blurted breathlessly. "Swallowed fresh water and a lot of rubbish, but she's just about alive. If we can just keep her going – "

Sandy Woodings allowed Brown, who looked astonishingly competent, to continue with the resuscitation, while he had a quick look along the length of the fields on the opposite side of the stream. It was already too dark to see more than fifty yards with any clarity and he could see no sign of any human figure. Calling Tom, who was still in the car, on Brown's handset, he gave him very specific instructions.

"Can you drive it?"

"It's not modified for me, but I think I can just about manage, if I start it in second with the clutch in."

"Okay, Tom. Take the car along the road to the bottom. Swing the headlights over the fields between here and the road – see if you can pick out somebody running." He turned to the impressively hard-working Brown. "Did you get a decent look at her attacker?"

"Blue trousers – maybe working-jeans. A black top. Medium build. Too dark to say more."

"Man or woman?"

"Sorry, sir, I couldn't say." Brown continued his resuscitation as he spoke and Sandy nodded, communicating what little description they had both to Tom and to Inspector Earnshaw, who by now was in charge of the manhunt. "Listen, Charlie," he added reflectively, "I think we should concentrate on this vicinity. If you find nothing round here, widen it out until you've covered the whole village."

Immediately he had given his instructions to Earnshaw, Sandy had the reception check urgently with their man at the Martins' house. Nobody had left the house since he had left. He pressed them to make sure this was correct but they confirmed it. Nobody had left the Martin house and Simon Martin was still missing.

Sandy was still thinking about that when he saw the car's headlights sweep across the fields that sloped gently up and away from him. He watched very carefully as the car's lights moved slowly over every sector of grass and hedge, but he could see no sign of a figure in blue and black. He realised it was a waste of time and asked Tom to turn in their direction. At least the lights would act as a guide for the ambulancemen when they arrived. There was nothing more he could do except patiently wait for developments.

Brown continued his efforts until the ambulance came down the field and parked no more than fifty yards from them. It was only as the ambulancemen, having fitting Mrs Pendle up with an air-way and oxygen, were lifting her into a carrying position on their stretcher that Sandy noticed the clenched right fist.

195

"Just a moment." He gently prised the fingers apart and saw there was something in her hand. "It might be important," he apologised to the ambulancemen, and got Brown to hold his clean white handkerchief under the hand as he prised the fingers open, so that their contents fell on to the outstretched square of linen.

"Ashes!" said Brown, staring down at what he had captured, in the light of the pocket torch held immediately over it by Sandy Woodings.

"Something white. Looks like lace." Sandy nodded, brushing gently with the blunt end of a ball-point among the ashes, before folding the handkerchief over several times for the benefit of forensics.

Back in his car again, after the comatose Mrs Pendle had been whisked away at high speed under a blaring siren, Sandy spoke once more to Inspector Earnshaw over the car radio set.

"Seal the lower end of Scragg Woods off, Charlie. Keep the men in the hunt a hundred yards clear of there. I want that whole site properly and comprehensively searched with dogs at first light."

"Okay!" said Earnshaw's phlegmatic voice.

"*Ashes*," said Sandy Woodings, sitting back against his seat once more deep in thought. "An altar with pagan signs and figures. And risking her life for a fistful of ashes – "

The car radio bleeped and Sandy answered it. He had forgotten the numbers on the melamine board, but now the sergeant on reception at the old school reminded him. The first number was that of a local newspaper, while the second was even more interesting, the home number of the paper's crime reporter, a troublesome young man called Palmer.

"I think we should have a word with Mr Palmer." Sandy nodded with narrowed eyes.

"I'll get hold of him tonight, if you want," said Tom determinedly.

"Not tonight – tomorrow! We'll both see him tomorrow.

Meanwhile, I want you to go back to the centre. Keep in touch. Any change in Mrs Pendle's condition, contact me immediately. If Martin turns up, do the same."

"Maybe we should go and have a word with Mrs Sheridan again?" suggested Brown helpfully.

"Later. There's someone else I want to go and talk to. A bit of a long shot – but the timing's right."

He drove alone to that odd-shaped cottage, with its single apple tree, now with tiny fruit beginning, against all the odds, to swell and ripen. Sitting once more in the wedge-shaped living-room, with the silhouette of the tree still visible through the uncurtained window, Sandy spoke with unusual gentleness to the tiny prematurely aged woman, who seemed to squeeze herself into a smaller volume of air than even her tiny bulk needed.

"Mrs Pendle is in hospital right now, Mrs Thorpe. I've just had word over the radio. On a ventilator. The odds against her – "

"Mrs Pendle? I don't understand. Mrs Pendle in hospital?"

"She was viciously assaulted. Attacked by someone with a knife. You must tell me the truth, now. I knew last time we spoke that you weren't telling me all that you knew." He sighed inwardly at that frail and battered face, the bruised hunch of the rounded shoulders. "You've done your best for him all his life. You can't just go on covering up for him, Mrs Thorpe."

"Covering up for him? What do you mean, Chief Inspector?"

Sandy Woodings leaned forward himself, from the edge of the uncomfortable and waterproof surface of the black vinyl chair. "What time did Paul leave here today? I must ask you again."

"Halfway through the morning. I am telling you the truth, Chief Inspector."

"And you have no idea where he is, when he will be back – whether today or in a week's time?"

She shook her head hopelessly. "I don't think he intends ever coming back again."

"What makes you think that?"

"I know."

He hesitated, digesting this new piece of information, fitting it into what he already half knew and half surmised. "Listen to me, Mrs Thorpe. Let me tell you what I already suspect. Last time I spoke to you I asked you if Paul had a knife. You told me he hadn't. But that wasn't the truth, was it? Paul has a knife, hasn't he?"

She was nodding her head again, with that same hopelessness in the gesture.

"What kind of knife?"

"His great-grandfather was a soldier. In the first war."

"A bayonet? A first-world-war bayonet? Is that it, Mrs Thorpe?"

She nodded, with her lips inverted and closed eyes.

"And you know where he normally hides it, don't you?"

"He took it with him. I've already looked for it."

"After Paul left here this morning? Is that when you looked for it?"

She nodded, with tears exuding between her closed eyes. "Why did you look this morning? What was it that made you go and look?"

"I don't know. I just felt – "

Even as he inhaled, the bleeper of his handset sounded and, staring down at the brown carpet with the black and yellow flowers, he took the call from the old school.

"It's Martin!" Tom declared flatly. "He's given himself up to our man at the house. He claims he was in his shed in the garden all the time we've been looking for him. Hiding from us," He added.

"Drunk?"

"Pretty close to it from the sounds of things."

"And?"

"*He's* asking to see *you*, Chief."

"Is he now." Mrs Thorpe felt his hand touch her shoulder, as, just for the briefest of moments, she caught the force of concentration in his eyes. His eyes disturbed her. They appeared to see too much. They weren't an ordinary blue, more a mauve-blue. Sandy Woodings would have been very surprised to realise just how his eyes could disturb people.

24

"I want simple answers to simple questions, Mr Martin. Where were you between seven o'clock and ten o'clock this evening?"

"I'm not prepared to talk to you in the presence of a third party."

"Inspector Williams stays. I must ask you again where you were during the time we were looking for you."

"Making amends to art and truth, pompous as that may sound!"

"I won't play your games with you. Either I get the simple truth or I'll try once more down at police headquarters."

"The simple truth! You know the creature doesn't exist."

"You're not drunk. You've had a few whiskies maybe but you're sensible enough to answer my questions. Would you prefer this conversation to take place at headquarters? You could play at being drunk, as on the last occasion."

"You're too smart for me, Woodings. I'm tired. I'm too tired for games. I'm not playing games, believe me. I want to talk to you here."

The three men were alone in Martin's office. The room was virtually unchanged since Sandy had last questioned Martin here, except that computer printouts had now been largely replaced by fantastic patterns of what appeared to be rock crystals, taken through all manner of lights and colours.

"Do you want to make a confession?"

"Father Alexander Woodings – give me credit for intelligence."

"You asked to see me?"

"I wanted to talk to you alone."

"Tell me what's on your mind – I'm listening."

Simon Martin did genuinely look tired. His shoulders inside his heavy navy-blue American shirt were slumped as if from exhaustion, and his legs were sprawled at awkward angles, in dirty stained blue jeans.

"I killed Angela. So there you are. Arrest me."

"*How* did you kill her?"

"What does it matter."

"It matters."

"Why won't you just take my statement as fact? From the horse's mouth instead of all that indirect rubbish you've been accumulating from interviewing every single member of my household and reading my private bank accounts."

"Have you been wearing these clothes all day?"

"What's up – can't you stand the smell?"

"We shall want the shirt, trousers and shoes for examination."

The lines between Martin's eyebrows had deepened into an omega. "For God's sake, didn't you hear what I just said? I *killed* her. So take me away and do your worst."

"Why did you kill her?"

A little spurt of the old confidence resurrected itself in Martin. He smiled drily. "Dostoevsky says, If God does not exist, then everything is permissible."

"You hid here in your workshop. You knew I was coming. I had made an appointment to see you. Why did you avoid seeing me?"

"I wasn't ready to talk to you just then."

"We searched the workshop pretty thoroughly. We found no sign of you – !"

"I know my own workshop better than anyone. I had to be alone. I made sure I was alone."

"Why did you want to be alone?"

"I don't remember. It seems years ago."

"Because there was something you needed to do? Because somehow – perhaps because a member of this household overheard my telephone conversation with Constable Brown – you knew that Mrs Pendle was in the vicinity of the house. Because you knew that Mrs Pendle had information about the killing of Angela Hawksworth which she had concealed from us and which you didn't want us to find out?"

It was impossible to say from Martin's face if he knew what had happened to Mrs Pendle. He murmured, "That old witch!" continuing to look Sandy Woodings straight in the eye.

"Tell me exactly when you first entered the workshop this evening."

"I've been in and out of my workshop all day."

"What were you doing in your workshop between the hours of seven and ten this evening?"

"I was drinking whisky and thinking. But I wouldn't expect you to believe that. I looked hard at my own creations. I felt sick quite a lot. I actually felt ashamed."

"I can believe one aspect of your story – you took whisky and probably also a shot of cocaine. I'll wager that we could prove both if we took a sample of your blood right now. That was how you came to meet Angela, wasn't it? Miss Lauderman didn't introduce her to you as a startling new find, as a model – we're surrounded by her work and there isn't the remotest interest in the human form. She met her as a supplier of cocaine. And you, the great Simon Martin, of world reputation, collected by all the reputable museums and the wealthy, had discovered that the creative process had gone into a state of decline. The initiative, the creative spark, gone! So she acted as messenger girl, between you and Thorpe. The cocaine came first, the modelling after. Did she blackmail you into it? Was that it? Her ambition to become a model – where better to get a start than to be the subject matter for one of the creations of the great Simon Martin?"

"That's right. Angela was a smart girl – smart rather than intelligent."

"Was it just a few minutes' erotic titillation? The old machismo turned on by a shot during the creative act? She would have been attractive enough to any man. And sufficiently ambitious and impressed by you to make herself available, I would suspect. Maybe she had other ambitions too, longer-term ambitions. An uneducated girl. She must have seemed almost simple in her mercenary naivety to you! What then went wrong? The influence of the drug maybe, you got careless. And maybe she didn't care? Maybe she wanted it that way. She wanted to get herself pregnant by you! A temporary lull in the modelling career if she actually went the whole hog and had the baby. Only that probably wasn't the idea at all? An abortion – which would pull the strings between you even closer. Then you would have to look after her. Your influence – her own very words to her mother on the night she was murdered: 'Everything is going to be all right.'"

"Is that what she thought? Poor little fool – !"

"All right – if you wish to be so co-operative – tell me exactly how you paid for the cocaine. Did you buy it in batches? Or did you buy it in regular small amounts? Was that to conceal any big unexplained movements of cash?"

"Do you know what youth is, Woodings?" Martin wasn't defeated at all: he was actually grinning, a humourless grin that was positively hideous. "Youth, Angela's kind of voluptuous youth, was nothing less than purgatory. Have you ever realised how beauty punishes the ugly, Woodings? Have you ever imagined the plight of us, the ungainly, when we know the nobility in our own hearts, and we see how easy it is for these shallow tormentors, with their perfect features, their lovely billowing hair and lithe grace! I've made a lifetime's study of it – I'm telling you they never relinquish the torment. They keep it up into old age – right to the mouth of the grave."

"What are you trying to say? That you killed her because she was beautiful?"

"Like awakening in the most foul stinking hangover and being blinded by the sunrise!"

"So she represented some kind of ideal to you. Until you discovered that the inner woman didn't match the surface attractiveness?"

"What shit you talk."

"You were annoyed by the youngster's petty ambitions. Such a simple little ambition. She wanted to be a model. That she could have used the likes of you, brought you down, for that simple little girl's ambition."

"You must be pretending to be so stupid just to annoy me."

"What happened then? You went into a paranoid rage. Whisky and cocaine are a potent mixture. You made an appointment to meet her. You kept that appointment and brutally murdered her?"

"A paranoid rage. Those are the very words. I hope your inspector's shorthand is keeping pace with this."

"Tell me how she presented the pregnancy to you. What was it, the little girl ashamed? It must have taken all of your patience to suffer that act. You, knowing what was taking place inside her calculating mind. What did you say to her? Did you play the concerned father? What did you say to her, Martin? Did you make a play of wanting the child, just to give yourself more time and to keep the knowledge of the pregnancy private, long enough for you to work out a plan of action?"

"There you have it – the whole unexpurgated sordid story. I confess. I'm prepared to sign to that effect."

"You haven't given me a single corroborative fact. If

you want me to arrest you, give me even a handful of hard facts. "

"Socrates was condemned for being wise enough to know nothing!"

"You're not Socrates. And I'm becoming increasingly irked by these pseudo-confessions. So I'm not arresting you. But don't think even of leaving the house. Don't try to go anywhere. Don't speak to anybody, including the press. Your movements will be watched, night and day."

They left through the back door and Sandy had a good look round the rear of the house. He could see a light on above, which came from a bathroom window, but otherwise the back of the house was in darkness. The scene inside Martin's studio caused them both to whistle in astonishment. There had been major changes since he had last been here. Several of the partially finished works, which had contained representations of Angela Hawksworth, had been reduced to rubble. Only the one finished work of Angela remained. That simple yet subtly erotic pose, Eve with the serpent and the apple.

"He could have been telling the truth in at least one respect, Tom," remarked Sandy. "There are no end of dark corners where he could have squatted with his bottle."

"I don't think he would recognise the truth if it sat on his tongue and scratched him," growled Tom, staring at the scene of destruction.

"What did you make of his reaction to the mention of Mrs Pendle?"

"I honestly didn't know what to make of it. He's very clever."

"Yes," murmured Sandy, with a curt laugh. "As to that story – Beauty and the Beast!"

He led Tom in the direction of the door, stopped to look for a final time at the youthful voluptuousness in the one creation that Martin had not had the heart to destroy.

Outside it was beautiful: a cloudless night sky, no moon but plenty of stars.

"Where to?" asked Tom, who looked a little uncomfortable sitting in the passenger seat.

"The hospital – Mrs Pendle."

"You're not a believer in philosophy, are you?" he asked Tom, as the car coursed from the village into the night streets of the city.

"I know there's a toad in the American desert that hatches out two kinds of tadpoles. Most of them are small and eat vegetables. The big ones have big teeth which they use to eat their smaller brothers and sisters – "

"So you are a philosopher after all!" smiled Sandy, glancing at Tom's long ski-lift of a nose jutting assertively over his Hapsburg lip.

"Is there a difference between a philosopher and a cynic?" asked Tom disingenuously, as the car turned through the main gates of the hospital.

They discussed Mrs Pendle with a Doctor Creasey, who was in charge of the intensive-care unit. He told them she wasn't able to breathe on her own, that they had already tried switching off the ventilator and had had to get her back on to it sharply.

"What about her brain, doctor?"

"If you're asking me if she's brain dead, then all I can say is I don't know."

"If you thought she was, you'd have unplugged the ventilator, wouldn't you?"

"There are some reflexes. But reflexes don't mean anything. Spinal reflexes."

"What about the knife wound?"

"We've transfused her but otherwise left it alone. No point in operating if she is brain dead. Give us twenty-four hours and we'll see."

Sandy looked the middle-aged doctor directly in the

eyes, then stared at the figure linked by a mask and corrugated black tubing to the noisy machine. "You could do me a favour, doctor. I didn't have a clear look at the wound where we found her. I'd like to see it in a good light."

The doctor sighed but he called two nursing sisters and between them they manhandled Mrs Pendle's body sufficiently for the two detectives to peer at the cleaned wound under the dressings.

"Satisfied, Chief Inspector?"

"Satisfied isn't the word, Doctor." He thanked the man and the nurses and then left them to their duties.

"A curved wound – !"

"I noticed – just like Angela Hawksworth," Tom muttered, shaking his head. "So where do we go from here, Chief?"

"We go home. Get some sleep. I'll meet you at first light – we'll see what turns up with the ground search."

There was always a strange and exhilarating restlessness at this stage, when he was at last close to understanding. Driving home under the peculiarly comforting warmth of night, he took his time, debated whether to go and see Josie, but then changed his mind, turning for home. He parked his car as a man does who knows he has all night. Sleep would not come. He would not even attempt it.

Simon Martin had remarked the fact that he had spoken to everybody else in that household, yet only once before to Martin himself. While it was true, at the same time Martin had studiously avoided drawing attention to the slow nature of the enquiry. A man who had lost his best model and possible lover – he hadn't even whimpered. He had sat back and got drunk and otherwise done nothing.

Martin: Mrs Pendle: Arber: Thorpe: they were all names now beginning to solidify in his consciousness. Their roles, those of the four others who lived with Martin. Thorpe was still missing. Thorpe was still unaccounted for. Possibly on the run, but there were other possibilities –

Sandy had improved a great deal in the year since Julie had first told him to pack his bags: he could cook now. He prepared himself a rice dish, using a tin of tuna, chicken stock, mushrooms, fresh cream, flour and seasoning. He enjoyed the mindless preparation of the meal, while he continued to turn things over in his head. He had them all in his head. Thorpe, Arber, Martin, Wadsworth, the three women who shared Martin's house and artistic vocation with him.

Something remained out of place. That strange business of Martin volunteering to confess and in reality confessing nothing. They were close. Sandy knew they must be very close indeed to a solution. Everything that had happened, both murders, the murder attempt – possibly yet successful – on Mrs Pendle, they were all connected. He felt sure that the solution would draw all of these outrages together.

On a sudden impulse he picked up his telephone and put through a call to the switchboard at the old school incident centre.

"Huntley was the man who stayed with the Martins – I suppose he has gone off duty?"

"Yes, sir. Would you like us to get a message to him?"

"Give me his home telephone number will you, please. I must have a word with him."

"Hello – is that you, Huntley?"

"Yes, sir – ?"

"You sound as if I've dragged you out of bed – sorry about that. But just one or two little things I'd like clarifying and I'm afraid they won't keep."

"Fire away, sir!"

"You were watching from outside the Martin place and nobody came in or went out?"

"Nobody except you and Inspector Williams."

"And then you were told to go into the house and keep Mrs Martin company, while keeping an eye open for any irregularities?"

"That's right."

"You reported that Mrs Martin did not leave your presence at all during the evening?"

"Perhaps for the odd moment. Putting the kettle on, or visiting the loo."

"And you're absolutely positive of this? She was in the same room as you all the time?"

"Definitely. She was with me all that time."

"She couldn't have changed places with her sister – or Miss Lauderman?"

"No chance of that at all."

Sandy considered this fact carefully, with several seconds of silence. "What about the others? The two women?"

"They stayed in the house. Nobody left."

"They stayed, like Mrs Martin, in the lounge with you?"

"No – or at least for part of the time, yes. But they didn't seem as nervous as she did. They saw that she was all right, then they retired very early – only ten or fifteen minutes after you left and I arrived."

"They went upstairs? To sleep?"

"To bed – I don't know about sleep!"

Ignoring Huntley's implication, Sandy pressed him: "And you're absolutely certain that neither of them came back downstairs?"

"I sat facing the open lounge door, with the stairs in full view. They didn't come down, I can guarantee it."

Sandy was silent another few seconds. "All right, Huntley – thanks. Sorry to have woken you."

"That's okay. Sorry if I seemed a bit dozy at first. But I'm wide awake now anyway. Just one thing, maybe of no importance, sir. Not something I'd put into my written report."

"What's that?"

"Well – them taking a shower! Sounds a bit silly, but it just struck me as a bit on the bizarre side."

"What struck you as odd?"

Huntley actually sounded a shade embarrassed. "Well, I mean – those two were in the shower together. Honest to God, I'd swear to it."

Sandy scratched his head, had a sip from his coffee, deep in thought. "How do you know they were in the shower together?"

"No – that's not really what I'm trying to say, I mean, well you know what I mean. I wasn't really just being voyeurish."

"I'm not criticising you, Huntley, but I'm curious about how you knew they were in the shower together when you didn't even hear Martin doing a demolition job out there in his shed."

"I don't think it's as surprising as you might think. The walls of that place are so thick, they're practically sound-proofed. I didn't hear a thing from outside but I could hear them talking together and the shower going at the same time. I could make that out quite clearly. I thought it was a bit comical, that's all. I remember thinking – 'Well, they don't give a damn if they waste money!' "

"Surely sharing a shower, whatever else you might think about it, would save rather than waste money?"

"Not if the same two women had another shower together, no more than an hour or so later – "

Sandy paused again, smiled a little wickedly. "Perhaps they had more than the usual amount of dirt to wash off?"

"I suppose that would be one way of explaining it."

25

At 5:45 a.m. seventy-two uniformed officers made their slow painstaking zig-zags down the slope of Scragg Wood under the direction of Inspector Earnshaw. On the road above the slope the men with dogs put them back into their two vans and went home, because Sandy Woodings had ordered them to do so. Dogs were wrong for Scragg Wood. The sun was twenty minutes up and already highlighting the undulating serenity of the Derbyshire hills, rolling away to the west below the slope under an opalescent blue sky. The men worked methodically, with good humour and without excitement. All the same, there was an air of something important happening.

At 8:00 a.m. precisely Sandy was joined in his vigil by Georgy, who nodded hello and lit his pipe. A few minutes later a stout man with a shore-line of red hair about his shining bald head arrived in a white Ford Sierra: Henry Jackson, forensic scientist, from the laboratory in North Yorkshire, who asked Sandy bluntly what he hoped to find.

"The murder weapon."

Georgy puffed contentedly on his pipe while the compulsively tidy Henry stared down the slope, to the point near the stream where Earnshaw was now conducting a hands-and-knees search. "But the old girl isn't dead!"

"Mrs Pendle has the omens on her side. Built of good resilient stock. There's a chance she might survive."

"The omens?" Henry looked puzzled, but Sandy was not

211

inclined to explain. "So what have you come up with on the charred piece of material we gave you last night, Henry?"

"It's a piece of burnt white satin."

A shout sounded from the bottom of the slope: Charlie Earnshaw was waving at them like mad.

"What do you make of this piece of white satin?"

"Could be a piece of a dress. A special dress, such as an evening-dress – or a wedding-dress."

"Thanks, Henry."

Charlie Earnshaw climbed the slope a lot faster than he had descended it. He looked jubilant, carrying something wrapped in a brown paper bag, tied off at the neck with two elastic bands.

"A woodworking tool?" surmised Henry, inspecting the object, which had a gleaming stainless-steel blade, eleven inches long and curved in its transverse section.

"Almost right," Sandy corrected him. "Not a wood chisel but a sculptor's chisel."

Henry put the chisel, resealed in its bag, into his briefcase for safety. "Looks as if I've got what I came for. I'll take it straight back with me."

"You'll be in touch?"

"Immediately I've got something on it."

Watching the white car pull away, Sandy nodded his congratulations to Earnshaw. Then, using the car radio, he called the sergeant at the incident centre to inform him he was coming in for breakfast.

"One other thing," he added, as an afterthought, "arrange for Sergeant Williams to pick up a Mrs Sheridan and have her meet me after breakfast at Mrs Pendle's cottage."

When he arrived at 9:30 the men from the RSPCA were already in the garden, herding the menagerie of animals into vans. Mrs Sheridan was waiting for him inside the cottage. She identified some of the weird paraphernalia round the altar. The Egyptian figure with the oval halo was the lady of the turquoises. The snake was a python, symbol of earth and related to the oracle at Delphi, as was the dolphin which represented Apollo. A male figure with one finger raised was an Etruscan haruscopist. The Chinese symbol was "chi", which meant something Mrs Sheridan called the cosmic breath.

"Could you please explain what it all means to me in simple words, Mrs Sheridan?"

"You've heard of necromancy, Chief Inspector?"

"Divination – astrology, that kind of thing?"

"Geomancy is simply predicting the future, or asking the divines for good omens, protection, the good versus the bad chi. I myself am a simple astrologer. I have learnt my trade. I follow strict guidelines – rules."

"Come to the point, Mrs Sheridan."

"I warned you that Emily Pendle was ambitious. Necromancy is the communication with the dead. Emily Pendle is a usurper. She used these powers of communication for no better reason than to impress everybody."

"To communicate with whom?"

"With the dead girl, of course."

"Hmm!" He wrinkled his brow. "In what way impress people?"

"Power – what else!"

"I think I am beginning to understand. Thank you very much, Mrs Sheridan."

"If you want a more detailed explanation of all this?"

"Perhaps later. I think for now that I've got the general idea."

He felt greatly disturbed, anxious, restless.

Chief Superintendent Barker was waiting for him at the incident centre. He wanted to know if it was true that Martin had confessed last night to the murder.

"He said he killed her. He couldn't – or wouldn't – say how or why or anything else."

"What more do you want?"

"I don't know, Georgy. You may be right. We may take him in today."

"It's going wrong. I don't like that attempt to murder Mrs Pendle. We should have prevented that. There's still something that is out of our control!"

"I feel it too."

Sandy wondered once more about arresting Martin there and then, if only to hold him for a while, as they waited for answers, the forensic examination of the chisel. Martin's chisel. Maybe he would become more factual in his confession when presented with the chisel? But with Martin no response could really be predicted. There was still more to it. Still it all felt wrong. There were important aspects that did not add up. Arber, Thorpe, Mrs Pendle! He didn't for one minute believe a word of all that necromancy business. That altar was new – put in the cottage to impress. If Mrs Pendle knew the identity of the murderer, it was through simple means, which she might well have claimed as a result of the occult. Yes, he could see that. Maybe not enough money coming in from herbalism, the conflict with the national health service was the equivalent of the corner grocery versus the hypermarket. But given some proof of her powers of divination –

"Get me Inspector Williams," he asked the switchboard. Even while waiting, he changed his mind. "Get hold of Inspector Williams – he left Mrs Pendle's cottage to check progress in the groundsearch at Scragg Wood – and tell him I'm on my way back into the city. Tell him to follow me in to the newspaper's offices. I intend to have a chat with both the reporter and his editor."

The reporter, Palmer, had curly red hair, parted neatly to the left of his pink face, and a thick little moustache soft enough to be combed to either side of his upper lip. Sandy had had several brushes with him in the past which was why he insisted the editor and Tom be present when he talked to him.

"Mrs Pendle very nearly died. There's a good chance she'll die still. I hold you, Palmer, and this newspaper partially responsible for that. Let me further warn you that I am also considering pressing charges of withholding evidence from the police in a murder investigation. So let's get one thing clear, right from the start – I want straight answers. I don't want to ask any question twice. No evasions. So let's start with what Mrs Pendle had to say to you."

"How was I supposed to know that what the old girl claimed was of any use? She made fantastic allegations – and she only made them over the telephone."

"What allegations?"

"That she knew who had murdered the girl and why."

"So who did she claim committed the murder?"

"That's just it – she refused to tell me."

"I don't believe you."

"No more than I believed her. I thought she was a nut case. She wouldn't even tell me who she was. I didn't know her name until you told me it was this Mrs Pendle. I've never met the woman in my life."

"What exactly did she say to you?"

"She asked if I was the crime reporter. When I said I was, she said she knew who had committed the murder and wanted to know whether, if she gave me this information, I would publish it as coming from her."

"How did you respond?"

"I thought she was crazy – and she sounded a bit tipsy!"

"So you refused her?"

"I work for a newspaper. There's always an angle. I played her along a bit. I asked her to tell me whatever she knew. She said she had spoken to the dead girl."

"Spoken to her? When?"

"She said she was one of the last to see her alive. Possibly the last before she was murdered. That gave her a special responsibility."

He nodded: so Mrs Pendle had admitted seeing Angela on the actual day of her murder. "Was that the word she used – responsibility?"

"No. She said something like: 'Puts me in a special position' – or something very close to it."

"Did she tell you what she meant by her knowing the reason for the murder?"

"Only that when I was told, it would be convincing enough for me to believe it."

"So what did you tell her to do?"

"Nothing."

"I'm warning you, Palmer. I shall only give you this one warning."

Hargreaves, the editor, answered for Palmer. "Mr Palmer called me immediately. He asked me what I thought."

"And what did you think?"

"Naturally we would have got in touch with the police immediately – if there had been a shred of evidence."

"Evidence?"

"That's correct, Chief Inspector. You get your crank calls and so do we. A woman, who sounded drunk, talking rather crazily about knowing something about a murder – "

"That's all that was said then?" Sandy looked from one man to the other in a manner not meant to reassure them.

"I asked her to call me back," Palmer continued sheepishly.

"After you had had a word with your editor?"

"That's right. I asked her to call back in ten minutes."

"And did she?"

"Yes. I tried, believe you me, to get some more information out of her. Who she was, who she thought had committed the murder. But she said that naturally I wouldn't take her word for it. Even given the reason why, that would only give a reason for murder and not evidence of who had committed it."

"You told her to get some evidence, didn't you?"

"I may have told her that nobody would listen to her without some kind of proof. Naturally – "

"And it was the attempt to get such proof that resulted in Mrs Pendle's attempted murder!"

The journalist said nothing.

"Let me caution you, gentlemen. Inspector Williams has written down a transcript of what we have just said. At the moment all I intend to do is to caution you. I may take it further – it will depend on the outcome, both of Mrs Pendle's state and the case itself. Either way, I shall discuss it with Assistant Chief Constable Meadows."

"Let me express my regret that we didn't involve you sooner, Chief Inspector."

Sandy Woodings heard the unconvincing apologies follow him through the open door.

26

At no time in the case had Sandy felt so uneasy. Accompanied by Tom, he drove round to the medico-legal centre only to find that he had to wait for Doctor Atkins's return to his office from a lecture at the university.

On the doctor's arrival, Sandy looked at him questioningly, for a moment wordlessly.

"What troubles you, Chief Inspector?"

"The nature of the wounds on Angela Hawksworth's body."

"I seem to recall having this conversation with you before." While speaking, Doctor Atkins had retrieved the folder containing his report, together with the detailed photographs.

"It isn't on the photographs. I'd like to go through the video sequence with you present – if you wouldn't mind?"

"Very well. It will only take five minutes to set it up in the darkroom." Doctor Atkins called his secretary to arrange this.

"One final favour, doctor. Would you mind if I called in Chief Superintendent Barker? He's just down the road at headquarters. I would particularly like him to be present – since he was with you at the actual scene at the time."

Doctor Atkins raised no objections so that, fifteen minutes later, Georgy sat with them and watched the start of the video film, Georgy limping into view in the company of Doctor Atkins. The figures rapidly approached between the trees, on the stretch from the path to the body of Angela Hawksworth. The cameraman had made an artistic point of showing the holly tree, perhaps in a mild personal protest – or to show he could produce something other than records of criminal activity. Next they saw Doctor Atkins pulling on his gloves, the soundless movement of his lips as he spoke into his dictaphone, describing the body, its position, surface appearances and the ambient conditions. They continued to watch for several more minutes.

"There!" said Sandy quietly but urgently. "Can we go back to the point where you are about to turn her over?"

Doctor Atkins rewound the tape and they looked again, with the sequence played in slow motion.

"I wondered, just looking at the stills. Now I'm certain." Sandy pointed to two areas with his ball-point. "The body had been moved. We already knew that because the first wounds were believed to have been inflicted on her back. The multiple wounds on the front of the body were believed to have been inflicted either post-mortem or at the very latest as she lay at death's door. That was your impression, was it not, Doctor?"

"Certainly!"

"No – not certainly. Look here – what is that?"

"Blood, Chief Inspector. She bled from the wounds in her back. She was lying on her back in that precise position when the frenzy took place over her chest and abdomen."

"Then how do you explain this second pool of blood?"

"Precisely that – it's another pool of blood."

"But it's a good three feet from the body – "

"We did notice. I presumed that in her death agony, the poor girl rolled about."

"You presumed that this blood must have also come from the wounds to her upper back – because the tissue reaction round the wounds to her chest and abdomen seemed to imply that these wounds were inflicted at or after death?"

"That was my conclusion – yes."

"What if there had been one single wound? One wound in the middle of all those thirty-odd? One wound to the lower abdomen. And that was the *first* wound. Let's think the sequence differently, think afresh. The first stab takes place with her facing her killer. She is still only just realising what is happening. She is astonished, then terrified. She tries to escape, but she's in pain and severely wounded. Her attacker pounces a second time after very little chase, this time a wound in her back. She falls. She lies face down after that wound and that explains the blood here. Immobilised and vulnerable, this is when the telling wounds are inflicted, from which time everything is precisely as you have already deduced. The tearing of the wounds. The one wound in the middle of so many would be lost. Even the bleeding from this wound would come straight out through the flimsy skirt and underclothes. She lay in a pool of blood, a pool which had originated from her lower abdomen. With the frenzy of the second and eventually fatal attack on her back, she moves – she moves as somebody does who is simply desperate to avoid the murderous rain of stabbings. She managed to move only a short distance – precisely the distance between the two pools of blood. Here she is turned over again. But this time it is her attacker who turns her over. Her attacker turns her over in order to inspect the part of her that initially excited so much fury. Her lower abdomen. Her three months pregnancy. By this time her attacker is thinking more rationally. Her attacker stabs her repeatedly over the front of the body, including the lower abdomen, thereby masking the importance of that first wound. It is during all this that the second pool of blood is formed, blood from the wounds in her back. Then, having finished with this gory exercise in deception, her attacker turns her once more, turns her for some reason which must be uncertain, perhaps because her attacker wants attention to focus on the wounds in her back – perhaps merely so as not to have to face her – "

"Then the frenzy might not have been such an uncalculating frenzy after all?"

"Not necessarily. There might well have been a frenzy of attack – but there was direction to the frenzy. And the frenzy was ultimately controlled sufficiently to allow for some deliberate deception."

"It's a theory which can no longer be corroborated since she has been buried for three weeks. Even if the body were fresh in the mortuary, it would be virtually impossible to be certain, given the surrounding carnage."

Henry Jackson picked this moment to telephone from the forensic-science laboratory and tell them that some smudged fingerprints on the chisel matched those taken from Simon Martin when he was brought into headquarters.

Sandy turned to the silently thoughtful chief superintendent. "At least let me arrest him myself, Georgy! I want to be there. I want to see his reaction!"

The jigsaw appeared to be falling into place all by itself. The difficult pieces appeared to be difficult no longer: on the contrary they appeared extraneous. The jigsaw would complete itself without them! He called from his car to discover that Martin had gone for one of his walks but their men had been given precise instructions and two of them were not so much following him as keeping him company. Apart from checking exactly where they had entered the woods and when, he did nothing. He could have had them bring Martin back to the picnic area, but he deliberately chose otherwise. As he had indicated to Georgy, he wanted to be there. In the woods – so much the better. He had to be there. He had to see the look on Simon Martin's face.

They parked their car and walked down the moderate slope of grass, between the young birches and hazels, now well advanced in leaf. Climbing over the little stone steps in the low wall, they advanced into the gloom of the wood proper.

Martin should be perhaps a mile ahead of them, a man dawdling, in no apparent hurry. A man with nowhere to go.

They had walked about eight hundred yards when they heard a sound, like distant thunder.

"Motorbikes!" exclaimed Tom, turning himself round to try and locate the sound. "This way!" He had started to run off the path to their left.

"No. Wait. Wherever they seem to be now, there's only one place they can be heading." Sandy spoke tersely into his handset, asked the switchboard to warn the two officers. "This way." He led Tom running along the path, in the direction of Simon Martin.

The sound of the motorcycles ebbed, went quickly past them and disappeared. In the distance they caught a glimpse of the three men, Martin and the two watchful detective constables. Sandy recognised Brown as one of the two. Suddenly he could hear the thundering again – the motorcycles had circled round and must be approaching Martin from the opposite direction. There was a stitch in Sandy's side. But he forced himself on, although more slowly. He jumped over the stream and landed with one foot in water, but it saved twenty yards. Martin couldn't be more than four hundred yards from him. He caught his first glimpse of the motorcycles. He recognised the quarter-ton of aluminium and metallic-blue that could only be Thorpe's bike. He was shouting now as he ran.

"Watch out behind you!"

All three of them had seen the danger. Brown had hold of Martin by the arm and was pulling him close to a tree, while the other detective – Sandy was close enough to identify Huntley – picked up something that looked like a length of bough. It seemed that within a few seconds the bikes were upon them. Huntley was thrown to one side. Arber had deliberately crashed into him and he lay in a heap where he had fallen.

Sandy couldn't run any further. He was still a hundred

222

yards from where Brown was circling behind the tree, with Martin still in his grasp. The bikes were also circling. Sandy saw the glint of something – it had to be the bayonet – in Thorpe's gloved hand. He put through a desperate call for help on the handset. Then he started to run again, with a dead weight throbbing in his chest and his legs stiffening under him.

Arber's bike hit Brown and knocked him sideways. Martin fell, but he wasn't injured. He stood up almost immediately. He had Huntley's piece of bough in his hand. He appeared to be standing his ground, facing the two riders, who were circling again, perhaps twenty yards from him.

"Run, Martin! For God's sake!" Sandy shouted at the top of his voice. He was no more than sixty yards from Martin and Tom was lagging a good twenty yards behind him.

But Martin just stood there determinedly as the bikes roared back towards him. He aimed a blow at Arber, which sent him wobbling off at an angle, but then there was a stricken sound as the bayonet went into his body up to the hilt. He was still standing, swaying, as the two bikes roared past Sandy, no more than feet from him on either side. Sandy ignored the bikes and ran as best he could to where Martin had fallen. Brown got there a second or two before him and Tom arrived a few seconds later.

Martin was clearly dying. Sandy didn't even bother to call immediately for an ambulance. He knelt down next to the man's face and he asked if he could hear him.

Martin's eyes flickered. There was a barely perceptible nod of his head.

"Listen to me, Martin. There's no time for anything other than a declaration. You could make a declaration. Under these circumstances it would still stand up in court." He hesitated to ascertain that the man could genuinely hear and understand him. "Did you kill Angela Hawksworth?"

Martin didn't even look at Sandy. His eyes were staring

223

blankly into the foliage overhead. Sandy had to repeat his question. Had he killed Angela Hawksworth?

Martin nodded.

"And Richard Belton? Did you kill Belton?"

Martin was still staring up at the trees. There was no nod this time. There was no reaction.

Sandy stood up and stared down at him.

Tom murmured quietly, "We saw it. We're both witnesses, Chief."

Sandy nodded to Tom, distant for a moment, then knelt down once more and ascertained that there was no longer a carotid pulse. Martin was dead.

"Damn!" he sighed deeply and audibly. "Call headquarters, Tom – not the incident centre. Get the patrols mobilised. Tell them I don't give a damn about the miners' strike. You know who and what we're looking for. Then call the incident centre. Send squads straight round to the homes of Thorpe and Arber."

27

There was sunshine every morning when Sandy awoke: the heatwave continued. It gathered strength, that milk-blue haze in the distance, each day hotter than the previous. Gardeners had established a ritual of hosing down their lawns and vegetable areas. Housewives stood on stepladders and daily gave their wall-baskets a good soaking. It was also a difficult week for the murder team, particularly so for the detectives under Sandy Woodings, who had expected after Martin's dying declaration that the case was virtually over.

The bayonet that had killed Martin matched the wound on the body of the drug addict, Richard Belton. The chisel found next to where Mrs Pendle had been attacked matched precisely the wound in her back – and just as precisely those odd crescent-shaped wounds inflicted in the frenzy over Angela Hawksworth's body. Paul Thorpe had killed Martin right in front of three detectives. They had seen the bayonet in his hand, his mother had admitted that the bayonet had been in his possession all along. Thorpe must therefore also have killed Belton. He had killed Belton because the drug addict, living rough in the wood, would have been brought in for questioning sooner or later and this would have drawn attention to the drug running. The fact that Belton had Angela's wristwatch probably meant nothing more than that he had come upon her body before Mrs Pendle. Belton had had nothing to do with

Angela's murder, except in the sense that Thorpe had killed him in a pseudo-frenzy, deliberately copying the style of Angela's killing. It was not difficult to surmise that Thorpe, even if he had not been responsible for Angela's death, would have wanted Belton's murder blamed on the same source, hence his simulation of her killing. Simon Martin had confessed twice to the killing of Angela, first verbally, when he had volunteered his statement after Mrs Pendle had been attacked, secondly and finally in the form of a dying declaration – this archaic form, the only indirect statement admissible as evidence in a court of law – which had three experienced detectives as witnesses. His strange behaviour could be explained by the fact that Mrs Pendle had survived the attack. It had been fear that she ultimately would name him that had caused him to stand there so invitingly when Thorpe had ridden against him on his motorbike like an obscene avenging angel, brandishing his bayonet.

The murder team had every possible explanation. They could not understand the chief inspector's mysterious and implacable persistence. All that remained was the capture of the two tearaways, who had managed somehow to evade the road-blocks placed round the village. They appealed to Georgy but Georgy remained as he had seemed throughout, strangely distant if still interested. Sandy drove the team to obsessional limits. Every person connected with the crimes was questioned again, their movements counter-checked, from minute to minute if possible. Every statement was compared and rechecked against those made by other unrelated parties. Whenever two statements corroborated each other, there they had a fixed point, from which the people already questioned several times over were questioned again.

The journalists who tried to catch his attention at all times of day for this difficult week found him equally unrevealing. This detective, whose team had earned the reputation of never failing in a murder enquiry, seemed reluctant to take any credit for establishing Martin's guilt. And Martin, an international celebrity, one of the most distinguished sculptors in Britain, dying violently in that same wood where his beautiful young model had earlier been murdered – ! It was news in a big way. The reporters never gave up trying.

Chief Inspector Sandy Woodings also had his ritual. Sleeping with his curtains and windows open, he found the sunshine a sufficient alarm clock. He rose early each morning, washed and shaved, then drove directly to the incident centre at the old school where he reviewed the previous day's statements over breakfast. He made notes, but mainly he took things in mentally. The establishment of times, people's movements, all were sifted through carefully, with such a queer determination that he seemed to be deliberately heaping fact upon fact, for reasons that were over and above any need for evidence in a court of law.

If Martin had been concerned that Mrs Pendle might wake up and tell them everything, he had had no cause to do so, Sandy thought. Mrs Pendle might never remember anything, even in the event that she did recover. Sandy had little doubt that she would eventually recover – she was made of recovery material – but he placed no faith that that recovery would help him further with his enquiries.

It was dogged, patient work: he used the computer technology recently installed in headquarters administration to establish their network of inter-personal contacts and timings. On the television news in the evenings, he observed a similar dogged determination on the faces of police lines and miners' mass pickets. The miners' strike was as durable as the heatwave.

Then their luck suddenly improved. On Friday June 15th Jacky Arber was captured after a high-speed chase down the M1 motorway. Although injured – with a Colles' fracture and a broken collar-bone – he was very much alive and talking. Sandy Woodings was waiting by his bedside as he recovered consciousness from having his wrist set.

"How are you, Jacky?"

"I'll survive."

"You should have listened to me last time we spoke."

"I'm listening now – does the same deal hold?"

"I make no deals on murder."

"Suit yourself then!"

Sandy regarded him calmly, thoughtfully. "But you could avoid adding failure to co-operate to these charges – and you're going to have more than enough of those already."

Arber stared back at him. There was already the sinking fear of prison in the youngster. Prison for life. He said, "Will you give me your word that you'll put in a good word for me? Say I wasn't the one with the bayonet?"

"Where is Thorpe?"

"Search me. We separated after we biked it out of the wood."

"And you haven't seen him – you haven't heard a word from him since?"

"I've been hiding in farmers' barns and empty garages."

"Maybe I believe you. Just maybe, Jacky. He won't get away. We have his picture, his prints. We know his habits and his contacts too. We'll get him. But I'd prefer it to be sooner rather than later."

"I've told you the truth. That's all I know!"

"Let's talk about Richard Belton."

"Who's he?"

"We know that between you and Paul, you murdered Belton. What I want to know is why?"

"I had nothing to do with it."

"He was killed by the same bayonet that killed Martin. He was dosed up with heroin first, so as to make him easy. A planned and pre-meditated murder, Jacky. Juries don't like that."

"I had nothing to do with it."

"Just as you had nothing to do with murdering Simon Martin? Or running down Detective Constable Huntley and knocking him unconscious, not to mention fracturing five of his ribs?"

"Paul killed Belton."

"To shut him up about the drug trafficking here in the village?"

I don't know anything about no drug trafficking! I don't know anything more than I've told you!"

"Something you haven't told me, Jacky. Tell me how you knew that Martin was in the wood. Let me tell you what I already know. You came prepared twice, not just the last time, but the time before too. The time when you played games with Inspector Williams. Thorpe had the bayonet then, but when you saw the inspector, he hid it. That was a trial run for the second time. On each occasion you knew Martin was in the wood. I want to know how you knew Martin was in the wood?"

"Paul said he got a call."

"I don't believe you."

"You can believe what you like. That was what Paul told me."

"A call from whom?"

"I don't know."

"Who could have called him? Who did he know who could have kept track of Martin's movements?"

"Maybe it was one of you – maybe it was a cop."

"Which cop?"

"I don't know. He didn't say."

"A lot depends on it, Jacky. Your future depends on the answer to that question. So let's try again. He must have given you some indication. You must have wondered yourself how he knew both times."

"I'm telling you the truth, Mr Woodings. I asked him the second time. He seemed so cock-sure of himself. I did – I asked him. Only he just laughed and he wouldn't tell me. But I could tell from the way he laughed, whoever it was it tickled him pink. You should have seen the look in his eyes when he laughed at me."

Sandy spent the weekend with Josie. She noticed his strange mood but she couldn't fathom it, any more than his detective colleagues. On the Saturday night they went to a night club, but, when they came back to Josie's place afterwards, they didn't make love.

"Not much longer, but I need just a little more time, Josie." He touched her cheek tenderly, in mixed apology and explanation.

"I'll give you until next weekend," she cautioned him, half smiling.

But then she was surprised at the way he looked at her – as if somehow she had hit upon something that was undecided in him. It was as if he actually took her caution seriously.

On the Monday he sat in his temporary office in the old school, getting the facts straight in his head. Then suddenly, on the Tuesday, he took it into his head to travel down to London. He spent the entire day in London and he gave no explanation. At lunch time on Wednesday he met Georgy in the Drunken Duck, a meeting that had become a part of this ritual, and told him what he had learnt in London.

The overweight chief superintendent nodded, sipping at his half-pint of beer, his lips harder pursed than usual.

"Have you arrived at your conclusion then?" he asked Sandy mildly.

"Yes, I have." Sandy looked out through the bow window into the village centre. "You aren't surprised?"

"I've known, as you have, Sandy. We both knew right from the beginning."

"You had no proof – but then I'm not sure I have proof enough, even now – "

28

Sandy awoke as usual without an alarm at 7:00 a.m. He stood in front of his bedroom window and gazed out at the blue sky. There migth have been something subconscious about it. Today was Thursday, June 21st: officially the first day of summer.

Shaving and showering were part of that same ritual, which was in itself a kind of protection. He knew it, although he hated the weakness it implied there must be in his character. He was ready. He no longer needed to think, his mind lay clear as to what he must do. As he ran his dusty car through the car wash at his local garage, his gaze was gentle to the point of vacancy. He watched the deluge of soapy water with his heartbeat audible in his own ears, then drove the gleaming black Capri out to the incident centre in the old school where he shared a light breakfast of toast and coffee with the duty sergeant. He looked at his watch – 8:20! An hour and ten minutes to kill before he met up with Tom here at the centre. He drove out to the picnic area, parking in the precise spot where Doctor Atkins had parked his Peugeot when he had arrived to inspect the body at the scene of murder. Climbing out, he traced those same asymmetrical steps of Georgy together with the doctor.

The sun was already warm. Today would reach the high eighties. Loosening his tie, he decided to remove it altogether, folding it neatly so it fitted into his inside pocket. Then he continued to walk stiffly down the slope between hazel and young birches, over the stone stile, before taking his first curious steps into the wood.

The wood was even more beautiful than he had remembered it, perhaps because the investigation was over. Sweet summer: a different beauty from showy spring with the blossom largely gone now, apart from the cottage cheese of the hawthorn. There was a heavy maturity in the hundred shades of voluptuous green, the density of that enormous semi-transparent canopy, reaching out into every crevice of light, only a matter of weeks before it entirely blotted out the sun.

Why the hell had he come here? Why when he had worked it all out? When he had picked the wood bare to its bones of anything that might have proved useful, why pause now at that same spot in the path, walk carefully along what was now worn as a path? But of course he knew very well, staring up once more at the holly that marked the spot. The evergreen must have preferred winter. It was a hopeless struggle now against all those richer, faster-growing, oaks and beeches.

He walked at the same sure and unhurried pace back to the path, before heading on deeper into the wood, to the spot from where he had seen Simon Martin cut down. He wanted to see it just as it had happened, the figure seemingly small and slightly tensed. Standing. Martin had seemed so frail and doll-like, the jerk as his body took the full thrust of man and heavy machine pushing the blade several inches out of the man's back. Only now did it all make sense. Only now, standing in the identical spot, remembering what he had seen as he watched helpless with breathlessness. Pity showed on his face as he retraced his steps along the path, only a matter of fifteen minutes or so until he emerged into the bright sunlight once more, and drove back to meet up with Tom at the old school.

In his mood of the morning, he had exaggerated. Later,

233

after his calm discussion with Tom and Georgy at the school, he noticed them in passing. There was still blossom to be seen in the village. Not so striking perhaps, the quiet purple of lilac, an occasional orange tongue of broom. At precisely 10:00 a.m. Tom parked his white Escort outside the six-foot drystone wall. Pushing the passenger door shut, Sandy left Tom waiting at the wheel, while he walked stiffly along the gravel drive, pausing for only a second before pressing the bell.

It was Eleanor who answered it and she made no effort to conceal her irritation at seeing him.

"Caroline is still extremely upset! Is it really necessary for you to disturb her further?"

"I'm afraid it is." He spoke politely, not waiting for her to invite him inside, but taking her as an adult leads a child from behind, his hand by one folded elbow, leading them both into the lounge where Caroline stood up to face him. Her face was very pale and there were deep hollows under her eyes. Yet still attractive. There was still that haunted vulnerability about the pale face and the contrast, today sharper than ever, between white skin and deep-brown eyes.

"Mrs Martin?"

Her eyes now showed how instantly she perceived the formality of his tone of voice. Her face was entirely without make-up so that the human being inside the woman showed through, the unpainted lips, pale skin, two lines about each eye from smiling.

"What is it you want, Mr Woodings?"

"The truth." His voice was firm but without menace.

"You're crazy. Everybody has gone crazy." Eleanor sat on the arm of her sister's chair. "I think you should go. Go on! Get out!"

He stared at the pair of them a moment in silence. In agitation the family similarity had strengthened.

"The convention should be to caution you – but I don't

pretend that this visit is conventional. I'm afraid my superiors will not approve of my coming here this morning. I'm breaking very many rules."

"What does that mean, Chief Inspector?" She ignored her sister.

"It means that, since I'm alone and I'm making no notes, this conversation will never become part of any formal statement. It will never be used in a court of law."

"Tricks!" Eleanor muttered contemptuously.

"We already know a great deal. I think we know everything that is important." His eyes were a soft deep blue, fixed on Caroline's. "After we found the evidence in Mrs Pendle's hand, we conducted an exhaustive search of the entire village. We knew exactly what we were looking for and we found it – fifty yards from this room, across the road, in the undergrowth immediately opposite this house. The remains of a fire. A fire in which a wedding-dress was burnt."

He had taken the liberty of sitting down opposite her: close enough to make out the tiny fissures over the backs of her hands.

When she didn't answer, he added, "You must realise how that would look to us. Neither of the other two women in this house would possess a wedding-dress."

"Anybody could have taken Caroline's dress out there and burnt it. Anybody. Simon? Surely it's obvious that it was Simon!" exclaimed Eleanor.

"I was married. I think it very unlikely that a man would burn his wife's wedding-dress."

"You didn't know Simon. Simon was quite capable of any grand exhibition. And hate – hate beyond bounds! After he had killed that girl."

"I believe I did understand Simon. In as much as any human being ever understands another. I doubt that the dress would ever have occurred to him. It's a basic difference between men and women. The burning of the dress had to be the act of a woman." His quiet voice continued: "Mrs Pendle understood the significance of the wedding-dress. For that she very nearly lost her life. But Mrs Pendle will recover. I expect that her memory will recover too. In parts. Little by little. She'll remember Angela Hawksworth coming to see her. Angela suffering from morning sickness asking for something safer than the pills she could obtain from her doctor or from the chemist. Mrs Pendle gave her a simple herbal salad. But of course Mrs Pendle then realised that Angela was pregnant."

There was a radiance to Caroline's face, a burning look in the eyes. He couldn't bear to look into her eyes a moment. He waited for it to pass.

"I don't know whether Simon or Paul Thorpe was the father. I do believe that Mrs Pendle was convinced Simon was the father. When exactly Paul Thorpe discovered the pregnancy, I can't be sure. But it seems likely that he knew early on. Whether he was the father or Simon – and maybe Angela herself might not have been sure which of the two it was – I know that Thorpe saw it as a chance for simple mercenary advancement. You drew ten thousand pounds out of your bank account six weeks before Angela's murder, Mrs Martin! Ten thousand pounds at a time when, by remarkable coincidence, Thorpe and Arber appear to have come into an identical sum of money. What did you do with that money?"

"Don't answer him, Carrie! You have no need to explain what you do with your own private money." Eleanor turned her full glare back on Sandy Woodings. "Both my sister and I were at home at the time of Angela's killing and of the attack on Mrs Pendle."

"In fact, when Angela Hawksworth was murdered Virginia Lauderman was in London and the same applied to Ronald Wadsworth at the time Mrs Pendle was attacked. Apart from Simon, you two were the only occupants of this house still in the village at the time of both murders. In the case of Angela's murder, the people in this household all gave each other alibis. A household which was held together not by mutual liking or respect but by Simon's prodigious earning capacity. If the household broke up, you would all lose your comfortable existence. Not a single person other than Simon was capable of making his or her living from art. At the time Mrs Pendle was attacked, Constable Huntley confirms that you, Mrs Martin, were in his company all the time, but not you, Miss Standon. You left the lounge within fifteen minutes of his arrival. You went upstairs and had a shower and then appeared to retire to your bedroom. You shared the shower with Virginia Lauderman. An hour later you shared a second shower. I've inspected the back of the house immediately below the bathroom window. The waste pipe would be very easy to climb, down or up. You're slim and fit. You could have climbed out of the window, leaving Virginia Lauderman behind to cover for you. When you returned, you needed a second shower. During the hour you were gone, had Constable Huntley climbed the stairs to check where you both were, the plan was for Virginia Lauderman to pretend you were both still in the bathroom. No doubt the trip took longer than you imagined it might. You also did not allow for the curiosity of Constable Huntley, particularly in relation to the second, apparently shared, shower."

"And Simon, who was missing all this time – where was Simon during all this?"

"You knew perfectly well where he was. The bathroom is at the back of the house from where you couldn't miss the noise of him breaking up his sculptures. Putting two and two together, you knew he was drunk, and you also knew that he had avoided our earlier search for him. It was an opportunity not to be missed. You hated him and the idea came to you in what must have been a moment of desperation how blame could be diverted on to him for both killings. Knowing where the chisel had been concealed after

237

Angela's murder, you retrieved it. You had heard me discuss Mrs Pendle's disappearance over the telephone. You must also have known exactly where to find her. I could hazard a guess that Mrs Pendle somehow witnessed the burning of the dress. That this was where she was when she did her first disappearing act. I interviewed her immediately afterwards and I noticed that several charms were missing from her bracelets. She gave us a story about falling and blacking out. I believe she did fall, but she did not black out. She fell somewhere close to the fire and left the charms as evidence of her own identity. Anyone in this village would have recognised those charms.''

Eleanor's face burned with hate. Her voice was almost a scream as she put her arm round her sister. "So you suspect that I killed Angela and tried to kill Mrs Pendle! You're demented!''

"Why did you come here today, Chief Inspector?'' It was Caroline's voice in that same quiet questioning tone.

"Don't say a word to him, Carrie! Can't you see what he's up to? He wants to destroy you and me.''

But that quiet voice continued, with that fire smouldering still in her brown eyes. "Why are you speaking to us in this way?''

"Because I want to help you, Mrs Martin.''

"Liar!'' exclaimed Eleanor.

"We already know so much. From the very beginning we suspected. We already had what for most people would have been considered sufficient motive. But not for you, Mrs Martin. You're not my idea of a murderess. Even allowing for your going through life with such different rules. That was what puzzled us. It puzzled me right up to the point when I witnessed Simon's death.''

"I don't understand,'' she murmured simply.

"Don't listen to him, Carrie. He's very clever.''

"When Chief Superintendent Barker took Simon in for questioning I realised why he pretended to be drunk and

238

incapable. I had an inkling from my first conversation with him, but he was playing such a good part. I believe now that he was drunk in a way. He was drunk from grief. Yet he played that part in order to defend you."

"No!" She shook her head, disbelievingly.

"I spoke to him as he lay dying. He actually made a statement exonerating you. Even then, Mrs Martin. In spite of everything, he made what is legally termed a dying declaration."

"He had such a strong sense – sense of duty. Caring." Her voice was little more than a whisper.

"He loved you."

"I wish I could believe that."

"What he did – it should have been enough. If it hadn't been for all of those little things. The wedding-dress. The way he talked to me about Angela. And that sculpture – how he looked when he talked about her sculpture! He couldn't bring himself to destroy it – not that one figure of Eve."

"No," she murmured. "No – he couldn't!"

"Yet he destroyed all the others. And they were sculptures of Angela too. Obviously this one was different. It was different because by the time he chiselled that out of the marble he loved her. He saw something special in her – didn't he, Mrs Martin?"

"Yes, he saw something special in her."

"Carrie!" Eleanor screamed with tears running down her face. She tried to embrace her sister, to stop her talking further. "You heard what he said. Nothing that is said here would matter a jot. Stop now. Can't you see what he's trying to make us do!"

"Yesterday you went to London and spoke to some of my friends from the Slade, Mr Woodings?"

"Yes. Initially it was to check up on that story Eleanor told me about your deprived childhood. I discovered your childhood was anything but deprived. Your parents were

wealthy and they gave you everything. The deprived childhood was Simon's."

"You shouldn't have invented that story, Lennie."

He added, "I had a second reason for talking to your
friends. I discovered something else in London."

"The fact that I am infertile?"

"Your marriage to Simon was the big event of your
graduation year at the Slade. I'm afraid anything to do with
you and your marriage remained news to your friends.
When you discovered you were infertile, you tried every big
name in gynaecology at the London hospitals."

"He has no right to pry into your life like this, Carrie. Tell
him he has no right."

"Somebody telephoned Paul Thorpe and told him that
Simon was in the wood. That somebody telephoned Thorpe
twice, expecting what that telephone call might lead to."

"Carrie doesn't believe you. You're inventing the most
horrible things."

A quiver of anguish caused Caroline Martin's eyes to
close. "It's true. Yes, it's true. I tried all of those gynaecol-
ogists – everybody!" She nodded. "And do you know what
they told me?"

He shook his head.

"Hostile! I am a hostile environment. No physical
barrier. Something chemical. Something in my very chemical make-up. What could I possibly do about that?"

"I'm sorry."

"Yes. I believe you are."

"Simon wanted a child desperately?"

"We both did. We tried so hard. You see, it was his
childhood. I think it must have been that. You say he told
you about his childhood, but I doubt if he really said how
very hard it was. There was no money and no love in his
family. And we had so much of both to give."

"You could have tried adoption?"

"I would have tried anything. But he couldn't. Oh, he

tried very hard. We would talk into the morning about it. He really did try his best. Simon!'' The tears coursed down her face from her eyes, which still burned with that barely sane fire. "Did he really try to save me? Did he say that when he was dying?''

"Yes, he did.''

She nodded. She made a determined effort to control herself. "Angela was the most beautiful model ever to sit for him. She was so beautiful. Young. It all helped. Simon wasn't wicked, you know. Only human and vulnerable. And she did have that simple thing. Even the most simple girl without a brain in her head has it. She could bear his child —''

"It was you who telephoned her at her home that evening, wasn't it?''

"Her number was in the book. Simon used to call her when he wanted her.''

He realised how Caroline Martin's alto voice, husky from urgency and emotion, might sound at a distance from the telephone receiver like that of a man's. "You made an arrangement to meet her?''

"Yes.''

"But that couldn't have been the first time! You must have met her many times. She sat for Simon only the day before, here at your house. Why then meet in the woods?''

"I was to have met her the day before — but she avoided me. I knew she was avoiding me and I panicked. It was her idea to meet in the woods. She was still very much a child. A childish notion of secrecy, I suppose.''

"You took the chisel — ''

"His best rounded chisel, with which he had carved — carved her — carved — !''

"You wanted to break up the developing relationship? You felt threatened by the pregnancy? Because you knew that Simon was planning to leave you and marry her?''

"The chisel was wrong. But I wasn't altogether in proper

241

control of my mind. It was so awfully unfair. She had taken my money – everything I had."

He stared at her, a new realisation only just starting to dawn on him. "The ten thousand pounds. You gave the money to Angela?"

"I can see now that it wasn't really sane from the beginning. It was mad. Oh, I can see how mad it was now! But she agreed to it at the time and it seemed to answer everything."

"She agreed to what?"

"She didn't want the baby. There was no doubt who was the father. Simon was the father. Simon was the reason she had become pregnant. I believe he may have wanted it, did it deliberately – at the very least subconsciously. She didn't want it at all. It would ruin her notion of a modelling career. I believe it was like a succession of shocks to me – I think from that moment I must have lost my reason. The idea was a desperate one – I saw this final opportunity. Simon's baby. I knew how much he wanted that baby. So I gave her all I had to buy her baby!"

Caroline Martin was sitting pale and still, while her sister sobbed in her arms.

"What happened in the woods, Mrs Martin?"

"I knew something was terribly wrong. I guessed when she started avoiding me. I told her the money was all I had – I couldn't give her any more. She said the money had gone. She had given it away – invested it, she claimed."

"Invested it on Paul Thorpe and Jacky Arber's cocaine running!"

"I could hardly understand what she was saying. Invested my money! She said I would get it all back! Oh, I didn't care about the money. All I cared about was the baby. To me, it was already my baby. And then – then – that look on her face! I knew then my worst fears were true. She said she was in love with Simon. The way her head seemed to turn away from me like a mechanical thing. Such a selfish girl – greedy

– and yet her mouth was so – so disgusted! A simple girl from the village school and I had disgusted her. I was a monster in her eyes. I became that monster – "

Eleanor dashed at him and attempted to claw his face, but he restrained her easily. Caroline Martin stood erect and did not face him.

"What should I do now?" she asked with ashen determination.

Sandy Woodings touched her momentarily, the merest brush of his fingers against her arm. His throat was dry as he said, "Inspector Williams is sitting outside in his car. Go out and tell him that you wish to make a statement. Ask him to take you into the old school where Chief Superintendent Barker is waiting."

She could see them through the car window, standing at the bottom of the steps, outside the door. He had his arm on Lennie's shoulder, but it wasn't so much a restraint as an attempt to support Lennie, who was crying. The inspector's earthy voice sounded strange and remote in her ears, speaking over the car radio to somebody who would be waiting for her at the village school.

How could she have explained to Lennie that nothing mattered any more. Not now. Not when Simon was dead. Especially not since Lennie had done that awful thing to poor Mrs Pendle. And it could only have been Lennie who had given Simon into the hands of those two horrible young men!

The car began to move and she had to turn her head to catch a last glimpse of him. Alexander – that was his name. She had known his name all along because Simon had told her. It was thinking of his name, thinking Alexander, that had helped her to believe him. He did want to help her. He was so much like the good side of Simon – or at least the image in her mind that had been Simon. The integrity in those frighteningly honest blue eyes. That she had found

243

herself liking him in spite of everything. She would have liked just to tell him that. That she found him sympathetic, kind, likeable. But of course she would never be able to speak to him like that. It would have been irrelevant, under the circumstances.

OTHER TITLES BY FRANK RYAN
AVAILABLE FROM SWIFT PUBLISHERS

IN FICTION

* GOODBYE BABY BLUE
  ISBN 1-874082-01-4   Price £6.99
* TIGER TIGER   ISBN 1-874082-25-1   Price £6.99

* THE SUNDERED WORLD (HARDCOVER)
  ISBN 1-874082-23-5   Price £16.99

* THE SUNDERED WORLD (PAPERBACK)
  ISBN 1-874082-24-3   Price £6.99

IN NON-FICTION

* TUBERCULOSIS; THE GREATEST STORY NEVER

  TOLD (HARDCOVER)
  ISBN 1874082-00-6   Price £16.99

If you would like to know more about these and other
exciting Swift titles, visit our interactive website at:

www.swiftpublishers.com

These titles may be purchased by credit card from our
website or, by post, by sending a cheque or postal order (not
cash) for the stated amounts to:

Swift Publishers Ltd, PO Box 1436, Sheffield S17 3XP, UK.

Please add £1 towards postage and packing for single
orders. If you order more than one book, please add an
additional 50p per additional book. Applies only to orders
to be delivered to addresses in the UK, Ireland or Europe.
If outside these territories, please enquire about availability
by letter or by e-mail to: *enquiries@swiftpublishers.com*